Life *with* Lily

Books by Suzanne Woods Fisher

Amish Peace: Simple Wisdom for a Complicated World
Amish Proverbs: Words of Wisdom from the Simple Life
Amish Values for Your Family: What We Can Learn from the Simple Life

LANCASTER COUNTY SECRETS
The Choice
The Waiting
The Search

SEASONS OF STONEY RIDGE
The Keeper
The Haven
The Lesson
A Lancaster County Christmas

THE ADVENTURES OF LILY LAPP

❧ Book One ❧

Life *with* Lily

Mary Ann Kinsinger and Suzanne Woods Fisher

Revell

a division of Baker Publishing Group
Grand Rapids, Michigan

© 2012 by Mary Ann Kinsinger and Suzanne Woods Fisher

Published by Revell
a division of Baker Publishing Group
P.O. Box 6287, Grand Rapids, MI 49516-6287
www.revellbooks.com

Printed in the United States of America

Library of Congress Cataloging-in-Publication Data
Kinsinger, Mary Ann.
        Life with Lily / Mary Ann Kinsinger and Suzanne Woods Fisher.
            p.   cm. — (The adventures of Lily Lapp ; bk. 1)
        Summary: Introduces Lily Lapp who, beginning at age five, finds opportunities for blessings, laughter, learning, and mischief as she explores her Amish community, welcomes a new baby brother, begins school, and spends time with family and friends.
        ISBN 978-0-8007-2132-9 (pbk.)
        [1. Amish—Fiction. 2. Family life—New York (State)—Fiction. 3. Schools—Fiction. 4. Friendship—Fiction. 5. New York (State)—Fiction.] I. Fisher, Suzanne Woods. II. Title.
    P27.K62933Lif 2012
    [Fic]—dc23   2012022920

Published in association with Joyce Hart of the Hartline Literary Agency, LLC.

Illustrations by Tim Foley

13   14   15   16   17   18   7   6   5   4   3   2

Mary Ann

To my parents,
for pouring their hearts and love
into their little family
and providing me with many happy memories.

Suzanne

To my four beautiful
and amusing children—
my source of constant new material.

Contents

Contents

Strange Goings-On

*I*t was still dark outside. Lily tried to keep up with Papa's long strides as he carried little Joseph across the yard to where the horse and buggy were tied to the hitching post. The wet grass swished against the hem of Lily's long flannel nightgown, making it slap against her legs as they hurried along. She felt wet and cold.

Only moments before, Papa had awakened Lily from a sound sleep and handed her a coat to wear over her nightgown. Something mysterious was going on that wasn't explained to five-year-old Lily.

Papa boosted Lily and Joseph up into the buggy and hurried to untie Jim, the buggy horse. Coiling up the rope, Papa tucked it under the seat before he climbed into the buggy. He gave a quick "tch-tch" to Jim and a light touch on the reins to guide the horse out the long, winding driveway.

The chilly night air had wiped all the sleepiness from Lily's

eyes. In the sky, stars twinkled and a full moon hung above the trees like a big golden ball. The only sounds she could hear were the clip-clopping of Jim's hooves and the crunchy sound of the buggy wheels as they rolled over the gravel road. The leaves rustled in the chilly night breeze and cast dancing moon shadows in the trees along the road. The lanterns that hung outside the buggy created little circles of light that shone on Jim's hindquarters. He twitched his ears forward and then back again, listening for Papa's voice.

It seemed to Lily as if they were the only people in the world who were awake. There were no lamps shining in the houses they passed. There were no cars on the road. No birdsong in the trees. The only sound of nature she could hear was the sweet sound of spring peepers, calling to each other in the creek.

As soon as they arrived at Grandpa and Grandma Miller's

house, Papa hopped off the buggy and led Jim over to the long hitching rail. He helped Lily and Joseph jump down from the buggy. Then he reached under the buggy seat for a suitcase. Lily hadn't noticed it until now.

Usually, Grandma and Grandpa Miller's house looked warm and inviting when Lily's family came for a visit. Tonight, in the dark, it looked cold and forbidding. Scary. Papa walked up to the porch and knocked on the door. His loud knock echoed in the quiet. Lily and Joseph stood quietly next to Papa, waiting. Finally, the dim glow of an oil lamp appeared in a window and moved toward the door. The door opened to Grandpa and Grandma, standing in their nightclothes with worried looks on their faces.

"How is she doing?" Grandma asked.

"She's doing fine," Papa said, "but I need to hurry right back."

Grandma nodded. She motioned to Lily and Joseph to come inside.

Papa paused on the porch for a moment. He bent down, gave Lily and Joseph a hug, and told them to be good little children until he came back for them. Then he ran to the buggy and hopped in. The buggy clattered down the driveway. As Lily watched the buggy disappear into the dark, a feeling of forlornness swept through her.

Grandma and Grandpa made a little nest of several thick blankets on their bedroom floor. Grandma tucked Lily and Joseph carefully into the nest, blew out the light, and climbed back into bed.

Lily lay there staring into the dark. She could hear Joseph breathing quietly in his blanket nest beside her. He had already fallen asleep! But then, he was barely four years old. He was just a little boy who didn't understand things like she did. Shadows from the moving branches of the pine trees outside of the window moved eerily across the wall and floor. The big grandfather clock in the downstairs hallway counted down the minutes in loud ticktocks. She could feel a big lump grow in her throat. She wanted to cry.

Something must be wrong with Mama. She hadn't even come to say goodbye before Papa had hurried them off to Grandpa and Grandma's house.

Lily would never sleep tonight. Never.

She turned over once, and it was morning.

❧✗❧

Aunt Susie still lived with Grandma and Grandpa Miller. She was almost as old as Mama, but she didn't seem that old to Lily. She was very patient, and spoke in a slow, thick way. Mama said that Aunt Susie had Down's syndrome. Lily didn't know what that meant, but she was glad that Aunt Susie was her aunt. She liked to play dolls and games with Lily. None of Lily's other aunts were as much fun to spend time with as Aunt Susie. When she came to the breakfast table in the morning and discovered that Lily and Joseph had spent the night, she clapped her hands in delight. Her whole face lit up like a beam of sunshine. Aunt Susie's happiness chased away Lily's worries about Mama.

Lily and Joseph sat on Grandpa's lap at the breakfast table. They combed his long gray beard, flowing like crinkled wires down his chest. "Looks like I will have some good little helpers today," he said. He had a fine voice, Grandpa did. Deep and thoughtful. "I could definitely use some help in my harness shop."

After breakfast Lily and Joseph followed Grandpa to the harness shop near the barn. Lily breathed deeply as she walked into the shop. It smelled like Grandpa—leather and saddle soap and oil. Horse harnesses hung on wall hooks. A big vat sat in the center of the room, filled with warm neats-foot oil. The farmers brought Grandpa their harnesses for dipping once or twice a year. After thirty minutes in the vat, the leather emerged like new, soft and supple. Grandpa lifted a big harness, made for a draft horse, and attached it to several large hooks that hung from cables. The cables were fastened to pulleys so Grandpa could lower the harness into the oil vat. "Stand back so you won't get splashed," he warned Lily and Joseph as he lowered the harness into the vat. He pulled his watch out of his pocket and checked to see the time.

Next, Grandpa took a piece of new leather to sew for a harness. Lily liked to watch Grandpa work at the sewing machine. Suddenly, they heard a *ker-splash!* Grandpa and Lily turned around to see Joseph sitting in the vat, covered with oil, a very surprised look on his small face. He had leaned over the edge to see the harness, lost his balance, and tumbled in.

Grandpa rushed over and scooped him out. Lily trotted behind Grandpa as he hurried to the house with a dripping-with-oil Joseph. Grandma's eyes grew wide as saucers as they entered the kitchen. She pointed to the bathroom. "Put him in the tub," she ordered Grandpa.

Joseph howled like a piglet stuck between fence rails as Grandma scrubbed him down with soap. A person couldn't hear herself think. Lily dashed off to play with Aunt Susie so she didn't have to hear Joseph's wails as Grandma washed his hair again and again and again. Even after Joseph had been scrubbed and dried and stuffed into the pajamas he wore last night, Lily was sure she caught whiffs of neats-foot oil whenever she stood near him.

Grandma took Joseph's greasy clothes and put them in

the trash. "They were soaked in so much oil that they could never be cleaned," she said, dusting her hands together the way she always did when she was making up her mind. Lily wished Joseph hadn't fallen into that vat. Grandma said that Lily and Joseph couldn't go back to the harness shop with Grandpa today. She said Grandpa had had enough excitement for one day.

Now Lily couldn't watch Grandpa hoist the harness out of the vat and help him wipe it with a rag to make it look shiny and new again. It was all because Joseph was too curious. Little boys were difficult that way.

There was a knock on the door. Grandma washed off her hands and went to open the door to see who had come to visit. And there stood Papa! He had a great big smile on his face. Lily jumped up from the chair and ran to meet Papa.

"We have a little baby boy," Papa said, reaching down to greet Lily and Joseph.

Lily jumped up and down in excitement. "Can we keep him?"

Papa grinned. "We'll keep him!" He stroked the top of Lily's head. "Let's go home and you can see him for yourself." He turned to Grandma. "We named him Daniel, but we'll call him Dannie."

"That's a fine name," Grandma said. She looked pleased.

Lily whispered the baby's name to herself. *Dannie*. She liked the name and not just because it was Papa's name.

The ride home was much better in the daytime than it had been in the dark. Jim trotted along briskly. His mane and tail blew gracefully in the wind. The buggy swayed comfortably. The birds sang their cheerful songs. Lily thought it sounded as if they were saying, "Dannie, Dannie."

"Where did you get the baby?" Lily said.

Papa glanced over at her. His cheeks colored up as he took his time answering. "God brought him to us."

Lily clasped her hands at that thought. How wonderful that God had taken time to bring a baby to them! "Is God still there?" she asked hopefully. But Papa said no, she couldn't see God today.

What a disappointment! Lily wished she had been home to meet God when He stopped by the house to bring a baby. The thought of meeting God was even more exciting than having a new baby.

When they reached home, Lily and Joseph helped Papa unhitch Jim from the buggy. Papa led Jim into the rickety old barn where he removed his harness and left him in his stall. Papa wanted to knock down this old barn and build a new one soon.

As they climbed up the porch stairs that led to the house, Papa cautioned Lily and Joseph to be very quiet. Lily removed her heavy black bonnet and hung it on a hook next to Joseph's little straw hat. After they had washed their hands, they tiptoed into Mama's bedroom. Next to Mama in the bed was a little bundle, all wrapped up in blankets. Lily peeked at the baby.

Why, it was the ugliest little baby Lily had ever seen!

His face was all red and wrinkly. His head was bald. Lily didn't know what to say as Papa lifted the baby carefully out of Mama's arms. He asked Lily to sit in the rocking chair next to the bed. Very gently, he placed the baby in her arms. "Say hello to your brother Dannie."

"Hello," Lily whispered. She looked at the tiny fingers, with tiny nails. The baby opened his eyes and started making funny whimpering little noises. He turned his head and tried to stuff his tiny little fist into his mouth.

"I think he's hungry," Papa said as he lifted the baby from her lap and handed him back to Mama.

Lily was glad to scoot off the rocking chair and go out to the living room to play with her own sweet little rag doll, Sally. What a huge disappointment! Of all the babies to choose from in the world, she couldn't understand why God had chosen to give them an ugly one.

Mama's Crabby Helper

*L*ily woke to the sound of someone working in the kitchen. Rubbing the sleep from her eyes, she climbed down the ladder of her bunk bed. Joseph was still sound asleep in the lower bunk. Lily tiptoed quietly to her closet to get her favorite play dress. It was light brown with five bright red buttons down the back. She could fasten the top button by herself, but Mama would have to help with the rest.

Lily loved getting up early to help Mama make breakfast. As she skipped down the stairs, she was surprised to see a stranger at Mama's stove. This woman was tall and skinny, with stooped shoulders and a red face. Lily paused at the door, watching and waiting, not sure if she wanted to go into the kitchen or not. Where was Mama? Then she remembered. Mama had a little baby. Quietly, she tiptoed away from the kitchen before the stranger could notice her. She hurried up-stairs to see if Mama was still in bed.

Lily knocked on her parents' bedroom door. She was relieved to hear Mama's sweet voice call out to her to come in. Mama was sitting up in bed. Baby Dannie was sleeping in a little white bassinet right beside her. His eyes were scrunched shut and his little wrinkly fist peeped out of the light blue and white polka-dot blanket. Lily walked over to Mama to have her button her dress.

"You're up early this morning," Mama said. "Do you want to come see the baby?"

Lily shook her head. "I wanted to help you make breakfast. But there is someone else in the kitchen."

"She's a helper named Frieda Troyer," said Mama. "She has agreed to stay with us for a while so that we can spend our time enjoying our new baby." Mama smiled at Lily. "I'm sure Frieda would be glad to have a little helper in the kitchen."

Lily hesitated. She had a funny feeling that Frieda might not be as glad to have a helper as Mama thought. But she went downstairs to the kitchen and found Frieda looking through all the cupboards. Shyly, Lily said, "I can set the table for you."

Frieda spun around and peered at Lily through her big thick spectacles. "I can take care of it myself. Run along and look at some books until breakfast is ready."

Lily went into the living room to get her doll, Sally, and sit on the couch. No one had lit the oil lamp yet so she couldn't see well enough to look at a book. Holding Sally close, she waited for Papa to come into the house after he fed Jim. From where she sat, she could see Frieda bustling around the kitchen, rearranging the things in the cupboards. She clinked and clanked and banged the dishes as she set the table.

Lily wanted to tell Frieda Troyer to go home and leave Mama's things alone. She was glad when Papa finally came in from the barn. He would tell Frieda to leave Mama's cupboards alone. But Papa didn't say anything. Not a word. He went over to the washbasin to wash his hands. After they were clean, he scooped up big handfuls of water and splashed it over his face. Frieda watched him, frowning, as little droplets of water splashed on the sink and floor.

When breakfast was ready, Papa filled Mama's plate with scrambled eggs, toast, and a big spoonful of liverwurst. Lily thought it was disgusting that Frieda would serve liverwurst for breakfast. She followed Papa as he took the tray to Mama in the bedroom. She told Mama what Frieda Troyer was doing to the cupboards. Mama exchanged a look with Papa.

She turned to Lily. "I guess you'll have to help me put everything back into place after Frieda goes home. But that will be our little secret. Okay?"

Lily smiled and nodded. It would be fun to keep a secret. Whenever she saw Frieda putting wrong things in the wrong cupboards, she would think of the secret she and Mama were keeping.

Every single day, Frieda told Lily and Joseph to get out of her way. She wanted to keep the house nice and didn't like it when they sat at their little table in the living room to color in their coloring books or put their puzzles together. She didn't like it when Joseph played with his toy animals or when Lily sat on the couch to play with her doll. She didn't even like it when they sang songs. Too noisy, she said. It hurt her ears.

Lily thought she had never seen anyone who didn't like so many things. The only thing Frieda liked to do was clean house and rearrange cupboards. And serve liverwurst for breakfast. Disgusting! Lily wrinkled her nose at the very thought of liverwurst.

So Lily and Joseph spent most of their days in Mama's

19

bedroom. Mama didn't mind if they played with their toys or talked and laughed and sang. She helped them sing songs and sat on her rocking chair to read stories to them. But best of all, Lily liked to help take care of baby Dannie. He was finally starting to get cute. She talked and crooned to him just like Mama did. Dannie would look at her with his big blue eyes and tuck his hands under his chin. Lily liked to hold his tiny hands and count his fingers.

On Sunday afternoons, visitors would come to the house to see Mama and baby Dannie. They would hold Dannie and say he looked just like Mama or Papa. Lily thought that was such a silly thing to say. Baby Dannie had no hair and no teeth. He looked like a baby, not like Mama or Papa. The visitors would bring a baby card and a few little toys. Mama would let Lily place the toys carefully on the dresser. There

were baby books, teething rings, rattles, homemade strings of pretty colored beads and little squeaky animals. Dannie was too small to play with them now, Mama told her. But when Dannie grew older, Mama would take the toys to church for him to play with while the ministers preached their long sermons.

At last, the day came when Frieda Troyer packed her suitcase. It was time for her to leave! Papa paid her and thanked her for helping out. She picked up her suitcase and walked out the door, down the walkway to where a taxi was waiting to drive her home. Lily climbed on a chair to look out the window and watch Frieda leave. As soon as the taxi disappeared around the bend in the driveway, Lily slid off the chair. She didn't know what she wanted to do first! She held her arms out and started spinning in happy circles until she was dizzy and collapsed, giggling on the floor. Joseph joined in and they both spun in circles. It was so nice not to have Frieda frown at them or tell them to stop! Lily was so happy she couldn't hold still! Mama smiled at Lily and Joseph from the rocking chair where she held baby Dannie. Lily wondered how Mama could remain calm. Lily felt as if her feet wanted to dance and jump and hop through the house.

Later in the evening, Papa sat in his big creaky rocking chair and held Lily and Joseph on his lap. Mama rocked Dannie in her rocking chair. It was wonderful to hear Papa and Mama laugh and talk again. Lily snuggled into Papa's strong arms and sighed with happiness. Everything in her world was right again. And tomorrow, she would help Mama start putting everything in the cupboards back to where they had been before Frieda had come.

Papa's Disappearing Shovel

On a warm, sunny April morning, Lily and Joseph were playing in the sandbox in the yard. A loud roar startled them. They looked up to see a big white truck come bouncing into sight at the bottom of the long driveway. Behind it rolled another truck, lurching around the bend. Stacked on the back of the trucks were piles of lumber.

Lily watched as the trucks came to a shuddering stop in front of the house. Papa walked over to talk to the truck drivers. He pointed toward Jim's pasture while he spoke with the men. Lily wished she could hear what Papa was saying! Something was going to happen and she couldn't tell what.

After Papa finished talking to the truck drivers, they drove the trucks over to Jim's pasture. One man climbed on the back of the truck and started handing lumber, one piece at a time, to the other man waiting below. The man on the ground carried the lumber over to Papa. He stacked the lumber in neat piles on the ground. After the men emptied the trucks, they said goodbye to Papa and drove back down the driveway. Lily was glad when the noisy trucks were gone. They had been so loud that she couldn't hear the birds sing in the trees. She couldn't hear Mama sing through the open windows as she moved about the house.

Lily dropped the little shovel that she had been using to dig a pond in the sandbox. She held Joseph's hand and the two ran to Papa. He was whistling a happy little tune while straightening the piles of lumber. He smiled at them. "Well, children, what do you think? Does this look like a barn?"

Lily giggled. To her, it did not look like anything but boards.

Papa pushed his hat back and wiped sweat off of his brow with his shirtsleeve. "Looks like a lot of work before it will be a barn. We'll have to see if we can organize a frolic."

"What's a frolic, Papa?" Joseph said.

Lily knew! She answered before Papa had a chance to explain. "It's when everyone comes to help you work."

Papa smiled at her. He understood. She was the big sister. She knew these things.

Later that day, Lily and Joseph were in the kitchen, watching Mama make molasses cookies. Through the window, Lily saw Papa hitch Jim to the little open buggy and tie him to the hitching post. He came into the kitchen. "I'm ready to go invite people to the frolic. Would Lily and Joseph like to come along?"

Lily and Joseph looked up at Mama. They knew Papa's question was directed to her, not to them.

"They had their naps already," Mama said, eyes smiling. "I think they might like to go."

Lily ran to get her black heavy bonnet off the wall peg. She tried to stand still as Mama tied the strings in a neat little bow beneath her chin, but it was so hard and the bonnet was so big. She skipped happily beside Papa as they walked to the buggy. Papa lifted Joseph to the seat and then boosted Lily up. Joseph had to sit in the middle, between Papa and Lily, so he wouldn't fall off while they were driving down the road. He was just a little boy. Barely four.

Lily loved riding in the open buggy. As Jim trotted down the road, she could see everything around her so much better than when she was in the top buggy. Big thistle plants grew in the ditches along the road. Goldfinches flew in funny little bouncing swoops from one thistle to the next, gathering seeds to eat.

Looking down, Lily could watch the wheels turn around and around. When Jim trotted, the spokes whirled into a blur, but when he slowed to walk up a hill, the spokes turned slowly. Papa whistled cheerfully as they drove along. Suddenly, Jim blew his nose in a loud snort. A wet spray blew back at Papa, Lily, and Joseph, splattering their face and arms. Papa's whistle died on his lips as he wiped off his face. Lily knew Jim didn't do it on purpose. Secretly, she thought it would be fun to be a horse and be able to blow her nose like that, whenever she wanted to.

As they reached the first Amish neighbor, Papa pulled the buggy up to the hitching post. He tied Jim's rope to the post and told Lily and Joseph to stay in the buggy. He was going to find someone to invite to the barn-building frolic.

As Papa disappeared, Lily gathered up the reins and pretended to drive the buggy. "Giddyup! Whoa!" she told Jim. Joseph wanted to drive too, so she handed him a rein. "Giddyup!" they shouted to Jim.

The gentle horse turned his head and looked back at them but didn't budge. Jim knew that Papa wasn't there. He was too well trained to try to leave without Papa.

When Papa returned, he took the reins back from Lily

and Joseph. He told them never to play with a horse's reins. "Even a nice horse like Jim might not like it."

All afternoon, Papa drove the buggy from one neighbor to another, until everyone in their entire church was invited to come to the frolic on Saturday.

Lily and Joseph sat on top of a little mound of dirt and watched as Papa and Mama pounded little wooden stakes into the ground. Papa wanted to square off the foundation of the barn before the frolic, so that it would be built straight and solid. Baby Dannie kicked his feet and cooed as he lay on his back in the baby carriage beside Lily. He tried to swat at strings of colorful beads that Mama pinned to the roof of the carriage for him.

Lily liked sitting on the little mound. It was several inches higher than the rest of the yard. There was another mound just like it closer to the house. Papa thought those mounds were a nuisance and an eyesore. Soon, he would try to level them. "Whoever did the landscaping around here must have been in a hurry," Papa said. "He sure didn't care what he was doing."

Papa pounded the last stake into the ground. After double-checking that the barn foundation was properly measured off, he picked up his shovel and walked to the house. Lily and Joseph ran ahead of him. As he stepped on the little mound where Lily and Joseph had been playing, his leg suddenly disappeared! Mama screamed and reached for Papa's hands. He managed to pull his leg out of the mound, but his shovel fell into the hole. *Ker-splash!* Lily could hear the shovel hit water far below.

Mama began to cry. Papa held her close to him and patted her shoulder. "It's all right, Rachel," he said soothingly. "No one was hurt."

Mama's face was white. "Oh, Daniel!" she whispered. "The children had just been sitting there! Think how often they've played on top of those mounds! How could we not have realized it was an old well? It was an accident just waiting to happen!"

"I must say it gave me quite a stir," Papa said in a soothing voice. "A man gets kind of used to having the ground stay solid under his feet." His face brightened. "But this solves the problem of how we will get water to the barn. I'll get this old well fixed up nice." He looked around at the mound. "Until then, I'd better do something to keep anyone else from falling through."

Papa removed the rest of the dirt and rotten boards. Hands on his hips, he stood gazing at the big, gaping hole in the yard. "I'm guessing there's an old well under that other mound too." He went into the basement to get another shovel. He started digging at the other mound. Once again, he found rotten boards covering an old well. This well, though, was bone dry. Not a drop of water was in it.

Lily and Joseph watched as Papa built covers for the wells and placed them over the holes. "That will have to do until I have more time." He tested each cover to make sure it didn't move and it could hold his weight.

Lily shuddered at how easily she and Joseph and baby Dannie could have fallen into the deep, dark, scary well. They might have disappeared and never been seen or heard from again. How sad! It was a dreadful thought.

❦

A few days later, Lily and Joseph sat on the back of the bouncing spring wagon as Papa drove Jim across the field. The grass came up all the way to Jim's belly. If Lily held her hands over the side of the spring wagon, she could brush the tops of the grass with her fingers. Papa was taking them to the edge of the woods for a big pile of rocks and stones. He wanted to fill the spring wagon with the rocks. He would use the rocks to fill up the dry well. If it was filled to the top with rocks, no little boy or girl could fall into it and disappear.

When they reached the rock pile, Papa hopped off the spring wagon and lifted Lily and Joseph down. He didn't have to tie Jim when he was working; he was such a good horse that he stood quietly wherever Papa left him. Besides, out in the field, if Jim wanted to take a few steps, it wouldn't matter.

Papa started throwing rocks on the back of the spring wagon. Lily and Joseph picked up smaller stones and tossed them into the wagon. Lily's hands felt dirty and grimy after the first couple handfuls, but she enjoyed being a help to Papa.

Papa whistled as he worked, and before long the spring wagon was filled with rocks. As they drove to the yard, Lily sat on the front seat with Papa while he held Joseph on his lap. Papa stopped Jim beside the dry well and removed the cover. He climbed into the back of the spring wagon and started pitching the rocks into the hollow well.

It took many trips to the rock pile before the dry well was filled to the top. Once it was full, Papa unhitched Jim and let him rest in the pasture. Then Papa filled a wheelbarrow with dirt and dumped the dirt on top of the rocks in the well. When he was satisfied that the well was filled and solid, he scattered some grass seeds on top. Soon grass would grow and no one would ever know that there had once been a well on that spot.

And no little girl would have to worry about falling into it.

A New Barn for Papa

On Saturday morning, Lily had eaten breakfast and helped Mama wash the dishes before the sun started to tint the eastern sky with its rosy colors. All that was left to do was to sweep the kitchen floor. Then they would be ready to have neighbors come for the frolic! As Lily held the dustpan for Mama to sweep the dirt pile into it, she heard the sound of buggy wheels in the driveway. She ran to the window and saw her cousins Hannah and Levi jump out of the buggy. Behind Hannah came Aunt Mary, Mama's younger sister.

Hannah was just a little older than Lily. She had blonde hair and dark blue eyes fringed with long, black lashes. Hannah was Lily's favorite cousin. They had special games they played with their favorite dolls. Levi had the same blond hair and blue eyes as his sister, but he didn't talk much, not like Hannah. Hannah did enough talking for both of them, Uncle Elmer—Hannah's father—always said. Levi was older than Hannah and Lily, but he had a slight stutter when he talked that made him shy around grown-ups. He was more comfortable with Joseph and ran off to find him.

Uncle Elmer drove the buggy out toward the lumber piles. He unhitched his horse from the buggy and tied the rope to a tree. Then he walked over to talk to Papa, who was stuffing nails into the nail belt around his waist. Uncle Elmer strapped his nail belt on and started to fill it with nails.

From the window, Lily and Hannah watched as more buggies started to roll up the long driveway. The men would stop to let the women and children off at the house and then drive out to where Uncle Elmer had parked his buggy. Soon there was a whole row of buggies lined up side by side in the yard. Horses were tied to trees. Some of the younger boys went to get several bales of hay. They dropped handfuls of hay in front of each horse so it would have something to eat. For the horses, it was going to be a long day of waiting.

In the kitchen, women started to prepare food. Potatoes needed to be peeled. Chicken needed to be fried. Fresh bread needed to be baked so it could be served hot from the oven at noon. Lily and Hannah watched the women cook for a while, then ran outside to see how much progress the men had made on the barn. The first wall had been pieced together. It lay on the ground, ready to be lifted. The men lined up along one side. Walking slowly toward the barn's foundation, they lifted the wall. The wall went higher and higher until it stood straight to the sky. A few men quickly ran to make supports and props to keep the wall from falling while others went to work on building the next wall.

Odd noises filled the air. Hammers pounded nails, handsaws cut pieces of lumber into proper lengths. Men called orders out to each other. Lily couldn't decide where the best place was to be: outside as the barn started to grow or in the house as food was prepared.

Mama came to the door and called, "Lily!" In her hands were large bowls. Lily ran to see what she wanted. Mama held the bowls out to Lily. "Set these bowls on the bench under the cedar trees and fill them with water. It's almost time to eat and the men need a place to wash up."

Lily and Hannah dragged a water hose to the bench and filled the bowls with fresh water. When they were done, they stacked several towels beside each bowl. It was time to go tell Papa that dinner was ready. She ran to find Papa. He stopped hammering when he saw her.

"Mama says it's time to eat!" Lily said.

Papa turned and hollered to the men that dinner was ready. The sounds of pounding hammers stopped as everyone started removing their tool belts and walked toward the house. "Sure smells good," they said as they passed Lily.

The men piled their straw hats on the ground under a tree and went to wash up. Their big hands scooped up water to splash over their faces. Lily and Hannah watched as they reached for towels to dry off. Water dripped from their long beards and trickled down the front of their shirts.

The men went into the house. The women bustled about, dishing up food and setting steaming bowls filled with mashed potatoes and sweet corn on the table, next to large platters of crisp fried chicken. Another platter held freshly baked bread, still warm from the oven. Beside each loaf of bread sat two little dishes. One held a round ball of homemade butter and the other was filled with sweet clover honey. On the kitchen counter was a row of pies: beautiful brown pecan pie, lemon and vanilla pie piled high with fluffy whipped cream, cherry pie with sugar sprinkled on the crust. Lily liked how the cherries peeped through the little holes in the pretty vine pattern that Mama had carefully made on each crust.

Lily's mouth watered as her eyes took in all the food. She wished she could sit at the table too, but there wasn't enough room. Only the men and the bigger boys could sit at the table. Once they found a seat, everyone grew quiet and looked expectantly at Papa. Papa bowed his head to pray a silent blessing.

As soon as he raised his head, everyone started talking and laughing as they passed bowls of food around the table. They spooned hearty helpings on their plates. Mama filled plates with food for the children and sent them outside to sit on the porch to eat. Once everyone was done eating, the men went back to work while the women started cleaning up the dirty dishes.

Papa stopped for a moment in the yard. He picked up a bench and folded one leg in. He set the other end on top of an overturned washtub. A slide! Lily loved playing on Papa's homemade slides. She hurried to line up behind the other children. One by one, they took turns sliding down the smoothly varnished bench.

After all of the dishes had been cleaned and put away, the women brought chairs and benches out into the yard under the shade of the cedar tree. They sat and chattered while keeping one eye peeled on the children. And they could watch the barn steadily grow.

As the sun began to set, the barn was finished. It looked beautiful with its shiny white sides and its dark green tin roof. It was time for the neighbors to go home, do chores, and get ready for Sunday church. The men hitched horses to buggies and drove up to the house to pick up their families. Lily waved goodbye as the buggies rolled down the driveway.

Papa and Mama stood in front of the house and looked toward the new barn. "Makes it feel like it's really our home now that we have a barn," Papa said. "Think we should go check it out?"

Lily and Joseph held Papa's hands and tried to match his steps. Mama followed with Dannie in her arms. Pausing at the barn door, Papa waited to let Mama step inside first. When they all stood inside, Lily thought the barn looked enormous! The stall for Jim had a nice manger for his hay and a little feed box where Papa could dump a scoopful of oats. Next to Jim's stall was a bigger pen with a low manger and a big wooden box on the floor. Next to that was a small pen with a long wooden trough.

"We'll fill those pens with a few piglets and a cow, and then we'll be set," Papa said. "We'll have a real farm."

Against a wall, Lily noticed a wooden ladder that led to a square hole in the ceiling. Papa said he would use the ladder to go up and throw hay bales down when he needed them. Lily saw a door near the ladder. She opened the door to discover a large room, with its floor covered in carefully raked gravel. "That room is for the buggies," Papa said. The little open buggy, the top buggy, and the spring wagon.

Papa and Mama walked through the barn one more time. "Why don't we get Jim's stall ready?" Papa said. He went outside and brought back a straw bale. He set the bale down, reached into his pocket and pulled out his pocketknife, and cut the twine that held the straw together.

Papa gave one slice of straw to Lily and another to Joseph. He showed them how to shake the straw until it fell apart to make a fluffy pile on the floor of the stall. Soon, the floor was covered in thick straw and Jim could have a soft place to stand, instead of the tumble-down barn he'd been in. Papa

put a few slices of hay in the manger and Mama put a scoop-ful of oats into the little wooden feed box. Everything was ready for Jim.

Papa went out to the pasture and whistled for Jim. The big horse trotted up to the fence to see what Papa wanted. Papa held out his hand, filled with sweet-tasting oats. Jim ate gently from Papa's hand as Papa reached for the halter and led him into the barn and into his new stall.

Jim went right to the manger to eat oats and hay as if he had been coming into this new barn every day of his life. Papa chuckled as he went to get the currycomb and brush. "Jim doesn't know how lucky he is to move into this nice barn before winter!" He brushed Jim down, then closed up the stall for the night.

33

As the family walked back to the house, Lily was surprised by how quiet the farm was after such a noisy, busy day. She heard an owl hoot once, then twice. Another answered back. It seemed to Lily that birds kept on singing as if they didn't know that anything special had happened that day.

But it had! It had been a wonderful day.

Jenny the Cow

Spring was in the air. As Mama dug a long, shallow furrow in the garden, the hoe made pleasant little clinking sounds. Whenever Mama hit a stone, she would pause to set it beside the furrow and Lily and Joseph would run to pick it up. They put the stones in the wheelbarrow that stood at the edge of the garden.

After Mama created a furrow, she showed Lily how to plant sweet corn seeds. She dropped two seed kernels, placed her foot in front of the seeds in the furrow to measure off a distance, then dropped two more. Step, drop, step, drop. High up in a tree, a big black bird squawked angrily and another one answered back. Mama shielded her eyes and looked up at the bird. "Lily, have I ever taught you a little planting rhyme that my mother taught me?

> One for the cutworm
> One for the crow
> One to rot and one to grow."

Mama handed the bag of seeds to Lily. It was her turn to sow! Carefully, slowly, Lily walked along the furrow, dropping seeds in front of her toes. She loved wiggling her toes in the soft, cool earth. Step, drop, step, drop. The warm sun shone on her back as she made her way along the furrow.

As Lily finished dropping seeds into the first row, Mama set the stakes for a new furrow. She left enough space between furrows so that Papa could easily get the tiller between the rows after the corn grew tall. She fastened a string to the stakes and pulled it taut, then dug another furrow.

Lily liked it when everyone helped Mama in the garden. Joseph's job was to pick up stones. Baby Dannie's job was to sit in his stroller and play with his toys. Mama started to hum "Jesus Loves Me," and soon they were all singing the words. All except Dannie. He only made "Bah, bah, bah, bah, bah" sounds. He thought he was singing.

Lily noticed a buggy turn into the driveway. She shielded her eyes from the sun and saw Grandma Miller in her open buggy, driving slowly. Ever so slowly! Grandpa Miller sat in the back of the buggy, legs hung over the edge. In his hands was a rope. At the end of the rope was a fawn-colored cow with big brown eyes, walking behind the buggy. Grandpa hopped off the back and brought the cow to Mama. He handed her the rope.

"Happy birthday, Rachel."

Tears filled Mama's eyes. "Oh, Daddy!" she said, her voice low and quivery. "A little Jersey cow. We've been hoping to get a cow someday!"

Mama led the cow into the barn, with everyone following close behind. Grandma Miller pushed Dannie's stroller. Mama put the cow into a pen Papa had made for the someday cow. "I think we'll call her Jenny," Mama said.

Jenny. Lily tried the name out loud a few times. The cow blinked twice and batted her big thick eyelashes at Lily when she heard the name. That settled it. Jenny had a name.

Grandpa climbed up the hayloft ladder and threw down bales of hay and straw. Lily and Joseph shook the straw into the pen to make a nice soft bed for Jenny. Mama put hay into the manger. They watched the cow settle into her new home, then they went back outside. Grandpa grabbed a shiny stainless steel milk pail he had hidden in the buggy and gave it to Mama. As Mama held it up, Lily and Joseph made faces into the pail and laughed at the funny way the pail twisted their reflections.

Then Grandma reached under the buggy seat and brought out a box. In it was a birthday cake covered with fluffy white frosting. Lily and Joseph exchanged a glance. It looked delicious! They were suddenly hungry. Practically *starving.*

Grandma noticed. She raised a thin eyebrow. "Not quite yet," she told them. She turned to Mama. "I see you're planting your garden. Can we help?"

"I have several rows of sweet corn to plant and I still need to set out the tomato plants," Mama said.

Oh. Lily and Joseph exchanged a glance. The cake eating had just been postponed.

Grandpa found a shovel and got right to work in the garden. It didn't take long to plant the rest of the sweet corn. Grandpa and Mama made the furrows while Lily dropped the seeds and Grandma followed behind her to cover the seeds gently with fine soil. Joseph ran around picking up stones in the garden and picking up the toys Dannie dropped from his stroller.

Now it was time for the tomatoes. Fifty tomato plants! Grandpa set several big pails, filled with water, beside the garden. He pushed the shovel into the ground and rocked it back and forth until there was a nice deep crack in the ground. Mama got a box of Epsom salt and showed Lily how to carefully measure a tablespoon into the crack. She covered the salt with a few inches of soil, then slipped the roots of a tomato plant into the crack. Joseph poured a cup full of water into the crack. Mama filled it up with loose dirt and packed it firmly and gently around the tomato plant. Over and over they planted, until all fifty little tomato plants were set in two nice straight rows.

When the last tomato plant was planted, Mama stood and brushed dirt from her apron. She laughed at the dirty

smudges her hands made on the apron. "It looks like we all need to go wash up."

Grandma gazed at the garden. "It's always such a good feeling to have the garden planted."

Lily stood beside her. The neat rows of tomato plants stood tall along the garden's edge. At the opposite end, green peas were already several inches tall, and rows of onions, lettuce, and radish were coming along nicely. Soon the sweet corn, beans, and potatoes would poke through the ground, and all of the brown dirt would be covered with a carpet of green.

Grandma said it was time to help start supper. "Uncle Elmer and Aunt Mary will be coming tonight to help celebrate your birthday."

Mama looked pleased.

Lily kept one eye on the window as she helped set the table. She couldn't wait until Uncle Elmer's horse and buggy arrived! She wanted to show Hannah and Levi the new cow. What was taking them so long? *Hurry, hurry, hurry!* she thought. *I have a surprise in the barn!* But there was no sign of them.

She went to the kitchen to see what Joseph was so interested in. He stood on a chair, watching Grandma mix something in a bowl. Lily peeped into the bowl. Oh, what a beautiful sight! Grandma was stirring sugary pink frosting. She watched as Grandma folded a square of waxed paper into a triangle and then rolled it up to make a funnel shape. After Grandma had spooned frosting into it, she folded the top and squeezed. She had turned it into a pen! A big fat pen with pink frosting for ink. She wrote pink letters on top of the white frosted cake.

"What does it say?" Joseph said. Of course, he was just a little boy and he couldn't read yet.

Grandma smiled. "Happy Birthday, Rachel."

"It should say: Happy Birthday, Mama," Lily whispered to Joseph.

Grandma chuckled and added "(Mama)" under "Rachel." Now it was perfect. The little ( )s looked like a hug for Mama.

Lily heard light footsteps clamber on the porch steps and turned to see Hannah at the door. She had been so interested in watching Grandma decorate the cake that she had forgotten to watch for Uncle Elmer's buggy! She ran to the door, grabbed Hannah's hand, and pulled her down to the barn to see the cow. Jenny kept her head bowed, blinking her huge brown eyes as if she was listening to Lily and Hannah's compliments about her.

After a few minutes, the girls grew bored, so they went up to the house, sat on the porch swing, and played with their dolls.

Lily couldn't wait for Papa to come home and discover there was a cow in the barn! It felt like a very long time before an old rusty pickup drove up the driveway. Papa hopped out of the truck and Lily ran to meet him. He always gave her his lunch box when he came home from his carpentry job. He saved a bite or two of his sandwich for her and Joseph to share. Today, there was even half of a cookie.

Papa lifted several large boxes from the back of the truck and set them on the grass. He waved goodbye to the driver of the truck. Then he turned to Lily. "Run into the house and tell Mama to come and see what I have."

When Mama followed Lily outside, she looked at the boxes with a question in her eyes.

"Go ahead and open them, Rachel," Papa said. "After all, it's your birthday." He was beaming, positively beaming.

Cautiously, Mama opened the boxes. Lily and Hannah

gasped in delight. In the boxes were black-and-grey-speckled hens. "First a cow and now chickens!" Lily said. She was thrilled. Their home was turning into a real farm. Then she clasped her hands over her mouth. Papa didn't know there was a cow in the barn yet. She had told! She had told Mama's surprise.

Papa laughed out loud at Lily's mortified look. "Well, it's about time we were settled in to stay."

Mama hooked her hands on her hips. "You knew? You knew about the cow?"

A broad smile creased Papa's face and his blue eyes twinkled. "Grandpa had told me he wanted to give you a cow for your birthday. It was a pretty big secret to keep, though." He saw Grandpa and Uncle Elmer on the porch. "I have a hunch they wouldn't mind helping me build a little chicken coop before supper."

Before supper? But what about eating the birthday cake? Lily sighed. Postponed *again*.

Behind the barn, Papa selected a few boards from a pile of lumber. He measured and cut the wood, Grandpa and Uncle Elmer pounded nails. It wasn't long before a brand-new chicken coop stood proudly next to the barn. Papa built a little ramp on hinges for the chickens to get in and out of the coop. At the side was a regular-sized door for Mama to use when she gathered eggs or fed the chickens. Papa fastened a narrow board inside the coop for the chickens to roost on at night. Tomorrow he would build some nesting boxes and fasten chicken wire all around the coop so Mama's chickens would be able to be outside without being bothered by dogs or cats. Or worse.

Lily and Hannah ran to the house to tell Mama her chicken coop was ready. She met them with the stainless steel milk pail. Her milking apron was already tied around her waist. She had another pail filled with warm, soapy water. Over her shoulder hung a clean rag. "It's time to go milk Jenny."

Oh no! The birthday cake eating had just been delayed *again.* Lily's tummy was rumbling. She couldn't stop thinking about that sweet pink frosting. What did pink taste like?

In the cool barn, Mama scooped two big cups of sweet molasses-coated grain into Jenny's feed trough. She plucked the three-legged milking stool from the nail on the wall. Mama sat on the stool and set the pail under Jenny, carefully washing her udder. Lily and Hannah's job was to hold Jenny's tail so she wouldn't swat Mama's face while she was getting milked. The first streams of milk made a pleasant zinging sound as they hit the bottom of the pail. As the pail filled with warm, frothy milk, the zinging sound disappeared. Out of nowhere, barn cats materialized, carefully watching Mama. Somehow, they seemed to know they would be getting a nice bowlful of fresh steaming milk once she was finished. That was the way it was with cats. Never around when you were looking for them, always around at mealtime.

Sweet and gentle, Jenny stood patiently as Mama milked her. After she finished eating her grain, she chewed her cud. When Mama had squeezed the last drops of milk into the pail, she poured milk into a dish for the cats. Lily liked watching their cute little pink tongues lap up the milk.

In the kitchen, Mama strained the milk through a piece of organdy cloth into a glass gallon jar. She set the jar in cold water in the sink so the milk would cool off quickly and stay nice and sweet.

Grandma Miller had supper all ready for them. The family gathered around the table and enjoyed Mama's favorite birthday dinner: crispy fried chicken with clouds of mashed potatoes and green garden peas. And afterward . . . they all enjoyed the birthday cake with the pink icing. Lily, most of all.

Pink, she decided, tasted just like she thought it would. Sweet and happy and soft. Almost as good as purple.

CHAPTER

6

The Mean Neighbor

One morning, Lily and Joseph were helping Mama pull weeds in the garden when a big car drove up. An old man wearing overalls jumped out of the car and marched over to Mama. He looked cross. He sounded cross. "There's a Jersey cow in my alfalfa field." He pointed across the field. "Is she yours?"

Mama sent Lily to see if Jenny was in her pen. When Lily ran into the cool, dark barn, she stopped abruptly, blinking fast. She couldn't see! She had been in the bright sunshine all morning. Soon, her eyes adjusted to the dim light. She ran to Jenny's pen. *Empty*.

Lily ran to tell Mama that Jenny had gone missing.

Mama told her to stay on the swing under the trees. "Watch Joseph and Dannie while I go fetch Jenny."

Mama grabbed a rope in the barn and went along with the angry man in his car. He drove a short distance and pulled

44

to the side. Lily could see the car beside a field. She could see Mama get out and walk into the field with the rope. But she still felt lonely and scared without Mama, even with Joseph and Dannie beside her. Lily gently pushed the swing to make it sway back and forth while they waited for Mama to get back. She wanted to cry, but she knew she had to be brave for Joseph and Dannie.

It wasn't long before Mama walked up the road leading Jenny by the rope. Jenny walked behind Mama, slow and steady, with a calm, innocent look in her big brown eyes. She didn't seem at all sorry about the alfalfa she had been eating in the man's field.

Then Jenny caught sight of the barn. Her head jerked up. She decided she wanted to get to her pen, fast, and see if any hay was waiting for her in the manger. She lifted her tail and kicked up her heels, broke into a gallop, and charged for the barn. The rope that Mama held on to Jenny with was wrapped around her hand. She tried to free herself, but Jenny was moving too fast. Lily and Joseph watched, wide-eyed. Lily screamed and jumped off the swing, running toward Mama, as Jenny dragged Mama over the hard ground and into the barn.

Inside the barn, Lily found Jenny in her pen. She was calmly munching hay as if nothing bad had just happened. Mama was leaning against the gate, her apron torn, trying to catch her breath. Then Lily saw Mama's arms. They were cut and bloody from getting dragged over the ground.

Mama limped into the house and sat on her rocking chair. She winced as Lily tried to clean her arms with a wet wash-cloth. Joseph brought a little tub of homemade salve to coat the cleaned cuts. Mama smiled weakly and called them her little heroes.

Later that evening, Lily and Joseph told Papa what had happened as soon as he came through the door. He checked Mama's cut and bruised arms, concerned, told her to sit and rest, to not worry about making supper. He said he was sure that he could cook a meal if Lily and Joseph would help him.

After supper, Papa went out to the barn and made a lock for Jenny's pen. A simple latch wasn't enough to keep a clever cow like Jenny penned up, if she had a mind to wander. On Saturday, Papa said, he would build a fence to pasture Jenny. "No more trips to the neighbor's alfalfa field for you," he scolded her as he double-checked the lock.

Jenny blinked, batting her thick eyelashes at him. It was as if she wanted to answer Papa back: "Who, me?"

Papa was up early on Saturday, digging holes for fence posts. Lily and Joseph had a quick breakfast and ran out to help him. Walking through the woods, Papa strung wire along the fence posts that he had set. Lily and Joseph followed behind. Lily carried a little pail filled with funny horseshoe-shaped nails. Every time they came to a post, she would hand a nail to Papa. He would take it and place it over the wire, give it several taps with his hammer, make sure the wire was fastened tightly to the fence post, then move along to the next one.

At the edge of the woods, Papa dug a deep hole and planted a large corner post with wooden braces. Papa fastened a fence stretcher to the end of the wire. He moved the handle on the fence stretcher back and forth until the wire was so taut that it made funny pinging noises when Lily and Joseph tapped it.

Suddenly, a man appeared, carrying a shotgun. It was the same cross man who had complained about Jenny moseying into his alfalfa field. Now he was angry that Papa was building a fence. He waved his gun and shouted at Papa. Lily grabbed Joseph's hand and hid behind a nearby tree. They peeped out to see what was going to happen next. Would the man shoot Papa? Would he shoot a little boy and a little girl? Lily could feel tears running down her face, but she stood still. As still as a statue.

Papa, though, didn't seem at all frightened. Calmly, he listened to the man. Once the man had finished shouting, Papa asked him where he thought the property line was. The man showed Papa a marked trail. Lily was glad when she saw that Papa's fence didn't touch the trail. But the man told Papa that he didn't like a fence so close to his land. He didn't want animals to reach through the fence and eat his grass.

After the man left, Papa loosened all the little nails that held the wire to the posts. He walked along the entire fence length and undid all the work he had done that morning. Then he pulled all of the fence posts out of the ground. It was hard work, and it was a warm day. Papa looked hot and tired. Still, he kept working. After all of the posts were removed, Papa dug more holes several feet farther away from the little trail. Then, again, he fastened the wire to each post. Now, even if Jenny stretched her neck as far as she could, she would not be able to reach a single blade of the man's grass through the fence. Not one single blade.

That evening, Papa told Mama about the angry man. Mama had spent the day baking and the house smelled of fresh baked bread. Papa said that he had an errand to run after supper and would need to drive past the man's house. "Would you mind if I took a loaf of homemade bread? I'd like to stop at the neighbor's house and give it to him."

Mama wrapped the bread in a nice towel and gave it to Papa.

On the front porch, Lily watched Jim pull the little open buggy with Papa on the wagon seat. The loaf of bread sat beside Papa. Lily felt worried. She hoped that the man had put his gun away before Papa stopped by. She hoped that Jim wouldn't try to eat any grass from the man's yard.

Finally, Papa came home. He said the man's name was Harold Young, and that he had been pleased to accept the loaf of bread. "Every time we think of Harold Young," Papa said, "we will try and think of something nice to say or do for him the next time we see him."

That night, lying in bed, Lily gave Papa's words some serious thought. She scrunched up her face and thought long and hard. She tried to think of one nice thing to say about Harold Young. But nothing came to mind. Lots of mean, horrible things, but nothing nice. Not one nice thought! She had promised Papa she would try. She would just have to try harder. Maybe tomorrow.

Joseph Wants to Fly

*P*apa was full of surprises. One afternoon he came into the kitchen and handed his big red handkerchief to Mama. He had tied the corners together to make a little basket. "Look what I found when I was checking the fence," he said, his eyes twinkling.

Lily stood beside Mama and watched her untie it. What was inside?

Out rolled five big, juicy, dark red plums. Mama looked up at Papa, a smile in her voice. "You found a plum tree!"

She went to get a knife and cut them open. She twisted the plum halves apart to reveal a juicy golden and pink flesh. Lily's mouth watered as Mama handed half of a plum to Papa to eat.

"That is the best plum I've ever tasted," Papa said. "If you have a few empty pails, I'll go pick the rest of them."

"Wait a few minutes and I'll go with you," Mama said.

"The bread is almost done baking and the rest of the work can wait."

Mama cut the rest of the plums into halves and handed them to Lily and Joseph. Lily took tiny bites, savoring the sweet sticky goodness. She tried to make her plum last longer than Joseph's. Joseph gobbled his plum and then watched as Lily slowly finished hers. Lily took even tinier bites. She couldn't help but feel a little smug as Joseph watched her, a hungry look in his brown eyes. Little boys had to learn to not be so greedy.

The oven timer went off and Mama pulled several loaves of beautiful golden bread from the oven.

"Lily, you had better get your shoes and socks on," Papa said. "There are brambles in the woods and I don't want you to hurt your feet."

Sadly, Lily put on her shoes. Papa helped her tie her laces. The shoes made her feet feel heavy and her toes penned in, but it would be a worse feeling to step on prickly brambles with her bare feet.

Lily loved to walk in the woods with Papa. Today, with Mama joining them, it would be even more fun. Mama held Dannie in her arms as they all walked along the new fence that Papa had made. When they came to the creek, they walked along the bank, stepping over fallen tree limbs and dodging bramble bushes. Lily liked to listen to the quiet gurgle of the creek as the water ran over the rocks in the creek bed. Ferns and other woodland plants grew along the banks. Usually, Lily would stop to gather a few ferns and wildflowers to take home to Mama. Today there was something more important to do. Soon, they came to a tree loaded with red plums. Lily thought she had never seen anything look so pretty.

Papa gently shook the tree. Plums dropped to the ground

like fat raindrops! Lily helped pick them up and put them into the pails that Papa had brought along. Lily wished she could eat plums right away, but she knew they had a job to do. The plums were to be gathered and taken into the house.

Joseph picked up a few plums too, but he was more interested in watching birds flit from branch to branch. "I wish I could fly like a bird," he said wistfully, gazing at a robin as it flew to the very top of a tall ash tree and peered down at them.

Papa chuckled. "Running and walking are the best ways for little boys to get around."

Once the pails were filled to the brim with sweet, juicy plums, they headed back to the house. Papa carried the pails into the kitchen. Mama put Dannie down for his nap and started right to work. She cut each plum in half, removed the pit, and dropped it into clean canning jars. She boiled sugar and water into syrup to pour over the plums. Then, she fit each jar with a lid and placed it carefully in the canner, filled with steaming hot water.

Mama saved a bowl of plums to eat fresh. She filled another bowl with plum halves and poured a thick layer of sugar over them. She set the bowl on the back of the kitchen counter. Lily wondered what she was going to do with those.

Mama noticed. "Watch and see, Lily," she said. "Soon, you'll find out."

Mama lit the burner in the oil stove and set the pot of sugared plum halves on top. She stirred and stirred as the plums turned into a thick jam. Mama spooned the jam into little jars and set them on the sink to cool. She took a big square of paraffin wax and carefully shaved pieces off of it into an ugly old battered bowl that she used for melting paraffin. Once it had melted, Mama carefully spooned a little bit of paraffin on top of the plum jam in each of the little jars. The paraffin would harden as it cooled, sealing the jam safely to keep it fresh until it was time to eat.

Lily helped Mama put lids on the jars and carry them to the cool, dark basement, lined with shelves for canned food. Lily thought the glass jars on the shelves looked so pretty. They were filled with sparkling red jam and pieces of plums. In a few days they would go back to the woods to gather more ripe plums. Lily hoped Mama would make more jam. Sweet jam on toast was the best thing to eat. The very best thing of all.

❧×❧

One afternoon in June, Lily and Joseph lay on their backs in the soft grass, watching fluffy white clouds float lazily across the sky. Lily liked imagining all the different shapes the clouds could be. If she squinted her eyes just right, she thought she could see a rabbit. And then a horse. Another cloud looked like a tree with a face.

"Do you see that tree with a face?" she said.

Joseph sat up and looked at the trees in the yard. "No, I don't. Which one is it?"

Lily laughed. "Not a real tree!" She pointed to the sky to help Joseph see which cloud looked like a tree.

"It looks like a big head of lettuce to me." Joseph lay back on the grass and folded his hands behind his neck. "I was watching those big birds fly instead of looking at the clouds. I wish I could fly like that. It looks like fun."

Lily watched the birds. It did look like fun to fly. The birds sailed effortlessly through the sky, hardly moving their wings at all. She yawned. She felt a little sleepy and her eyelids started to feel droopy.

Suddenly, Joseph jumped up. "I'm going to do it!"

Lily's eyes flew open. "Do what?"

"I'm going to fly! I've watched the birds long enough that I think I know how."

"But you don't have any wings," Lily pointed out. "Or feathers, either."

Joseph didn't pay her any mind. He ran behind the barn, so Lily jumped up and ran after him. She caught up with him as he started to climb the pile of lumber that Papa kept stacked behind the barn. Joseph stood at the edge of the stack. He flapped his arms wildly, jumped, and landed on the ground next to her.

"I don't think I flapped my arms fast enough." He clambered up the stack of lumber and tried again. Flap, flap, jump, land. He tried again. Flap, flap, jump, land. He looked disappointed. "I need to find something higher to jump off." He went off to search for something else to climb.

"But you weren't made to fly!" Lily called after him.

Joseph wasn't listening to Lily's logic. He had found just what he needed: the roof of the new chicken coop. It was much higher than the pile of lumber had been. If he could only find a way to climb to the roof, he was convinced he could fly.

"You would need a ladder to get on top of the chicken coop," Lily said.

"Can you help me carry it over here?"

Lily wished she had not said anything about a ladder. "Joseph, I don't think you can fly even if you jump off the chicken coop."

"I'm sure I can. The stack of lumber was just too close to the ground. I couldn't start flying before I landed."

Lily helped him lift the ladder and carry it over to the chicken coop. It was heavy and clumsy and banged their shins as they walked. Every few feet, they had to set it down, rest for a little while, then pick it up again. It took a long time

to carry it to the back of the chicken coop. Once they had it propped up, Joseph climbed up.

Lily watched nervously as Joseph stepped out on the roof. He looked so small up there. His blue shirt was almost the same shade as the sky that framed him. He was a long way from the ground. She was relieved when she heard Mama call out from the house, "Joseph! Hold still until I come. Don't move!" She ran to the coop.

Joseph obeyed and stood quietly until Mama reached the bottom of the ladder. "Hi, Mama! I'm going to fly like a bird today." Flapping his arms, he threw himself into the air, headfirst. Flap, flap, jump, land. This time, he landed on his arm. He crumpled into a heap and let out a wail.

54

Mama gathered him up into her arms. "Oh Joseph, why did you jump? I was coming to help you down safely."

Joseph kept on crying. Lily noticed that his arm seemed to be dangling at an odd angle. Mama saw too. She told Lily to run to Harold Young's house and ask if he could take them to the doctor.

Lily ran as fast as she could. Harold Young's house wasn't very far away, but it seemed to take a long time to get there. Lily was scared. What if Harold Young pointed that big shotgun at her? What would she do? But Mama and Joseph needed help. When Lily reached the door, she knocked, gasping for breath. A plump older lady with warm brown eyes opened the door. Lily peeked around the lady, hoping Harold Young wasn't behind her. She tried to tell the lady what happened, but her breath was still coming in fits and starts and the words jumbled together.

"Slow down and take your time," the lady said.

Lily breathed in and out for a long moment, then tried again. "My brother Joseph hurt his arm and Mama needs to take him to the doctor to get fixed."

"Wait right here," the lady said. She disappeared into the house. Lily waited until she came back outside with her purse and car keys.

The lady held open her car door. "You can ride with me."

Lily slid inside and sat on the seat. The lady said her name was Helen, and that she was married to Harold Young. It was hard to believe that such a friendly, nice woman could be married to Harold Young.

It only took a moment before the car turned into the driveway. Mama was waiting outside the house with Dannie and Joseph, who was still crying. Mama asked Helen Young if she could take them to the doctor, and would she mind if they stopped by Grandpa Miller's so Lily and Dannie could stay there until Mama and Joseph got back. Helen Young didn't mind a bit.

When the car arrived at Grandpa Miller's, Grandma hurried out of the house. She knew something was wrong.

"I think Joseph broke his arm," Mama said. "Can Lily and Dannie stay here while I take Joseph to the doctor?"

Grandma clucked her tongue sympathetically. She looked at Joseph, tears running down his face. He had stopped wailing but was still whimpering. "My, my, Joseph. What a brave little boy you are. The doctor will make you better and I'll take good care of Lily and Dannie until you get back." She took Dannie from Mama's arms. Lily hopped out and closed the car door. The three of them stood for a while, watching the car drive away.

Grandma had Dannie on her hip. "Well, what do we want to do this afternoon?"

For once, Lily couldn't think of anything. She was too worried about Joseph to think of having fun. She felt guilty that Joseph had been hurt. She had helped carry that ladder to the chicken coop.

"Why don't we go bake some chocolate chip cookies for Joseph?" Grandma said.

The whole day brightened. Making something that Joseph would enjoy helped Lily feel less guilty. She followed her grandmother into the house. Grandma found a few toys for Dannie to play with on a blanket on the floor. Lily held the measuring cups, filled with flour and sugar, as Grandma mixed the cookie dough. She gave Lily a few chocolate chips to sample before adding the rest to the mixture. Then they spooned little piles of dough on a cookie sheet. Grandma slid them into the oven. Lily could hardly wait to taste the cookies, hot from the oven. When they were finished baking, she and Grandma sat together at the kitchen table with a tall glass of fresh cold milk and a warm cookie.

"Can I take a few cookies to Grandpa?" Lily asked.

"He would like that." Grandma put a few cookies in a bowl. "Dannie and I will go with you. I don't think Grandpa knows you're here."

Lily carried the cookie bowl carefully as she followed Grandma out to the harness shop. Grandpa was sitting at his big sewing machine, making a new horse harness. He sewed the pieces of leather together carefully with strong thread. Lily took a deep breath as they walked into the shop. She loved the smells of leather and polish.

Grandpa looked up in surprise when he noticed Lily and Dannie with Grandma. "Well, well. Look who came to see me," he said, a wide grin on his face.

Lily handed the cookie bowl to him and said, "I helped Grandma make these cookies."

"You did?" he said. He took a big bite and closed his eyes in delight. "Mmmm!"

Grandma explained to Grandpa what had happened to Joseph. "Joseph will get better and be fine again," Grandpa assured Lily as he stroked her hair. "Don't worry about him. The doctor will take care of him. His arm will heal quickly and be as good as new."

In the kitchen, Lily helped Grandma pick out a nice little dish and place some cookies on it to give to Joseph. They had just finished putting the dish and cookies into a little paper bag when Helen Young's car drove into the driveway with Mama and Joseph.

Lily ran outside to greet them. Joseph's arm was covered with a heavy white cast. In his other hand, he held several stickers. He gave a little kitten sticker to Lily. She smiled and carefully slipped it in her pocket. Grandma joined them at the car with Dannie in her arms. As they drove away, Lily turned in her seat and waved goodbye to Grandma until she couldn't see her anymore. When they arrived at Lily's home, Mama offered to pay Helen Young for taking them to the doctor.

"No, no, I don't need anything at all," Helen Young said. "That's what neighbors do for each other. I was happy to be able to help you."

Mama thanked her again. After Helen Young drove away, they went into the house. So much had happened since this morning! Finally, finally, Lily had some nice thoughts to think about Harold Young. She still didn't think he was a nice man, but he did have a nice wife.

Mama and Her Sister

Clip clop, clip clop. Jim's hooves pounded a steady beat on the hot asphalt. The storm front of the top buggy was open so Lily was able to lean over to braid Jim's long tail as he trotted down the road. Mama held Dannie on her lap. Joseph stood between Mama and Lily, watching Jim's feet. Lily felt hot and sticky. The trees were silent. No birds wanted to sing on this muggy July day. Even the leaves on the trees hung hot and listless. Only the dragonflies were out today, darting about with their big googly eyes and glassy wings.

They were on their way to help Mama's sister, Aunt Mary, in her bulk food store. Lily looked forward to playing with her cousins, Hannah and Levi, while Mama helped Aunt Mary measure out flour and sugar into little bags to sell.

Hannah ran out of the house when she saw Mama drive Jim to the hitching rack. Lily jumped off the buggy. Hannah grabbed Lily's hand and they ran to play with their dolls on the porch swing. Joseph and Levi could find something to play with of their own. Little boys didn't play dolls very well.

Aunt Mary came out of the house to meet Mama and Dannie. Lily thought she looked wilted, like the leaves on the big maple tree next to the house. Lily decided this summer heat must make everything and everyone uncomfortable.

All afternoon, Lily and Hannah played while Mama worked in the little store with Aunt Mary. Too soon, it was time to go home. Lily was sorry to leave Hannah. In the buggy, she chattered to Mama about her day and how much fun she had. Mama seemed extra quiet. Lily peeked around Mama's big black bonnet and saw tears streaming down her cheeks.

Despite the heat, Lily felt a shiver. "What's wrong, Mama?"

"Mary is sick," Mama said quietly. "She has cancer."

Cancer. Lily didn't know what the word meant, but if it made Mama cry, it must be something very horrible.

❧⚬❧

Lily and Joseph loved playing in the barn while Papa worked. Each evening, he would curry Jim or sweep the hay from the hallway. A new litter of kittens had been born recently. Lily thought there was nothing as cute and fun as baby kittens. Every evening she and Joseph would sit on the barn floor and hold the kittens in their lap, stroking them gently as they purred. Sometimes, the kittens were in a playful mood and didn't want to be held very long. They would chase each other around the ladder and hay bales. Lily and Joseph would laugh and laugh, until their sides hurt. Even Papa would stop his work to watch the silly kittens play.

One evening, the kittens ran into the barn where the buggies were kept. Lily and Joseph ran after them. Lily picked a

kitten up in her arms and noticed another one under a wooden pallet. Only its tail peeped from under the pallet. Lily tried to coax it out by stroking its big black tail. My, it had a big bushy tail. Bigger than the kittens' tails. "Here, kitty, kitty, kitty." The cat wouldn't budge. Lily went to find Papa and ask him to help her.

Papa took one glance at the cat's tail that stuck out from the pallet and grabbed Joseph, hoisting him into his arms. "Follow me, Lily! Now!" Papa turned and ran from the barn. The tone in Papa's voice was alarming. Lily ran after him.

Once they were outside, Papa let out a big "Whew! That was close!" He looked at Lily, chuckling. "You are the only little girl I know of who has petted a skunk."

61

Lily's mouth opened in a big O, but not a word came out. She was too shocked to speak. That tail did seem a little different from their other cats, but she had no idea it belonged to a skunk. Oh, how dreadful if she and Joseph had been sprayed with a heavy choking cloud of stink. The very thought made shivers run up and down her spine.

In the house, Papa told Mama the skunk story. He thought he might ask around to see if he could find a dog. "Too many varmints have been coming around the farm," he said. "A good dog would make those varmints think twice before calling our barn a home."

Later that week, Papa came into the kitchen to find Mama. Lily and Joseph were helping Mama can peaches. His blue eyes were twinkling like they did whenever he had a surprise. "I found a nice dog in town," Papa said. "Let's go out and meet her."

Everyone followed Papa outside. A big black dog was tied to a tree near the house. Its wet pink tongue hung out of its big mouth. Lily spotted some big sharp teeth. As big as fangs and sharp as razors.

Mama seemed pleased. Didn't she see those big teeth?

"I think we should call her Stormy," Mama said as she stooped down to pet the big ferocious-looking dog.

Papa knew that if Mama named an animal, it could stay. "We're happy to have you live with us now, Stormy." He stroked the dog's big head. "I'll make a nice bed for you out in the barn. In a few days, we'll let you run anywhere you like on our property. You can play with the children and keep critters away."

All Lily could think about were those big sharp teeth. She did not want to play with that dog. She didn't want to get anywhere near it.

Papa smiled at her. "Would you like to come pet Stormy?"

Lily shook her head. Tears prickled her eyes. The dog was too scary! Lily's tears made Joseph cry too. That often happened. If Lily cried, Joseph cried. If Joseph cried, Dannie cried. Soon, they were all crying. Papa was surprised that they didn't like the new dog and told them that they didn't have to play with it today. He assured them that once they grew used to Stormy, they would find the dog would be a lot of fun. Maybe one of their best friends, even.

But Lily was sure she could never be friendly with a dog that had such great big pointy teeth.

⧉⧉⧉

As summer deepened, Aunt Mary grew weaker and sicker. Several times a week, Papa would hitch Jim to the buggy for Mama so she could help with Aunt Mary's laundry, cooking, and cleaning. Lily and Joseph would go along to play with Levi and Hannah. On days when Mama stayed home, Grandma Miller would tend to Aunt Mary.

Lily felt sad. Hannah wasn't fun to play with, like she had been before her mother had become sick with this cancer. Hannah looked sad all the time. Each time Lily arrived, she would find Hannah at the sink, washing breakfast dishes. Her blue dress was on backward so the buttons ran down the front. Her mother was too weak to help her get dressed and Hannah couldn't reach the buttons in the back. Mama would help Hannah dress properly, then start the day's work.

Uncle Elmer spent a lot of time sitting on a rocking chair next to Aunt Mary's bed. He would read to her or just sit quietly as she took little naps.

Lily tried to shake the feeling of dread that covered Hannah's house like a scratchy wool blanket. How she wished they could laugh and sing and play like they used to! Even when they stayed at home, Mama wasn't bubbly with laughter like she had been.

A few nights later, Papa had just finished asking a silent blessing for supper when a buggy rolled up the driveway. Lily saw Uncle Elmer jump out of the buggy and tie his horse to the hitching post. He walked back to the buggy and gently lifted a big box. He carried the box to the porch. Papa went to open the door for him. Lily wondered what Uncle Elmer had in the box. He set it down in a chair in the kitchen and carefully lifted out a tiny baby wrapped up in soft white blankets.

"Mary is in the hospital," he told Mama and Papa. "Since the baby has been born, the doctors want to do something about the cancer right away."

A baby? Lily didn't know that Aunt Mary was going to have a baby! That was good news. Very good news! No wonder she had been sick and tired. But now that the baby was here, everything would be better. Babies always made people happy.

"Hannah and Levi will stay at Grandma and Grandpa Miller's," Uncle Elmer said. He was in a hurry because he wanted to go to the hospital to be with Aunt Mary. He ran the back of his fingers over the baby's soft cheek. He handed the baby to Mama and turned to go. He opened the door and took a step outside as Lily called out, "Wait! What is this baby's name?"

Uncle Elmer stopped abruptly. Lily felt her cheeks grow warm. It was bold to question a grown-up like that. Children must be seen and not heard. Wasn't Mama constantly reminding her of that? But Uncle Elmer wasn't cross. He smiled at her.

"I almost forgot to tell you. We named him Davy."

As Uncle Elmer drove off in the buggy, Lily looked at baby

Davy. His skin was white and creamy. His head was covered with thick fuzzy black hair. Lily wanted to stroke it to see if it felt as soft as it looked. His face wasn't red and wrinkly like Dannie's had been. He wasn't ugly like Dannie had been. In fact, Lily thought Davy was the cutest baby she had ever seen.

❧✳❧

Lily liked having two babies in the house. Davy couldn't do anything but wave his hands and feet and make funny little noises when he was hungry. Mama said she never knew a baby who cried as little as Davy. Lily liked sitting next to Davy's bassinet and talking to him. Sometimes Mama would let her hold the bottle to feed him.

Uncle Elmer brought Hannah and Levi over several times a week so they could see their new little brother. They never stayed very long. Lily wished that she and Hannah could play with their dolls like they used to do, but Hannah didn't want to play. She only wanted to hold Davy.

Lily heard Uncle Elmer tell Papa and Mama that the doctors were doing everything they could to make Aunt Mary better. That news made Lily happy. She hoped it wouldn't be much longer before Aunt Mary could come home. Then, everything could be like it used to be. That's what Lily prayed for each day.

CHAPTER

9

Stormy's Puppies

"Stormy had puppies last night," Papa said one morning as he washed up at the sink before breakfast. "They're the cutest little things. I'll take you out to see them after we're done eating."

Lily ate as fast as she could, then sat and waited until everyone was done. *Hurry, hurry, hurry, Joseph!* she wanted to say, but knew she shouldn't.

When Papa finally took them out to the barn, she couldn't believe what she saw: eight tiny puppies. They made funny mewling sounds as they crawled over each other to get close to Stormy.

Papa told Lily and Joseph that they couldn't play with the puppies until after their eyes were opened up, not for a few weeks. For now, too much handling might make the puppies sick. "Stormy will take good care of them," he said. "She's a good mother."

66

After Papa and Joseph went back into the house, Lily stayed in the barn, watching the puppies with Stormy. She could hardly wait until they were big enough to play with. Stormy lay quietly, proudly looking over her babies. As she nuzzled her tiny puppies, she didn't look scary to Lily. Not scary at all.

❦

It was a beautiful afternoon. Lily lay on her top bunk bed and looked longingly out the window. The sun was shining and the leaves in the big oak tree danced in the light breeze. She could hear birds sing merry songs as they flitted from branch to branch. Under the tree, Stormy snoozed peacefully as her frisky puppies tumbled around her, chasing each others' tails. The puppies were bigger now. Lily and Joseph were allowed to play with them.

Lily could hear the sound of Papa's ax as he chopped firewood on the other side of the house. The steady *thump, thump, thump* from Papa's ax should have made her sleepy, like it had made Joseph. He was sound asleep in the bottom bunk. Even Mama was taking a little nap after she put Dannie and Davy to sleep in their cribs. The house was quiet. Too quiet.

Lily thought taking naps was a waste of time. From the window, she watched the puppies romp in the yard. She crept quietly out of bed and tiptoed outside to play with them.

Lily thought she might watch Papa chop piece after piece of wood from the huge pile. But then she thought again. Too risky. Papa might tell her to go back to bed. She gathered up her two favorite puppies and slipped into the barn before he could see her. She held the ends of her apron to make a basket and carried the puppies up the ladder into the hayloft.

Lily sat down to play in the back corner. Not much later,

she heard Mama call her name. A twinge of guilt prickled her. She squeezed behind a bale of hay and hoped the puppies wouldn't bark to give away her hiding place. Puppies thought everything was a game. She heard Papa call her name. She knew she should answer, but she didn't want to have to go back to bed. She held her breath as Papa and Mama kept calling her.

Her heart started to pound as she heard Papa climb the ladder into the loft. He had noticed the missing puppies and figured out her hiding place! When he saw her, he had a stern look on his face. She had never seen him look so cross.

"Lily!" he said. "Why didn't you answer when we called?"

"I didn't want to take a nap."

Papa helped her down the ladder and took her to the porch. When Mama saw her, a look of relief flooded her face. "Where was she?"

"Hiding in the loft with a few puppies," Papa said. "I think she should probably go to bed again so that she'll remember to answer next time we call her."

Lily could see that she had made Papa and Mama upset. She wished she hadn't slipped outside when Mama had told her to take a nap. She wished she had answered Mama when she first heard her calling. She certainly should have answered Papa when he called. And now—to have to go back to bed! What a *terrible* punishment.

Mama helped Lily wash her hands, then sent her back to bed, just as Joseph woke up and went into the kitchen. She could hear Joseph and Mama laugh and talk. She could hear Mama feed Dannie and Davy. She wished she could be with them. Having to stay in her room by herself, all afternoon, was much worse than taking a nap.

Finally, suppertime came. Papa came into Lily's room to

ask if she was hungry. She was famished! Practically *starving*. The whole day brightened.

She bounced out of bed. It was wonderful to sit at the table and be with everyone again. Mama and Papa seemed to have forgotten how naughty she had been. They talked and laughed like they did at every meal. Lily decided, from now on, she would always answer when she heard Mama or Papa call. Too many interesting things had happened and she didn't want to miss out on them by having to spend another afternoon in bed. Too risky.

☙❧

Autumn was coming. The floorboards in the morning felt cold to Lily's bare feet. The leaves on the maple trees were starting to turn bright red. Soon, they would turn orange, then yellow, and then they would fall from the trees.

Late one day, there was a familiar knock on the door of the farmhouse. Uncle Elmer had come to visit and, this time, he seemed like he was back to his normal self. He looked happy. He told Mama that Aunt Mary had come home from the hospital. The doctors said she would be fine. The cancer had been cured.

Uncle Elmer wanted to take baby Davy home. Lily was glad to hear that Aunt Mary was better, but she was going to miss baby Davy. He was starting to lift his head and wave his hands at colorful strings of beads that Lily dangled over him. She would miss giving him his bottle and seeing his smiles. He always made cooing and gurgling sounds when she was near him, as if he was trying to let her know he loved her best.

Lily helped Mama pack all of Davy's clothes and toys. Uncle Elmer wrapped him up in a blanket and carefully laid him in a big box. He set the box on the floor of the buggy so Davy would be safe on the ride home.

After the buggy turned onto the road, Lily sat between Mama and Papa on the front porch swing. Joseph sat on Papa's lap and Mama held Dannie in her arms. Papa gently rocked the swing back and forth, back and forth. Everything was quiet except the katydids and crickets. In the woods a few night birds trilled their sweet songs.

Mama broke the silence. "I like hearing those birds sing. With all these trees around the house, it seems there are always birds singing somewhere. This summer was hard with Mary being sick and with having two babies to care for. There were days when I didn't feel like singing. Then all I had to do was to listen to my singing trees and I knew everything was going to be all right."

Papa put his arm around her shoulder. "Rachel, you are a strong woman. Not many women could have taken care of two babies like you did. It will be nice just having to look after your own family."

Mama looked at the trees in the yard. "I think we finally have a name for our little farm. Singing Tree Farm." She laughed. "How about it, Lily? Would you like to be Lily of Singing Tree Farm?"

Lily tried out the sound of it a few times and decided she liked it. She snuggled close to Mama and listened to the wood thrush sing its evening song. She was happy that the birds had helped Mama this summer, and that they gave her a name for their farm: Singing Tree Farm.

CHAPTER

10

School for Lily

*L*ily had known this day was coming. School was what happened to little boys and little girls after they turned six. They were sent off to school. She had been worrying about this day ever since her birthday.

And now the day was here.

Lily sat on the front seat of the buggy beside Mama and Dannie. Joseph sat in the back. Lily was wearing a new green dress that felt stiff and uncomfortable. She held a shiny new lunch box in her lap. She had watched Mama pack it this morning: a nice egg sandwich made with thick slices of soft homemade bread. A cute, little pink bowl with a lid held several slices of Mama's canned peaches. And two oatmeal cookies.

Lily was pleased with her lunch box. She looked forward to eating the lunch Mama had packed. Mama talked as she drove Jim.

"School will be so exciting for you, Lily. You will learn to read and to speak English. The teacher will teach you new songs and then you can come home and teach them to us."

Lily wished she had Mama's confidence. Her tummy felt like it was doing flip-flops.

As they drove up to the schoolhouse, Mama got out of the buggy to tie Jim to a tree while Lily held Dannie. Mama helped Joseph climb out of the buggy, then took Dannie out of Lily's arms so she could hop out. They all walked into the schoolhouse. All the desks were lined up in rows. The desks had black iron feet and curved seats, with curving backs that were part of the desks behind them. The tops of the desks had grooves to hold pencils and shelves underneath them for books. A large heating stove stood on the side of the room. Almost all of the seats were empty. Lily didn't know where she should sit. Another wave of worry rolled over her.

Mama helped Lily place her lunch box on a shelf as the teacher came to meet them. "My name is Teacher Ellen," she said with a big smile. "And you must be Lily Lapp."

Lily nodded shyly. She thought she had never seen anyone as beautiful as Teacher Ellen. She had auburn hair, bright sparkly blue eyes, creamy skin, and rosy cheeks. Her smile looked like it came from deep inside and made little dimples appear in her cheeks.

"We have a lot of fun things to do today," Teacher Ellen said. "First, let's find your desk." She led Lily to the front of the room and showed her a desk with her name attached to the top. "This will be your very own desk where you can keep all your books and pencils and where you will be sitting to do your work."

Lily slid into the seat and opened the lid to her desk. There was a pile of books inside, as well as a box of new crayons, a pair of scissors, and glue. Joseph's eyes grew wide. He wanted to start school today too, but he would have to wait. Lily hoped Teacher Ellen would let her start writing in those books soon. Mama had taught her the alphabet already.

Mama crouched down by Lily's desk. "It looks like you're all settled in. It's time for me to take the boys home now. I'll come pick you up after school."

Lily stood at the door and watched as Mama drove away and left her there. She wasn't sure what she should do next. A group of children played a game on the playground, but she didn't know what game they were playing. Everything was so strange and new. She saw her cousins, Hannah and Levi, playing with a girl named Mandy Mast and some other children she knew from church, but no one seemed to notice her. She didn't know what to do with herself. Maybe, if she hurried down the road, she could catch up with Mama and go home. She could try school another day.

Teacher Ellen put a hand on Lily's shoulder. "Would you like to help me ring the bell to start school?"

Lily changed her mind about running off to catch Mama. Ringing the school bell would be fun! And wouldn't Joseph be envious when he heard what she had done? Teacher Ellen showed her how to pull the rope and make the bell ring. Lily pulled it hard, twice. The bell echoed loudly, so loudly that a family of crows startled and flew out of a nearby tree.

All the children came running to the schoolhouse. They stopped at the pump to get a drink of water before they went inside to sit at their desks. Lily was relieved when cousin Hannah sat across the aisle from her. Levi, a year older and in the second grade, sat behind her.

Teacher Ellen stood at her desk and looked over the classroom, smiling at each student. "I am so happy to be here with all of you," she said. "It won't take long to get to know each other. I'm sure we will have a very nice school year filled with learning new and exciting things. Before we get started, let's introduce ourselves." She took a few steps forward. "I am Ellen Weaver. My home is in Wisconsin, but I am happy to come to New York to be your teacher." She pointed to the back rows. "Now, let's start with the eighth graders. Each person can take a turn saying his or her name."

As Lily listened to the big eighth graders introduce themselves, her worries returned. She wished she were at home with Mama and Joseph and baby Dannie. She wondered what Mama was doing right now. A big lump started to rise in her throat. Tears prickled her eyes. She bit her bottom lip to try not to cry.

Mandy Mast raised her hand and waved it wildly in the air. In a loud voice she announced, "Lily Lapp is going to cry!"

Lily's lips started to quiver and a tear leaked down her cheek. She wanted to disappear. Teacher Ellen hurried to Lily's desk.

"As soon as we're done with introductions, I have a very cute picture I would like you to color for me," she said. "It's a little kitten on top of someone's birthday cake. You look like you would know how to color very nicely. Would you mind coloring it for me?"

Lily nodded. Teacher Ellen patted her shoulder to encourage her before she walked back to the front of the room. After each scholar was introduced, Teacher Ellen handed out assignments. As she passed Lily's desk, she handed her a paper. Lily got her crayons and started coloring. The kitten looked cute with its paws covered with frosting. She colored it yellow so it would look like her favorite kitten at home. She took out her pink crayon and started to color the frosting. It would be pink like Mama's birthday cake.

"EEEKKK!"

Lily's head snapped up. Teacher Ellen pointed to the trash can. The children jumped from their seats to see what was so frightening. Just then a little brown mouse darted across the floor and Teacher Ellen shrieked again.

Lily shivered and quickly drew her feet up off the floor. She did not like mice. She didn't want that mouse to run up her legs. Mice did that sort of thing. The boys started to chase the mouse, hoping to catch it. Some of the big girls joined in. Before long, the entire schoolroom had broken out in pandemonium.

Teacher Ellen hopped up on top of her desk in the front of the room. She noticed Lily cowering in her seat and motioned to her to join her. Lily jumped up on the teacher's desk and held on to Teacher Ellen as the terrified little mouse scurried around and around the schoolroom. Twenty children ran behind it, yelling and screaming.

Teacher Ellen shouted out for someone to open the door so the mouse could escape. The mouse made a few more laps around the classroom before it found its way to freedom and dashed outside to safety.

As the children settled down in the seats, Teacher Ellen hopped off the desk. "That was quite enough excitement for one day, don't you think so, Lily?" she said as she helped Lily down. "I'm glad I had someone to be with me while the mouse was chased outside."

Lily smiled up at her. School was going to be more fun than she had thought. It was exciting! And she already loved Teacher Ellen.

CHAPTER

11

The Trouble with Mandy Mast

Gray morning light filled the house. Mama gave Lily and Joseph a small piece of cloth to dust the furniture in the living room. Lily loved helping with the Saturday cleaning. She sang happily as she swished her cloth back and forth over the slats in the back of Mama's hickory rocking chair. They wanted the house to sparkle for Sunday. Not one speck of dust would be allowed to stay. Not one speck.

After every little piece of the rocking chair had been dusted, Lily helped Joseph finish dusting Papa's rocking chair. Then they dusted the little lampstand that stood between the two chairs.

Mama carried the oil lamps to the kitchen. She trimmed the wicks, filled them with oil, and washed the chimneys until they were clear and sparkling. Lily helped her put each lamp back where it belonged.

Next it was time to refill the kitchen canisters. Lily scooped flour into the big canister while Mama filled the others: white sugar, brown sugar, and cocoa powder in the little one. Lily placed the lids on the canisters. Mama wiped the outside surface and set them in a neat row along the back of the countertop.

Mama checked the woodstove to make sure the fire had died down. Only a few little red coals glowed in the ashes. She raked them carefully to the side and asked Lily to pull out the ash handle. Lily grasped the wooden handle at the bottom of the stove and pulled it out. *Whoosh!* A little pile of ashes dropped down into the ash pan at the base of the stove.

With the wood poker, Mama pushed the rest of the ashes into the little hole in the bottom of the firebox. After all of the ashes had fallen into the ash pan, Lily pushed the wooden handle back in and closed the little hole. Mama carefully spread the remaining ashes and red coal over the bottom and added a few scraps of wood to start the fire again.

Now it was time to clean the stove top. Mama got several pieces of emery cloth. She set a chair at the back of the stove for Lily to stand on, then folded an old rag and placed it on top of the emery cloth. Together, Mama helped Lily press as hard as they could in one direction. They rubbed the emery cloth across the stove top until it was shiny. If they rubbed the wrong way, they could make ugly scratches. Lily rubbed and rubbed until her arms felt tired. She didn't like the sound of the emery cloth on the stove top. Its screechy noise made her teeth shiver.

Next came Lily's favorite part of Saturday cleaning: time for Mama to sweep and mop the floors. Lily and Joseph were allowed to sit in Papa's big rocking chair and look through picture books. It was the only day they got to sit in Papa's chair and the only time they could look at those particular books. Lily wished the floor would take a long time to dry, but it never did.

Because then came the worst part of Saturday cleaning. "Time for your hair, Lily," Mama said, too soon.

Every morning Mama would comb Lily's hair back to make the part that was visible nice and neat. It was only taken down on Saturdays. All that combing back done during the week made awful snarls. Lily dreaded having her hair brushed out. Sadly, she slid off the rocking chair, put the special books away, and walked into the kitchen. Joseph ran to his room for this part because he didn't like to watch Lily get upset. If she cried, then he would cry.

In front of the sink, Mama placed a tall stool. She handed Lily a box filled with toys that were only played with while Lily had her hair done. A big matchbox filled with pretty pink and purple pop beads. Little books filled with pretty pictures and cute stories that Mama read while Lily turned the pages. A small Rubik's cube that Lily twisted and turned but never could get all the colors lined up. A little beaded purse filled with different cute key chains. Best of all, a tiny porcelain doll with blue eyes, pink cheeks, and a bright red mouth. Mama had sewed a tiny purple dress for the doll. It was so tiny there had not been any room for buttons, so the back of the dress was sewed shut. Lily wrapped the doll into one of her flowered handkerchiefs and held it while Mama unwove her braids. Lily's hair fell down to her knees in a river of crinkles.

And then came the terrible, awful part. It had been a week since Mama had brushed out Lily's hair. It was filled with snarls and tangles. Lily tried to ignore how much it hurt to have her hair brushed out. She tried to concentrate on the special toys, but before long, she couldn't think of anything else. She started to cry. Big tears splashed down on the porcelain doll in her arms.

To help distract her, Mama sang a funny song about a little boy and his dancing colt. Lily tried to choke back her tears so she could listen, but the brush hurt too much. She wailed even louder.

Finally, after Mama was satisfied that every snarl had been removed, Lily hopped up on the countertop to have a shampoo. She leaned her head over the sink as Mama poured warm water on her head, then gently added shampoo. Lily liked this part of getting her hair done. It felt good. Mama rinsed the shampoo out of Lily's hair and soaked up the extra water with a towel. Lily would sit back on the stool and Mama would brush out her hair again. Lily felt as if her hair had re-snarled and re-tangled, clinging even tighter to her scalp. Tears prickled her eyes.

Mama saved a special story about a horse for this second brushing out. This little horse pulled a milk wagon and sneezed every time he trotted by flowers. *Kerchoo! Kerchoo! Kerchoo!* Lily tried not to cry too loudly so she could listen to Mama pretend to sneeze like a horse. Mama finished by braiding Lily's hair and fixing it into a tidy little bun on the back of her head.

"There! You're all done," Mama said as Lily slid off the stool. Mama sounded as relieved as Lily felt. Lily put away the special box of "hairdo" toys, happy to think it would be a whole week before she had to have her hair done again. A week seemed like months and months to six-year-old Lily.

By the time Lily had put away the toys, Mama was already making bread dough and Joseph had come back to the kitchen. Mama let Lily and Joseph stand next to her and help punch and knead the bread dough until it was just right. Sometimes, she would give Lily and Joseph a piece of dough to make into a little loaf. If it was the Saturday before church, Mama baked six loaves of bread. Everyone brought food to share for lunch after church. Lily and Joseph took turns punching the dough until it turned from sticky to elastic. Mama covered the bowl with a towel and set it on the floor next to the stove. It would stay warm and start to rise in that little nook.

One Saturday morning, a knock came at the door. When Mama opened it, Nate Mast stood there with his daughter, Mandy. She was thin and fair and pale, with freckles sprinkled over her nose and cheeks like a dusting of cinnamon. Mandy was just a little bit older than Lily but she liked to act as if she was the boss of everybody. Mama said Mandy needed extra patience and understanding because she didn't have a mother. She meant, "Lily, you need to be nicer to Mandy." So Lily tried to be sweet and patient with Mandy, but it wasn't easy.

Nate Mast asked Mama if she had any extra eggs to sell. "I think we should have plenty for you," Mama said. She turned to Lily and said, "Keep an eye on Dannie while I go to the basement to wash and crate the eggs."

Nate followed Mama to the basement to help her while Mandy stayed in the kitchen with Lily. "Let's go to your room to play with your dolls," Mandy said.

Lily wasn't sure if that was a good idea. Mama had told her to keep an eye on Dannie. She peeked into the living room and saw Dannie playing with his wooden blocks beside the toy box. He seemed happy. Lily decided that if he started to cry, she would hear him upstairs and could hurry down to take care of him.

Mandy followed Lily upstairs to her room to play with the

dolls. Lily opened her closet and took out her dolls. The two girls sat on the bed and played with the dolls.

"It will be our turn to have church at our house soon," Mandy said. "Bring your dolls along so we can play with them after church. I found a secret place where we can play."

"Where?" Lily asked.

Mandy put her fingers to her lips. "You will have to wait to find out."

"Mandy!" Nate Mast's voice bellowed up the stairs. "I've got the eggs. Let's go."

Lily and Mandy bolted off the bed and galloped down the stairs. Lily stopped so abruptly when she reached the kitchen that Mandy bumped into her. Flour was everywhere! Dannie had crawled into the kitchen, straight to the jar of flour on the floor. Lily might have forgotten to put the lid on the jar. Flour was in his hair, on his face, all over his clothes. Then he had crawled to where Mama had set the bowl of bread dough to rise in the warm corner behind the stove. He was happily sitting beside the bowl of bread dough, pressing his wooden blocks into the dough. Mama was still in the basement, but Lily knew she would not be happy.

Mandy pointed to the mess, laughing and laughing. Her father frowned and hurried Mandy out the door. Lily wanted to slap Mandy. She thought it was partly Mandy's fault that they had gone upstairs instead of watching Dannie like they were supposed to.

Lily moved the bowl of bread dough away from Dannie. She pulled the wooden blocks out of the dough and set them on the sink. Dannie squealed, happy to have a playmate. Lily had to laugh at him. He looked more like a snowman than her little baby brother.

Lily turned around and saw Mama standing at the top of

the basement door, staring at the mess in the kitchen. Without a word, Mama began to clean up. Lily wished she would say something. Oh, but the silence was terrible!

It took Mama and Lily a long time to get the kitchen and Dannie clean again. When Mama finished, she turned to Lily. "Didn't I ask you to watch Dannie?"

"Mandy wanted to go upstairs to play dolls!" Lily said.

Mama looked sad. "Lily, you have to learn to say no to a friend if she asks you to do something that you know you shouldn't."

Lily looked down at her bare toes. Mandy was a friend who often had exciting ideas that got Lily into trouble. She knew she had to say no to Mandy's ideas sometimes, but it was so hard!

Mama glanced at Dannie again and started to chuckle. "For such a little boy, he sure made a big mess, didn't he?"

Lily was relieved. Mama was laughing again! They dumped the bowl of dough out and started all over again. The bread for tomorrow's church service didn't get baked until late that evening. Lily went to sleep that night to the sweet smell of baking bread. Her dreams were filled with snowmen that looked like Dannie.

Train Tracks and Little Girls

onday through Friday, Lily waved goodbye to
Mama and Joseph as they dropped her off in front
of the little red schoolhouse in the morning. The school
day passed swiftly. At recess and noontimes she played with
Hannah and Mandy. She liked school and she loved Teacher
Ellen.

Teacher Ellen made learning about numbers and letters
fun and easy. During recess, she would join the children
on the playground and teach them new games. Best of all,
Friday afternoons were devoted to art. Teacher Ellen would
give several suggestions for pictures and the children would
draw, paint, or sketch. The finished pictures would hang
on the wall to be admired. The schoolroom looked cheerful and happy. Lily was glad that Teacher Ellen had come
all the way from Wisconsin to be the teacher for Pleasant
Hill School.

Lily enjoyed school so much that she was sorry when Saturday and Sunday came along. She wished every day was a school day.

❦

"Time to wake up, Lily."

Lily sat up in bed and rubbed her eyes when she heard Mama's voice. She still felt sleepy.

"Hurry and get dressed," Mama said, jiggling Dannie on her hip. "Breakfast is almost ready. Soon, we need to leave for church."

Lily jumped out of bed and slipped into her dress. She spun around so Mama could button the back. She followed Mama and Dannie downstairs to the kitchen. Papa had come in from the barn and was washing up at the sink. Joseph sat at the table, waiting to eat. Joseph was always ready to eat.

Papa spread butter on a piece of bread and cut it into small strips so Lily and Joseph could dip the bread into their egg yolks. "Looks like it will be another beautiful day today," he said.

Lily glanced out the window. The sun was beginning to light the sky. No clouds! She was glad it would be a sunny day. She liked playing outside with her friends after church. Today, church was going to be at Mandy's house and she would discover the secret place where they could play with their dolls. She hadn't stopped thinking about that secret place.

As soon as breakfast was over, Papa gathered the dishes from the table while Mama swirled soap into hot water in the sink. Lily stood on a little bench next to the sink. Mama washed and Lily dried and Papa put the dishes in the cupboards. When the kitchen was sparkling clean again, Mama went upstairs to help Joseph and Dannie into their Sunday clothes. She told Lily to change into her purple dress. Lily skipped into her bedroom and carefully removed her purple dress from the hanger in her closet. She loved purple. She wished she could wear this dress every day, but it was saved for church Sundays.

Mama brought Lily's stiffly starched white apron into her bedroom. She helped Lily slip into it.

Lily went to the living room and opened the little drawer in the table beside Mama's rocking chair. In it were pretty flowered handkerchiefs. Lily was allowed to bring two to church. She chose two with purple flowers to match her dress. She lifted her apron and tucked them carefully into her pocket on the front of her dress.

Mama came to the living room to inspect Lily's face. Lily had already washed it, but Mama wet a washcloth and washed it again. She tied Lily's prayer covering in a neat little bow beneath her chin and handed Lily her big black Sunday bonnet to wear on top of it. It was heavy. Lily couldn't see anywhere except right in front of her when she was wearing it. She didn't like it. She often wondered if this was how Jim felt when he had to wear blinders.

Papa had hitched Jim to the buggy and drove to the house where Mama and Lily and the boys were waiting. Jim's ears were twitching and his tail was up. He seemed happy to be going out. As Lily joined Joseph in the back seat of the buggy, she wondered if Jim enjoyed seeing his friends at church, just like she did. Mama climbed into the front seat, next to Papa, and held Dannie on her lap. Papa clucked to Jim and they started down the driveway.

Usually, Lily and Joseph liked to kneel on the seat and

peer out of the back window of the buggy. Not on church Sundays, though. Mama didn't want them to wrinkle their clothes before they got to church. Lily could only see the sky and the treetops through the little window by her seat. She listened to the steady clip-clop of Jim's hooves on the road and the rolling sound of the buggy wheels. Lily listened to the wheels to find out how close they were getting to Mandy's house. She could tell what kind of a road they were on by the sound of the wheels. If they rolled over a gravel road, the wheels made a crunchy sound. It changed to a nice singing sound when the buggy turned onto an asphalt road.

Papa began to sing a church song in his deep clear voice and Mama joined him with her sweet soft soprano. Lily liked hearing them sing and hummed along. Their voices faded as they neared Mandy's home.

Papa guided Jim right to the house and turned him so the buggy wheel wouldn't be in Mama's way. Mama got the bread she had baked yesterday and took it into the house. She hurried back out to fetch Dannie and her satchel filled with diapers and pretty toys. She opened the back door of the buggy for Lily to hop out. Joseph would stay with Papa.

As Lily and Mama entered the house and removed their heavy black bonnets, Mama tipped up Lily's face to inspect it one more time. Satisfied, they went to shake hands with the rest of the women who stood in the kitchen, waiting for the bishop's wife to give the signal for the women to find a seat. In the living room were rows and rows of backless benches. The women and girls filed in and sat on one side of the living room. As Lily sat down, she leaned forward to look at Hannah, seated next to Aunt Mary, on the other side of Mama. Hannah returned Lily's smile, but then they both

looked away. The ministers were coming in and everyone had
to be quiet and serious until after church was over.

The bishop slowly made his way through all the benches
filled with women. He shook each person's hand. The two
ministers followed behind him. Lily felt so grown up as she
held out her hand to greet them.

After they sat down, the men and boys filed in and sat on
benches that faced the women. The deacon stood, held his
left arm straight and stiff, and piled songbooks on it from
his hand all the way up to his shoulder. Lily wondered how
he kept them from falling as he made his way through the
room to give each person a songbook.

One of the men announced a song number and everyone
began to sing. The ministers rose and went upstairs while
everyone else kept on singing. Mama followed the words with
her finger so Lily could try to follow along. She thought the

squiggly German letters looked funny. Voices rose and fell all around her, singing in high German.

The ministers came back into the room—the silent signal that the time of hymn singing was over. Everyone tucked their songbooks under their bench as the first minister rose and started to preach. Lily's legs soon grew tired of dangling from the bench. She wanted to swing her legs but knew she had to hold still. She reached into her pocket to bring out a handkerchief. She folded it into a triangle, then folded the ends into the center. She rolled it up and twisted it around to make a little mouse with a tail. She tickled her nose with the tail. She unfolded the handkerchief. This time she folded it a special way to make a little cradle with twin babies inside it and gently rocked the cradle back and forth. She glanced over to see what Hannah was making with her handkerchief, then sighed with envy. Hannah looked so pretty with her satiny blonde hair and her blue eyes. Lily wished her own hair looked like Hannah's. Even if her hair was straight dull brown instead of blonde, she wished she could have at least had waves. She reached with her finger to trace a scallop line along the front of her hair. Maybe that would help her hair look wavy. Mama nudged her and frowned, so Lily quickly dropped her hand to her lap and played with her handkerchiefs.

Mama placed her hand on Lily's. It was time to kneel and pray. Lily slipped her handkerchiefs back into her pocket and knelt with everyone else. She rested her head in the cradle of her arms and then very quietly lifted her head to peek at the women who sat behind her. After a time of prayer, the next minister started to preach. He had a singsongy voice that made Lily sleepy. Leaning against Mama, she fell asleep. Before she knew it, Mama nudged her awake. It was time for church to be over. Finally, finally, Lily could go play with her friends!

In the blink of an eye, the men converted the benches to tables. Women sliced bread and filled bowls with sweetened creamy peanut butter to set in the center of the tables. Seated next to Mama, Lily ate a nice thick slice of bread with gooey, sticky peanut butter spread on top. Of all the food served at church, nothing was as good as church peanut butter.

After everyone had eaten, the men took the benches outside and set them up so the children could slide on them. Lily loved sliding on the benches. She was waiting in line to take another turn when Mandy called the girls over.

"Let's go play with our dolls," Mandy said. "The boys can play on the slides by themselves."

Lily and the other girls ran to get their dolls. Mandy led the girls to a big willow tree behind the house. Not far behind the tree there was a railroad track. The girls sat under the long sweeping willow branches for a long time, playing with their dolls.

"This was a nice secret," Lily said. She didn't think it was a terribly exciting secret place, but she remembered that Mama told her to be extra nice to Mandy.

Mandy dismissed that comment with a flick of her hand. "This tree isn't my secret. This is what I use for my playhouse. The secret place is over there." She pointed to the railroad tracks. "We can sit on the train tracks to play church."

"But what if a train comes through?" Lily asked. She didn't think they should be playing on the tracks.

"Not on Sundays," Mandy said. "The engineers have to go to church so they don't drive their trains on Sundays." She lifted her chin. "Everybody knows that."

Lily didn't know that. Nor did the other girls, but they all followed Mandy out to sit on the tracks with their dolls and play pretend church. Mandy acted like the deacon and the minister and the bishop, all rolled into one. She started to sing a church song and everyone joined in. They knew the songs by heart. They had been singing them all their lives.

Suddenly, Lily felt the tracks wiggle, then rumble. Something seemed odd. She stopped singing to listen more closely. There was no mistake. A train was coming!

Just then, the train came into sight. It blew its whistle to make the girls move off the tracks.

"Train!" Mandy yelled.

The little girls bolted off the tracks and ran to the willow tree. All but Lily! She couldn't move her feet. She was frozen! The train kept speeding toward her. The engineer kept blowing the whistle. The girls were screaming and screaming, but Lily couldn't budge! The big blue engine came barreling toward her. The engineer was trying to get the train to stop. The wheels of the train made strange screeching sounds as the engineer leaned out of the window to wave his arms.

"Get off, get off!" he yelled.

Suddenly, Papa's big strong arms whisked Lily away just before the train went thundering by.

The breath Lily hadn't realized she was holding whooshed out of her. As Papa held her close to his chest, she burst into tears.

"There, there," he said, trying to comfort her. "You're not hurt."

She buried her face against his shoulder and sobbed. Papa carried Lily up to the house and told Mama that it was time to go home. His face looked tight and pale.

Mama didn't ask Papa why he wanted to leave so early. Papa hitched up Jim as Mama found their bonnets and joined him in the buggy. Papa drove the buggy past clumps of men who were visiting with each other. He drove past the boys who were sliding on the benches. He drove past the little girls, holding their dolls under the willow tree.

As they left Mandy's house, Papa told Mama what had happened. Lily didn't hear Mama's response, but she knew she would never again play on a railroad track no matter what Mandy Mast said.

CHAPTER

13

Teacher Ellen's Accident

*L*ily's only disappointment with school was that she was the youngest child in the entire schoolhouse. Mandy Mast liked to point that fact out, often. Lily's turn always came last: choosing the game to play at recess, or picking the hymn to sing in the morning, or standing at the end of the line of scholars when they lined up. The last one to get a drink of water at the pump before going inside after the bell rang. The last one to wash her hands at lunchtime. Always, always last.

But other than Mandy Mast, Lily looked forward to her days at school. And most of all, she loved art. They had art every Friday. Sometimes, if they did very well with German class on Wednesdays, Teacher Ellen might let them have an extra hour for art.

On a crisp, autumn Friday afternoon in late September, Teacher Ellen stood in front of the classroom with a big smile on her face. Her eyes swept the room as the students waited eagerly to see what she had planned for today's art project. Every week she had something new planned and Lily never could guess what it might be. Sometimes Teacher Ellen wanted them to draw a picture. Other times, they painted. Lily stretched her neck to see what was on Teacher Ellen's desk, but she couldn't see anything.

"Today we will be doing something a little different for art," Teacher Ellen said. "I have a stack of old calendars here. Isaac, please come up and pass them out so that everyone has one."

Isaac was the nicest boy in school, so Lily didn't mind that he was always given the job of passing out papers. That was another thing Lily was too little to do: pass out papers. Only the big boys and big girls were given the task of passing out papers. Lily couldn't wait until she was a big girl and could pass out papers.

Lily watched Isaac walk from desk to desk, handing each student a calendar. He handed Lily a beautiful calendar filled with pictures of mountains and lakes and other scenery. Lily glanced over at Mandy's calendar. It had birds on it. It was nice, but not as nice as hers. She thought Isaac might have given her the prettiest one.

After everyone had a calendar, Teacher Ellen told them to choose their favorite picture and carefully tear it out. Lily chose a meadow filled with wildflowers. A big snow-covered mountain loomed in the background. She tore it out carefully as Teacher Ellen explained the next step.

"I have brown and black construction paper," Teacher Ellen said. "I want you to cut strips of paper. We'll glue the paper strips around the picture to make a frame, and one through the middle. It will seem as if we are looking out a window."

As the students cut and pasted, Teacher Ellen walked up and down the aisles. She put two small pieces of fabric, plus a needle and a thread, on everyone's desk. "After you are done making your window frame, I want you to make a curtain for your window with the fabric pieces. You can stitch the fabric right to the paper. I have some ribbon in a basket on my desk. You can line up and choose a ribbon to make little tiebacks to draw the curtains back from your windows."

Not another lineup! That meant that Lily had to choose last from the basket. She was happy to see there was one purple ribbon, but she was sure Mandy would choose that one. But amazingly, she didn't! The last ribbon left in the basket was the purple one. Lily sighed with happiness.

Lily did not like to sew by hand. She did not like it at all. But she wanted Teacher Ellen to be proud of her picture. The schoolhouse was quiet except for the sound of scissors and pasting, and needles and thread swishing through layers of paper. Teacher Ellen helped Lily tie her purple ribbon tiebacks into a bow because she wasn't good at tying bows yet. And then, her beautiful window picture was done.

Isaac and two other big boys helped Teacher Ellen tape the windows along the wall. Hers really did look like a window with soft white curtains—outside was a flower-filled meadow and mountain. Lily admired each one, even Mandy's bird picture. Everyone's window looked different. Lily thought it was the best project they had ever made during art period.

❧❧

During recess, the scholars divided up into two teams to play softball. Teacher Ellen said she would pitch for both teams. Today the batting lineup started with the youngest. Even though she would finally be first in line for something, playing softball was never good news to Lily. She didn't like playing softball because she could never hit the ball. The rest of the time she had to wait for a turn at bat, bored. It was much more fun to play tag or some other running game. Lily looked forward to the day when it would be her turn to choose the game at recess. They would not have to play softball *that* day!

Lily stepped up to the plate with the bat. Teacher Ellen took a few steps forward and pitched slow and gentle. Lily swung and missed. Strike one. She swung and missed again. Strike two. As Lily swung and missed for the third time, she dropped the bat and walked over to the rest of her teammates. Softball was no fun. No fun at all.

It was cousin Levi's turn at bat. As he picked up the bat, Mandy Mast whispered loudly, "It's L-L-L-Levi's t-t-t-t-turn!"

Teacher Ellen overheard. She stopped the game and walked up to Mandy. "We do not make fun of anyone in our school," she said sternly. "I want you to go apologize to Levi."

Mandy mumbled a quick "sorry" to Levi, but Lily didn't think she sounded at all sorry. Just sorry Teacher Ellen happened to hear.

Lily felt badly for Levi. His stutter wasn't nearly as obvious as it had been when school started. She thought it seemed that the less nervous Levi was, the less he stuttered. She hoped that someday his stutter would disappear for good.

Teacher Ellen wound up her arm to pitch to Levi. He swung the bat and *Thwack!* he hit the ball way out in the field. Levi dropped the bat and ran all the way to first base. Second base. Third base! He looked so pleased! Lily was happy for him.

Levi might have a little trouble talking smoothly, but he made up for that in almost everything else. He could hit a ball farther than any boy his age. He could run faster than any boy his age. He was always friendly and willing to help anyone he could. All of those things, Lily thought, were much more important than a little stutter.

❧

Rain came down like a curtain of water. Lily stood inside the schoolhouse and looked out the window, watching for Mama to arrive in the buggy to pick her up. Mama was late and Lily was one of the few students left in the schoolhouse. Isaac and his younger brothers had brought umbrellas to school. They could walk home in the rain.

Lily watched as Isaac and his brothers walked across the school yard to the road. Isaac led the way while his younger brothers followed behind him, like baby ducks following the Mama duck. Lily wouldn't mind walking all the way home in the rain if she had a pretty umbrella. Maybe a purple one with polka dots or flowers.

A buggy turned into the school yard. It was Mandy Mast's neighbor, Naomi, coming to give Mandy a ride home. As the horse passed Isaac and his brothers, it stopped abruptly

and snorted. The horse tossed its head angrily and jumped forward a little. Then it reared up and pawed at the air with its front hooves.

Isaac realized that the umbrellas were scaring the horse, so he yelled to his brothers to close them. "Fast!" he yelled.

Too late.

The horse dropped back down on all four hooves and broke out in a run. Nostrils flaring, it dashed past the schoolhouse. Naomi held on to the reins as hard as she could to try to stay in control. Lily's eyes went wide as she watched the horse go crazy. Mandy started to cry. The horse and buggy rounded the schoolhouse. The buggy tipped dangerously on two wheels as it rounded the bend. Then the horse galloped out the school yard, across the yard, and into a farmer's hayfield. Poor Naomi!

Lily saw Jim pull Mama's buggy into the school yard. She grabbed her bonnet and lunch box, then ran outside and climbed into the buggy. She told Mama what had happened and pointed to poor Naomi, stuck in the hayfield.

Mama jumped out of the buggy and tied Jim to the hitching rail. "Lily, you stay here. I want to make sure Naomi is all right before we start for home."

Lily wasn't sure what Mama could do with a scared, frightened horse. She watched Mama cross the road to go to the hayfield. In the pouring rain, Mama held the horse's bridle and gently stroked his nose. Lily could see that the horse was jumpy and nervous. Mama guided the horse back to the schoolhouse and waited until Mandy was safely in the buggy. The horse trotted out of the school yard and started down the road, but it was still twitching its tail more than usual. Lily hoped Naomi and Mandy would get home safely without passing any more umbrellas.

Poor Mama was soaking wet. On the way home, she said, "Isn't it nice that our Jim doesn't mind umbrellas? Sometimes, little things can spook a horse. Your Papa is very good at training horses and I'm glad for it!"

Lily was glad too. And now she wasn't sure she would want to walk home from school with an umbrella after all. Too risky.

❧

Lily's mouth watered as she eyed the bowl in the middle of the table. It was filled with steaming hot corn that Mama had canned from her summer garden. Next to the bowl was a plate filled with red and orange tomato slices—the last of the season. The bread platter was piled high with fresh homemade bread. There was a cup of milk beside everyone's plate. When sweet corn was the main entrée, Lily was allowed to eat as much as she wanted to. Papa had just sprinkled salt on Lily's mound of corn when a knock at the door stopped him. Papa wiped his hands on his napkin and went to see who had come to visit.

Papa opened the door to find Nate Mast, hat in his hands. He stood stiffly, with a somber look on his face. Papa invited Nate to join the family for dinner, but he didn't want to sit down.

"I stopped by to let you know that Teacher Ellen is in the hospital," Nate said. "She was on her way home from school when a car smashed into the back of her buggy. Careless teenagers. They were driving much too fast." He looked down at his feet. "She has been badly hurt. There won't be any school tomorrow. Maybe not for a while."

Sweet, pretty Teacher Ellen couldn't be hurt! She had to get better and be the teacher again. She simply had to! Lily

99

was no longer hungry. She pushed her corn to the side of her plate. Big tears started to roll down Lily's cheeks. Soon, she was sobbing.

Mama picked Lily up and held her on her lap, hugging her tightly. "Everything will turn out okay, Lily. Teacher Ellen is in God's care. Once she is feeling a little better, we'll take you to go visit her."

Day after day, school was canceled. Day after day, news from the hospital was the same. Teacher Ellen remained unconscious. Her parents stayed with her at the hospital. Lily overheard someone say that as soon as Teacher Ellen could travel, her parents wanted to take her home to Wisconsin.

If Teacher Ellen left Pleasant Hill School, who would be their teacher? It was a continual worry to Lily.

CHAPTER

14

Squeaky Cheese

Once a week, Mama made cheese and butter. First came the cheese making. Mama would allow the extra milk to sour a little. Then she would heat the sour milk on the stove.

Mama clipped a thermometer on the side of the milk pail. She needed to keep a careful watch on the temperature. The milk should not get too hot, just hot enough. While the milk was heating, Mama would break a rennet tablet in half and put it into a little bit of warm water to dissolve. Then she would pour the water into the sour milk and stir. After the milk reached the right temperature, Mama took the milk pail off the stove and placed the pail into a tub of lukewarm water.

While they waited for the milk to thicken, Mama would start the butter making. She poured fresh sweet cream into the butter churn. Lily and Joseph took turns turning the crank. The paddles made a pleasant *slap, slap, slap* sound

101

as they hit the cream. After a while, the sound changed to a muffled *slap, slap, slap.* If Lily looked inside the churn right now, she would see mounds of whipped cream. She knew that to be true because she had peeked inside many times. But it wasn't butter yet. She kept on cranking the handle, until she heard just the right sound: *slappity thump, slappity thump.* Now it was butter!

Mama carefully poured the buttermilk liquid—separated from the solid butter—out of the churn into several glass jars. One jar for Papa, who loved to drink fresh buttermilk. She would use the rest for baking. She put the butter into a bowl and kneaded it with the back of a wooden spoon to squeeze every little drop of buttermilk from the butter. Not one drop of liquid would be left. And then Mama would sprinkle salt into the butter and knead some more. Finally, she would shape the butter into little balls and place them in a glass dish in the refrigerator. That delicious sweet butter would feed the family all week long, until the next cheese and butter making day.

The sour milk, thickening in the pail, was ready. Usually, Mama used it to make cottage cheese, but sometimes she made a soft cheese that spread on bread like honey. Today, she wanted to make hard cheese to slice for sandwiches. She made long cuts all the way through the thickened milk, then made cuts the other way. Mama rolled up her sleeves as far as they could go and washed her hands to make sure they were perfectly clean. She gently lifted the cut pieces of thickened milk with her fingers, then broke them into smaller pieces as they fell back into the pail. Over and over she gently sifted the cheese with her fingers, until it was all crumbly. They were called curds.

"It's time to get the other pail ready, Lily," Mama said.

Lily opened a drawer to get a large piece of cheesecloth and a box of clothespins. She fastened the cheesecloth to the top of a big white five-gallon pail tightly with many clothespins. "It's ready," she said as she set the pail next to Mama.

Mama poured the curds into the big pail. The curds stayed in the cheesecloth but the liquid whey dripped through it, pinging into the pail. *Ping, ping, ping.* Mama left the cheese alone until the whey had completely drained. The cheese curds were nice and chewy and squeaked when Lily bit into them. Lily and Joseph loved to sample them, but Mama only let them try a few bites. She needed the rest to make a big block of cheese.

Mama sprinkled salt over the curds on the cheesecloth, stirred, and placed the curds into the cheese press. She screwed the top weight on the press, and turned the crank to squeeze the curds together. Mama turned and turned and turned the crank. As the crank turned, the cheese squeaked. It really did. Lily didn't like hearing the squeak. It sounded as if the cheese was getting pinched. Mama said that was silly—cheese could not feel anything! But still, Lily covered her ears.

When Mama couldn't turn the crank one more time, she knew the cheese was squeezed as much as it could be squeezed. Mama set the press on a shelf in the pantry. It would take a week for the curds to form into a nice chunk of hard cheese.

The last thing to do was to feed the pail of whey to the pigs. Those pigs seemed even happier for cheese and butter making day than Lily and Joseph. Whey was a treat for pigs. Lily and Joseph would laugh as they listened to the pigs' happy greedy snorts as they slurped down the whey. Lily picked Dannie up to carry him out to the barn with Mama and Joseph.

It had rained during the night and the porch steps were slick. Mama slipped on the top step and tumbled down to the bottom. Lily and Joseph watched, horrified, as the big pail of whey bounced behind her and spilled all over her. Mama was soaking wet with whey! She lay at the bottom of the steps for a little while to catch her breath. Then she got up and limped slowly and painfully up the stairs to get cleaned up.

Poor Mama.

The pigs would not be getting their treat today.

Poor pigs.

Lily's New Teacher

*D*ay after day went by and there was no teacher to be found for Pleasant Hill School. Lily didn't mind too much because she liked to stay at home with Mama and Joseph and Dannie.

This morning, Lily and Joseph had played a game with empty thread bobbins. They tied the bobbins to Joseph's toy horses with a piece of thread. As they guided the horses along, the bobbins would roll behind it. Usually, Lily liked to play horse and bobbin with Joseph, but this afternoon, she sat on a little stool beside Mama's sewing machine. Mama was sewing a little tan shirt for Joseph. She made it look easy as she carefully guided the pieces of fabric under the needle while slowly pumping the treadle up and down with her feet.

Joseph came over and watched Mama sew. "I want some chocolate milk."

"I'm almost done with your shirt, Joseph," Mama said.

"Then I'll mix up some chocolate milk for all of us." She stood and asked Joseph to hold his arms out to measure the sleeve length before she sewed the cuffs on at the end of the sleeves. Satisfied, she went to sit at the sewing machine to finish the shirt.

But Joseph was upset that he had to keep waiting for chocolate milk. Right as Mama was about to sit down, Joseph yanked the chair away. Lily watched in horror as Mama fell to the floor. Joseph's eyes went wide. Mama got right up and brushed herself off. Her mouth was set in a tight line.

"Little boys have to learn to be patient," Mama told Joseph. "I don't think anyone will be getting chocolate milk today." Without another word, she sat back down at the sewing machine to finish the shirt.

Later, after Dannie woke up from his afternoon nap, Mama called Lily and Joseph into the kitchen. She filled cups with plain cold milk and gave each one a cookie. But they would have to wait until tomorrow to have chocolate milk. Lily was very disappointed, but she knew Mama needed to teach a certain little boy to be patient.

❦

A month had passed without school. The school board still hadn't found a new teacher, but Teacher Ellen had regained consciousness and soon would be ready to go home.

As promised, Papa and Mama took Lily to go see Teacher Ellen in the hospital. Lily was shocked when she saw her. All of her pretty auburn hair had been shaved off. Her legs were held in ugly contraptions. It looked as if there were big screws that were fastened right into her legs. The sight of those big screws made Lily shudder.

Teacher Ellen's face lit up when she saw Lily. Lily was glad to see that her smile was still the same.

"I'm sorry I won't be able to be your teacher any longer," Teacher Ellen said, "but the school board will find someone else and you can keep on learning. And we can still be friends. I will send you letters and you can write to me too. I want to hear everything that you're learning in school and anything else you want to talk about."

That sounded like fun! Lily had never received a letter of her own in the mail. She was still sorry that Teacher Ellen had been hurt and wouldn't be her teacher anymore. But Lily would write to her often. Every day! Maybe twice a day.

~✺~

One week later, Nate Mast stopped by Singing Tree Farm to tell Papa that the school board had found a new teacher. School would start again on Monday. Lily was excited! She hoped the new teacher would be just like Teacher Ellen.

On Monday morning, Lily sat at her desk and studied the new teacher. This teacher looked older than Teacher Ellen. She had coal black hair and big bushy eyebrows, as big and fuzzy as

107

wooly caterpillars. Lily thought she might look pretty if only her mouth wouldn't pinch together into such a stern firm line.

Lily felt her stomach turn into knots as the teacher glared at the scholars. Lily glanced over at cousin Hannah. She looked as scared as Lily felt.

The teacher stood. "Good morning, children. My name is Katie Zook. I will be your teacher for the rest of this school year. We go to school to learn, not to have fun. The first thing that needs to be done is to get rid of all these ridiculous pictures on the walls."

Lily's heart dropped. All of their pretty artwork was coming down? Teacher Katie directed the upper grade boys to remove the pictures. One by one, the pictures were removed and stacked on Teacher Katie's desk. The wall looked bare and sad. Teacher Katie tore the pictures up and tossed them into the trash can. "That's the last of such nonsense!"

Lily felt like crying. She thought of all the happy Friday afternoon art periods with Teacher Ellen. It was all gone. All in the trash now.

The scholars were quiet and sober as Teacher Katie handed out assignments to each class. She walked grimly between the aisles to make sure everyone was doing their work properly.

Lily was glad when it was time to go home. She hadn't smiled at all today. Not once. She couldn't wait to be at home with Papa and Mama and play with Joseph and Dannie.

⤞⤝

Teacher Katie was very stern. From the first day, she ruled with a firm hand. The schoolroom felt as if a heavy gray rain cloud hung over it, even on sunny days. No one dared to disobey Teacher Katie. Lily tried her best to write and color neatly in her books. She didn't want to upset the teacher.

Because Teacher Katie liked to yell.

She yelled at someone every day, for the smallest things. Missing a spelling word, not sitting up straight, daydreaming. Teacher Katie didn't like to have to explain anything more than once. If she had to review a difficult arithmetic lesson because a scholar couldn't understand it, she would get cross. She kept a ruler tucked inside her apron belt and used it to whack a scholar's hand whenever she became frustrated. *Whack, whack, whack!*

Cousin Levi was a source of great frustration for Teacher Katie. Levi wore new shoes, and they squeaked when he walked to the chalkboard. The squeaky sound made Teacher Katie cross. She thought he was making them squeak on purpose.

Poor Levi. His face was as red as a ripe tomato. Tears welled in his eyes. His hands twisted in his lap. Lily would not want to be in his shoes.

❧×❧

Teacher Katie was not the kind of teacher who went outside to play with the children at recess and Lily was glad for that. Recess was the only fun part of the day. When Teacher Katie said to put away books for recess, you never saw such good children. They quickly put their books away and sat up straight, eager to be free from Teacher Katie's cross words, at least for a little while.

Today, Lily quietly closed her book and placed it carefully inside her desk. She laid her pencil on the special little tray along the side, closed the lid, and waited until Teacher Katie told everyone to stand to be dismissed. Teacher Katie peered up and down the rows at the scholars. The way she scowled made her two big thick eyebrows meet in the middle, like two caterpillars kissing. Finally, she gave a brief nod, a signal for permission to leave. Lily joined the girls on their side of the room to get her coat and scarf and then hurried outside to join a huddle. She wondered what they would be playing today. It was Isaac's turn to pick.

The children gathered around Isaac to listen to his idea. Isaac always had the best ideas. He was a wonderful boy, a big eighth grader, with sun-bleached hair, almost white, and eyes the color of a blue sky on a cloudless, summer day. Isaac had a grin that lit up his whole face. Lily thought he was beautiful.

"Do you remember the book Teacher Ellen had been reading to us before her accident?" Isaac said. He meant a book about a pioneer family who had traveled west in a covered wagon and built a log cabin. "I think it would be fun to play pioneer. We could build a few little cabins in the woods right here beside the school yard."

Everyone followed Isaac as he climbed through the fence and into the woods. "Look for fallen tree limbs or branches that are lying on the ground," he said, pointing out some brush. "We can pull everything over here to make our cabins."

The older children started to drag branches into a pile. Isaac directed them to prop the branches up to make a little cabin. Lily and Hannah and the other little girls weren't strong enough to pull the fallen limbs by themselves, so Isaac thought of something else for them to do. He suggested they gather cattails along the swampy area near the creek. They would use the cattails for pretend food. Isaac was thoughtful like that.

Lily helped carry armload after armload of cattails and dumped them under a tree near the little cabin. Too soon, Teacher Katie rang the bell and it was time to go back to the schoolhouse. Lily wished recess would last much longer. It was fun to play with the other children and not worry about Teacher Katie's bad temper.

But the next hour of school flew by and soon it was noon. The children gulped down their lunches and ran to the woods to work on the cabins. It was taking a long time to build them. Lily couldn't wait until they could start playing inside. She helped the other little girls gather more cattails. On her way to the cabins, she noticed acorns under a big oak tree. The little girls gathered up the corners of their aprons into one hand to fill them with acorns. The acorns could be more pretend food. Lily twisted the tops a little and the acorn popped right out. The hull could be used for tiny plates.

Day after day, the children worked on the cabins until Isaac decided they were complete. They didn't really look like log cabins to Lily. There seemed to be more cracks than logs in the walls of the cabin. The roof was made out of wild grapevines. Lily could see the sunlight through the grapevines, but she decided it would still be fun to play in the cabin. As long as it wasn't raining or snowing.

Lily helped the other girls gather stones to make a round fire pit. They would pretend to cook food over the fire pit. The boys made funny little bows and arrows with sticks and twine. The arrows only flew for a few feet, but the boys thought they were expert marksmen. They would pretend to go hunting for food while the girls stayed in the cabins to cook and clean.

The boys returned with skunk cabbage leaves. Pee-yew! Lily could see how the cabbage got its name—the leaves smelled like skunk. As Lily and her friends tore the cabbage into pieces for pretend salad, she almost gagged. She was glad they wouldn't have to eat it.

Playing pioneers became everyone's favorite game. It helped to make the school day go faster. At recess, they rushed from the schoolhouse to the cabins to play. Lily thought she would never get tired of it, though the weather was starting to change. Her nose was red. Her hands were cold. She had to clap them to stay warm. Soon it would be winter. The thought made her sad. They wouldn't be able to have recess and lunch outside very often during cold winter days.

Then the day came when Mandy Mast announced that playing pioneers wasn't fun anymore. "It's getting too cold," she said. "Every day, we do the same thing. I'm tired of it! I want to play something else." She sat in the cabin, sulking.

Mandy had a point, Lily thought. It was chilly. Lily's breath came out in puffs of white. The other children wanted to keep playing, so Mandy was overruled. She joined in with the others, but with a sour look on her face. "Maybe if we could only build a real fire, it would be more fun," she said. "That way, at least we could be warm."

The next day, during the first recess, Mandy pulled Lily away from the other little girls. "Look what I brought," she said. She glanced around to make sure no one could hear. She opened her coat and drew a box of wooden matches out of her coat pocket.

Lily was shocked. "But we're not allowed to play with matches until we're much older!"

"Don't be such a scaredy-cat." Mandy dismissed Lily with a wave of her hand. "I light matches all the time and nothing ever happens. Besides, in many important ways, I'm practically ten." Mandy was only six, just like Lily.

For the first time, Lily was glad to hear Teacher Katie ring the bell. It was time to go back to the schoolhouse. She hoped Mandy would forget about her matches before lunch's recess.

After the little girls ate their lunch, Hannah decided they needed a fresh supply of cattails. Everyone ran to the edge of the swamp to gather more cattails. Lily filled her arms with cattails, and suddenly realized that Mandy hadn't come to the swamp with the girls. She caught a whiff of smoke in the air. *Oh no!* Lily dropped the cattails and ran to the cabin as fast as she could. As Lily saw the cabin, she could see little wisps of smoke curling out of the holes in the walls and roof.

Lily stopped abruptly at the cabin door. "Mandy, put out that fire!"

Mandy didn't pay any attention to her. She kept heaping more dry grass and twigs on the little fire, like kindling. The flames snapped and popped and crackled, licking at the grass. Large sparks flew up into the air. Mandy kept feeding the fire with more grass and sticks.

Lily didn't know what to do! The girls were down by the swamp gathering pretend food. The boys were out pretend hunting. She wished Isaac were here. He would know what to do.

Lily heard the girls' voices, coming up from the swamp with their arms filled with cattails. She ran to them. "There's a fire at the cabin! Come quick!"

The girls followed her back to the cabin. Now Mandy stood outside of the cabin. Even she looked worried. The fire had grown much bigger. The walls of the cabin were smoldering.

Lily saw the boys returning. A great shout went up from the boys when they caught sight of the fire. Isaac took off his coat and started to beat the flames. The other boys tried to help him, but the fire was too big. It seemed to be growing bigger every minute. Their coats were scorched and had little holes burned in them.

The boys started yelling, "Fire! Fire!" and the girls joined in. Uncle Elmer's field was next to the schoolhouse. He heard the children's shouts and came running through the woods. He saw the fire and told the children to get to the schoolhouse while he ran to the phone shanty to call the fire department.

Reluctantly, the children walked back to the schoolhouse. The big boys were covered with black smudges. Their coats were ruined. Even Mandy was very quiet. Lily wondered what Teacher Katie would have to say.

This was not good. It wasn't good at all.

They had barely reached the schoolhouse when Lily heard the fire whistle in town. Soon, the siren sounded from the fire trucks, closer and closer. The children stood outside the schoolhouse and watched as the fire trucks drove right through the school yard and up to the fence. A police car followed. Uncle Elmer cut the wire fence so the firemen could drive through to get closer to the fire. Firemen jumped out and grabbed hoses from the side of the truck. They ran toward the fire. Soon the dark clouds of smoke turned white, then became smaller and smaller, until the fire was put out.

The firemen waited until they were confident the fire was out, then they drove the fire trucks out of the woods. The policeman came over to the children and asked if they knew how the fire started. Lily looked at Mandy. Mandy's eyes were fixed on her shoes. Lily was afraid the policeman would take all of them off to jail in his police car. She didn't want to go to jail. She nudged Mandy with her elbow. Mandy refused to look at her. The policeman stared with suspicion at them all, especially Lily. Her heart was pounding. *Ba bump! Ba bump! Ba bump!* She was sure the policeman heard her thumping heart.

The policeman talked to all of them of how important it was to never play with matches. He gave them a very long lecture, grazing Lily with his spectacled gaze. He told all kinds of stories about how fires can get out of control very quickly. When he finally ran out of frightening stories and severe warnings, he got into his police car and drove off. Lily was so relieved! Jail seemed like a horrible place and she didn't want anyone to go to jail. Not even Mandy.

Then it was Teacher Katie's turn to lecture. Her face twisted into an angry scowl as her caterpillar eyebrows formed one long line—never a good sign. Her eyes closed to a pair of dangerous slits. She gave them a lengthy scolding about the dangers of fire, and ended it by having every scholar write: "I will not play with matches." One hundred times.

Lily's hand started to ache after writing only ten lines. She didn't think it was fair that they all had to be punished. It was Mandy's fault! And Mandy didn't seem to mind one little bit that everyone was in trouble. In fact, she looked happy.

The next day, the children went out to the woods. The cabins were only charred pieces of wood. There was a big black area where the fire had been. Lily looked up and saw a few snow flurries drift slowly from the sky. A flock of geese honked overhead. They were in a hurry to go south. The cabins were gone, the snow was coming. Playing pioneers was over.

Chubby the Miniature Horse

inter had arrived. The days were growing shorter, and frost was crawling up on the windows at night. Soon, the snow would come. The creeks and pond would freeze. Mama's garden was already brown and withered. She had worked hard to can the fruits and vegetables she had grown all summer long. Lily loved to go down to the basement with Mama and see the colorful jars of peaches and cherries and applesauce and green beans and corn, all lined up on shelves Papa had built. Lily thought the beautiful food in the jars looked as pretty as a rainbow.

One chilly morning, Papa circled an advertisement in the newspaper. "Someone is selling a miniature horse," he said, folding up the paper. His eyes were twinkling. "I'm thinking of taking a look at it. It would be nice to have a horse for the children."

"Is there enough room in the barn for another animal?" Mama asked.

"We'll be butchering the pigs before long," Papa said. "We could keep it in their pen. I'll stop on the way home from work tomorrow. If the horse looks like a good buy, I'll ask if they could keep it until we have some room in the barn."

Lily hoped Papa would like the miniature horse. It would be nice to have a horse even smaller than a pony. It would be just her size.

The next evening, Papa came home with a broad smile. He had bought the miniature horse! The man had given him a little cart and harness too. In just a few weeks, Papa said, they could bring the horse to Singing Tree Farm.

Lily thought a few weeks' wait seemed like a very long time. She wanted the miniature horse to come home right away. "What does he look like, Papa?"

"He's somewhere between two and three feet tall. He's coal black and a little chubby." Papa chuckled. "So they named him Chubby."

Chubby. What a fine name for a little tiny horse. Lily hoped Papa and Mama wouldn't want to change it.

Finally, the day came when Chubby would come to Singing Tree Farm. On a Saturday morning, as Lily and Joseph helped Mama do the cleaning, Papa hired someone with a cattle trailer to deliver Chubby. When the trailer turned into the driveway, Mama helped the children into their thick winter coats. Then they hurried out to the barn.

Papa was in the pen with Chubby, currying him and talking gently to him. "Well, what do you think of this little guy?"

Lily wasn't sure what to say. Chubby was so small. Why, he was even smaller than Joseph! "Can I pet him?"

"Sure," Papa said. "Hop in the pen. Chubby is very tame. He likes little children."

Lily climbed over the side of the pen and hopped on the soft straw. She started to pet Chubby. He was much more wooly than Jim. It seemed funny to be able to look down into a horse's face, instead of up.

"I put the cart over by the buggies. Let's take a look at it." Papa swung the door of Chubby's pen open and held out his hand for Lily. They walked over to look at the cart. It was just as tiny as Chubby. Just the right size for her and Joseph.

"Can I drive Chubby this afternoon?" Lily asked.

"Not yet," Papa said. "I want to be sure he is safe for you to drive. I'm the only one who will be driving him for a while."

Every evening, Papa hitched Chubby to the little cart and drove down the road. Every evening, Lily wished she could drive Chubby by herself. She wouldn't go out on the road, but it would be fun to drive him around the barnyard. When spring came, she would drive Chubby all over the yard and in the pasture. And when her friends came to visit, she would give them rides too.

Later that week, Lily watched Papa drive Chubby down the road. She stood at the window to watch for Papa to return, but it was taking much longer than usual. Finally, she saw Harold Young's station wagon drive up to the house with Papa in the passenger seat. Papa jumped out and hurried to the house. Where was his hat?

By the time Papa reached the porch, Mama held the door open for him. "Whatever happened, Daniel?"

Papa was shivering and dripping wet, head to toe. His teeth chattered. "Let me get into some dry clothes and I'll tell you all about it." He bolted up the stairs to change. "And some hot chocolate would be nice too," he added over his shoulder.

Papa left a trail of water drops everywhere he walked in the house. Lily ran to get a rag to wipe up the mess. Mama heated some milk on the stove for Papa. Lily found the can that held the hot chocolate powder. She carefully spooned several tablespoons into a mug, just the way that Papa liked it.

Papa drew a chair next to the stove to warm up. He sipped at the hot chocolate as he told them what had happened. "I was driving down the road when Chubby decided he wanted to turn right into the Youngs' house. I pulled on the reins to try to get him to turn back out on the road, but he kept going. The next thing I knew we were both in the creek that ran alongside the Youngs' property. My hat popped right off my head when I hit that cold water and went floating down the creek. I didn't have time to worry about it, though. I got up right away and tried to help Chubby. He is so small that he had to tip his head up as far as he could to keep his nose above water. I unhitched him and tried to drag him out. Even though he's small, he was too heavy for me to get him out by myself. I wasn't sure what I was going to do. I didn't want Chubby to drown. Thankfully, Harold Young came home about then and saw us floundering there in his creek. He helped me get Chubby out and offered to let the horse warm up in his garage. He brought me home so I could get out of those wet clothes." He finished his last sip of hot chocolate so Mama hurried to refill the mug. "The cart is still in the creek. I hate to think of getting back into that cold water to drag it out, but I don't want to leave it there until spring."

Lily shivered. She was glad Papa and Chubby weren't hurt. And she was pleasantly surprised that Harold Young would allow Chubby to stay in his garage to warm up.

Later that evening, Harold Young stopped by the farmhouse

to say that Chubby was nice and dry. "He's as fluffy as a teddy bear by now," he said in his gruff way.

Papa went out to the barn to get a halter and rope. He would go back to the Youngs', pull the cart out of the cold creek, and lead Chubby home.

That month, Papa spent a great deal of time training Chubby until he was confident that the horse would behave safely for Lily and Joseph.

One Saturday afternoon, Papa came in the house. "Get

your coat, Lily, and come outside. I have Chubby hitched up for you to drive."

Lily pulled on her coat and scarf. She skipped out the door beside Papa. She would finally be able to drive Chubby! Lily had to bite on her lip to not laugh out loud when she saw that Papa had hitched Chubby to her pink sled instead of the cart. She hoped Chubby thought it was a cart. He might be embarrassed if he knew he was pulling a pink sled. Papa helped her get situated on the sled and handed her the reins.

"Don't make him trot today," he said. "I want you to get used to driving him. Only walk him for now. There will be plenty of time to go faster."

Lily sat on the sled, held the reins, and then clucked to Chubby just the way Papa always did to Jim. Chubby started walking slowly around the barnyard. She pulled on the right rein and Chubby turned right. If she pulled on the left rein, he would turn left. Lily drove around and around the barnyard. This was fun! Getting pulled on her sled was so much better than dragging it all the way up a hill only to have a short ride down. Now she didn't have to pull the sled anywhere. Chubby could do that for her.

And as soon as spring would come, she could give Joseph a ride on the cart that Harold Young had helped Papa pull out of the creek. She hoped that Hannah and Levi would come over often to play. Then she could take them on rides with Chubby too.

She might even offer Mandy Mast a pony cart ride. Maybe not.

Teacher Katie's Horrible Gift

It was the first recess for the school day. All the children had removed their sandwiches from their lunch boxes. Some of them were wrapped in foil already, but Teacher Katie kept a roll of foil in her desk in case anyone forgot. Lily checked her sandwich. Mama had made another egg sandwich for her. Lily took it up to Teacher Katie's desk and asked for a piece of foil.

Teacher Katie tore a piece of foil off the roll and helped Lily wrap her sandwich and then handed her a black marker. Lily carefully wrote LILY on the foil and then placed her sandwich on the register. The hot air from the coal furnace in the basement would heat her sandwich by noon and it would be a treat to have something hot to eat.

Lily looked at all the other foil-wrapped sandwiches. Everyone was going to have a good lunch today.

At noon Lily got her sandwich off the register. It was almost too hot to hold with her bare hands so she folded the corner of her apron to carry it back to her desk. She carefully opened the foil and let some of the heat escape before trying to eat it.

While Lily waited for her sandwich to cool down enough to eat, she noticed that most of the other children had cheese sandwiches. They looked so good! Thick yellow melted cheese oozed out between two slices of bread. Mama's homemade cheese was good, but it didn't melt like the store-bought cheese in those sandwiches.

After everyone had finished their lunch, they went outside to play. Mandy Mast gathered the other little girls around her. "Let's exchange our sandwiches tomorrow," she said. "It will be fun to have something to eat besides the same thing everyday. I'll make the sandwich myself to be sure it's just right."

The other girls all thought it would be fun to exchange sandwiches. Lily hoped she would get a good cheese sand-wich. She knew that Mandy Mast always had store-bought cheese and, even better, store-bought bread. Her mouth fairly watered at the thought. Maybe she would be the one to get Mandy's lunch.

During first recess the next day, everyone put their sand-wiches on the register. Lily looked at Mandy's sandwich. It was wrapped in new foil with her name written neatly on it. Compared to Mandy's, Lily's sandwich looked crinkled and sad. Mama always smoothed out and reused foil until it was too torn to use any longer.

At noon Mandy ran to the register and picked up her sand-wich. "Here," Mandy said, thrusting the sandwich into Lily's hands. "I want you to have my sandwich."

Lily was thrilled! She would get to eat an oozing cheese sandwich! She gave her own sandwich to Mandy and went back to her desk. Carefully, Lily unwrapped Mandy's sandwich. She sat there staring at it in disbelief. It wasn't a cheese sandwich at all! It was a peanut butter and jelly sandwich. It was hot and gooey and slimy. Lily didn't even want to try to eat it. It was a gooey mess.

Mandy Mast burst out laughing. She laughed and laughed until Teacher Katie told her to stop.

Lily blinked back tears that prickled her eyes. She refused to give Mandy the satisfaction of seeing her cry. She took her peaches and cookie out of her lunch box and started to nibble at her cookie.

"Here. You can have part of my sandwich."

Lily looked up. Isaac was standing next to her desk. He held out a melted cheese sandwich. His blue eyes twinkled as he smiled kindly at her and placed half of his sandwich on her desk.

"Oh, thank you!" Lily said.

She was getting a sandwich after all! A real cheese sandwich. She watched Isaac walk back to his desk to finish his lunch. She thought he was the nicest boy in school. Nearly as nice as Papa.

❧❧

December had come, and snow covered the ground. One morning, Teacher Katie stood in front of the class to make an announcement. "It's time to exchange names for our Christmas program here at school. I have everyone's names written on a slip of paper. If one of the boys will bring me a hat, we can start drawing names."

Isaac jumped up and went to the back of the room to pluck his hat off the wall peg. He handed it to Teacher Katie. She scooped a pile of small folded papers into the hat, then put her hand in the hat to mix them up. She drew out a piece of paper and put it into her pocket. Then it was Isaac's turn to draw a name. He put it into his pocket and carried his hat from desk to desk so that every student could pick a paper.

Teacher Katie spoke to the class as Isaac made his rounds. "Remember to tell no one but your parents about whose name you drew. That way it will be a surprise when we open the presents at the Christmas program."

Presents? That sounded like fun! Isaac paused beside Lily's desk to let her draw a piece of paper from his hat. She carefully opened it to see whose name she drew. *Teacher Katie.* Her excitement fizzled like a popped balloon. She folded the paper and slipped it into her pocket to give to Papa and Mama as soon as she got home.

Every day in December, the scholars prepared for the up-coming Christmas program. Parents and siblings were invited to come to it and to stay for lunch. Teacher Katie instructed the scholars to walk to the front of the schoolroom and file into three rows. The biggest boys and girls stood in the back row and the smallest stood in the front. They sang Christmas songs and recited Christmas poems and read a few Bible verses about Jesus's birth.

Every day.

The same fifteen songs.

Every single day.

Lily's legs grew tired of standing for such a long time. She grew bored with the songs and the poems. She was even bored with the same old Bible verses, though she knew it was wrong to think such a thought.

Mama helped Lily memorize the snowman poem Teacher Katie had assigned to her to recite at the program. Lily didn't like the poem. It wasn't a real Christmas poem like Hannah and Mandy's. Everybody knew that snowmen were around all winter—not just Christmas. Everybody knew that.

The evening before the Christmas program, Mama helped Lily wrap Teacher Katie's gifts. Mama had bought a beautiful big candy bowl filled with candies and nuts. She included two pretty pink towels with dark pink roses on them. Lily thought she had never seen such pretty towels. She hoped her gifts would make Teacher Katie happy. Maybe Teacher Katie would be nicer if she liked Lily's gifts. Lily set the beautifully wrapped gifts next to the door so she would remember to take it to school in the morning. Oh, but how terrible it would be if she forgot!

As Lily changed into her nightgown to get ready for bed, she wondered what all the other school children would bring for presents. And she thought about who might have drawn her name. Wouldn't it be wonderful if it were Isaac? She smiled and snuggled deeper under her covers. Tomorrow, school would be fun.

Papa was in no hurry to leave for work in the morning. Lily worried he might be sick, but Papa only laughed. "I won't be going to work today," Papa said. "I wouldn't want to miss my little girl's first Christmas program."

"Oh thank you, Papa!" Lily said. What a wonderful surprise! It would be such a treat to have Papa come to school. He could see her desk. He could see her books and her pencils. Lily knew she wouldn't mind reciting her dumb snowman poem with Papa sitting at the back, smiling at her in his encouraging way.

After breakfast Mama told Lily to hurry and change. "Today is a special day, so you can wear your purple Sunday dress."

Oh, this day was the best day, the very best! Papa was

coming to school and Lily was going to wear her favorite dress. She ran up the stairs, two at a time. She took her purple dress out of the closet and slipped into it. Then she covered it with her white organdy apron.

Lily hurried downstairs so Mama could button up the back of her dress.

When Mama saw her, she grinned. "I should have told you to wear your purple apron. The white one is only for church."

Lily removed her white apron and hung it carefully back in her closet, a little disappointed. She wanted to wear her Sunday best to school today. Even Papa was dressed up. He looked so handsome in his nice Sunday visiting clothes. Papa went outside to hitch Jim to the buggy as Mama scurried around getting everything ready. Lily helped Dannie with his socks and shoes, though she needed Mama's help to tie the laces. Just as Papa brought Jim up to the house, they were ready to go.

Lily carried the wrapped gifts for Teacher Katie out to the buggy as if they were made of spun sugar. After everyone was settled, Mama tucked a thick buggy robe over their laps. The buggy robe was warm and cozy, but Lily couldn't sit still. Too excited! She turned around and knelt on the seat to look out the window. Now she was glad she could wear her purple apron. She wouldn't have to worry about wrinkles.

Joseph turned around to look out the window too. It was fun to see the tracks the buggy wheels made in the fresh snow that fell last night. They rolled out like ribbons behind the buggy.

When they arrived at school, Papa guided Jim up to the hitching rack to wait with the other horses. Papa reached under the front seat and got Jim's horse blanket. He tossed it on Jim's back and fastened the straps underneath his belly.

The blanket would keep Jim nice and warm until they were ready to go home.

Mama had packed lunch for them in a big brown paper bag. All but Lily's. Her lunch was packed in her lunch box, like a usual school day, even though nothing about the day felt usual.

"Can I carry your lunch box?" Joseph asked.

Lily handed it to him and carefully carried Teacher Katie's gifts into the schoolhouse.

Rows of benches had been brought into the schoolhouse and pushed up against the walls of the schoolhouse. Most of the parents had already arrived. They were seated and visiting with each other. The students were huddled near the front of the room around Teacher Katie's desk. Her desk was piled high with presents of every shape and size, wrapped in pretty Christmas wrapping. One box was very big. What could be inside? It was almost as big as Lily was tall. She placed Teacher Katie's gift very carefully on the edge of the desk so it wouldn't be squashed, and then stood next to Hannah. Together they eyed the packages and tried to guess what was inside them and who would be getting them. Lily couldn't stop thinking about what was in that big box and for whom it was meant. Maybe it would be for Lily! Maybe it would be a new doll. Sally would like to have a doll friend.

Teacher Katie rang the bell for the students to sit down. She stood in front of the classroom. "Since we are having a program we will be doing things a little differently this morning," she said. "I would like to ask Nate Mast and Daniel Lapp to read the Christmas Scriptures for us."

Papa? Teacher Katie wanted Lily's Papa to read! Mandy sat up straight and proud in her chair, so Lily did too.

Nate Mast and Papa rose from their benches and walked to the front of the schoolhouse. Nate Mast read the second chapter of Matthew. Then it was Papa's turn to read. Lily loved to listen to Papa's deep voice, so smooth and clear, as he read the second chapter of Luke. When he finished, he closed the Bible and went back to sit next to Mama and Joseph and Dannie.

Teacher Katie nodded her head—the signal for the scholars to rise from their desks and file to the front of the schoolroom. The children stood in rows, just as they had practiced so many times. This time, they didn't use songbooks. Teacher Katie had made them sing the fifteen songs so often that they had everything memorized. Lily thought she could sing them in her sleep.

After singing several songs, it was Isaac's turn to recite. His poem was about the innkeeper in Bethlehem. Several other children recited their poems and then they sang more songs. Lily's turn to recite came last because she was the youngest. Always, always last. She looked out at the sea of faces. There were so many people! They were all looking right at her. Suddenly she couldn't remember any words to the dumb snowman poem. Her mind was like a white sheet flapping on a clothesline—blank and restless. Her heart thumped loudly.

She was sure others could hear it. *Ba bump, ba bump, ba bump*. It was echoing through the quiet room!

As she clutched the sides of her apron, she tried to think harder. *Think, think, think, Lily!* Everything was so quiet. Everyone was waiting. Everyone was watching. The room was full of watching eyes. Lily wanted to run right out of the schoolhouse and keep running. Just then she caught Papa's eyes. He winked. And just like that—snap!—Lily remembered. She quickly said her poem without a single mistake. And then the scholars sang the final song. Number fifteen.

At last, it was time to exchange the gifts. The children went back to their desks, watching with anticipation as Isaac and another big boy passed out the gifts. Lily watched as Teacher Katie opened her gift. She took a long time admiring the rose pattern on the towels and she started to eat the candy in the candy bowl. Lily thought she seemed pleased, but it was hard to tell because Teacher Katie never smiled. Not once.

Isaac placed a lumpy-looking package on Lily's desk. She turned it over and saw that it was from Hannah. She carefully unwrapped the funny-looking package. Inside was a paint-by-number set. Lily's favorite thing! Next to playing dolls. And there was also a cute red and yellow apple-shaped glass candy bowl with a few pieces of homemade chocolate candy and three packs of Smarties. Lily smiled at Hannah. Smarties were her favorite candy of all. The gifts were perfect, just perfect. She didn't even mind that she was not going to get the great big box. She placed her gifts on the corner of her desk and watched the other children open their gifts. Balls, books, candy. All of the gifts were wonderful! Very, very wonderful.

Isaac passed out the last gift and sat down at his desk where his gift was waiting to be opened. It was the giant box! Lily couldn't wait to see what was inside. She kept her eyes on Isaac as he opened it carefully. Inside the box was another box, wrapped in colorful wrapping paper. After he opened that box, there was another box inside of that one, and another and another. Each box was smaller than the one before. Finally, there was only a thin little box left to open. Inside was a coloring book—something Joseph or Dannie might like. But not something a big eighth grade boy would want. Lily felt sorry for Isaac. Everyone received special gifts except for him. She wondered who had given him a joke gift. A rusty snorting sound came from the front of the classroom. Lily looked up and saw it was Teacher Katie, watching Isaac and laughing.

The big girls gathered up the wrapping paper so the mothers could take it home to iron and reuse. After the room was cleaned up, it was time to eat.

Together, the students and parents sang a short song of thanks to God for their food. The children ran to get their lunch boxes. Mothers set out the food they had packed. The schoolhouse with filled with happy sounds of laughter and chatter.

When Lily had finished eating, she gathered her gifts into her arms and went to sit next to Papa and Mama. She stopped beside Isaac's desk. She had to know. "Who gave you that silly coloring book?" she whispered.

Isaac glanced around the room. He lowered his voice. "Teacher Katie."

Teacher Katie? *Teacher Katie!* What a mean trick! And then she had laughed at him too. How could a grown-up be so mean, especially at Christmas? It was a mystery to her. "You can have some of my candy." It wasn't an easy thing to part with her Smarties, but Lily would do that. She would do that for Isaac.

Isaac shook his head. "No, that's okay. It's yours."

Lily went back to Papa and Mama. She gave Joseph and Dannie each a pack of Smarties and then opened the last pack for herself. As the Smarties candy dissolved on her tongue, it tasted like Teacher Katie: sour and tangy.

The Stranger and the Steer

The room was warm and full of flickering firelight. Papa and Mama sat on their rocking chairs. A big pile of grapevines lay on the floor between them, near the small table that held the oil lamp. The owner of a nearby vineyard had brought the big bundles of vines for Papa and Mama to prune. One by one, they would take a long vine and carefully count the little knobby buds before they cut the vines into little pieces. Only one or two buds should be on each piece.

After they had finished trimming them, the owner would use the little pieces to grow more big grapevines. In several years, these little sticks would end up producing big juicy grapes. It was hard for Lily to imagine. Right now, they just looked like a big pile of twigs.

Lily sat on the couch playing with her doll, Sally. Joseph played on the floor with his stuffed animals. Dannie was already asleep in his crib. Lily wished she could help Mama and Papa cut the vines. It looked fun and easy. They made a quick snip with the pruning shears and tossed the cut piece in the box. The box was slowly filling up.

"Can I cut a few grapevines?" Lily asked.

"We only have two pruning shears," Papa said. "And it is much harder than it looks. Maybe when you are a little older, you can help us."

Papa started to whistle. Mama hummed along and soon Lily and Joseph chimed in. The little farmhouse was filled with the sounds of their sweet voices.

A wailing sound floated down the stairs. Their beautiful singing must have woken Dannie up. Mama went upstairs to rock him back to sleep. She laid her pruning shears on the floor beside her rocking chair. Lily eyed the pruning shears. It looked so pretty with its bright blue handles and its shiny little scissor-like blades. She was sure she could snip the vines just like Mama had been doing.

Lily scooted behind Mama's rocking chair and got a vine. She carefully counted two buds and cut. Snip! Suddenly the pruning shears slipped and cut a gash into her hand. Lily screamed as blood seeped out of the cut. Papa bolted from his rocking chair and yanked his big red bandana out of his pocket. He wrapped it around Lily's hand and took her to the kitchen sink to wash the blood away.

Mama heard Lily's scream and rushed downstairs to see what had happened. She peered over Papa's shoulder to see how deep the cut was. They decided it didn't need stitches, so they cleaned it carefully, covered it with ointment, then taped a neat little gauze bandage over it.

"I think it's bedtime now," Papa said.

Oh, no. So early! Lily wished she hadn't tried to cut the grapevine. Her hand was sore and now Papa was sending her to bed early. After Papa read a short prayer from the little black prayer book, Lily and Joseph went upstairs to bed. As Lily lay in her bed, she listened to the cold winter wind moan through the trees and whistle at her windows. She could hear the murmur of Papa and Mama's voices as they continued to snip the grapevines. She yawned and wiggled farther down the mattress. Soon, she fell asleep.

Early one Saturday morning in March, someone knocked on the door as Lily and Joseph gathered breakfast dishes from the table to take to Mama at the kitchen sink. Mama wiped her wet hands on her apron. She reached up to tuck a stray wisp of hair behind her ear before she went to see who was at the door.

Mama opened the door to a stranger. Lily didn't know who the man was and tried to listen as he talked to Mama.

"I have come to pick up your steer," the stranger said. "Where do you want me to put the trailer to get him loaded?"

"Along the far side of the barn," Mama said. "I'll be right out to help you load him." She closed the door and turned to Lily. "I have to run out to the barn for a little bit. Keep an eye on Dannie for me and I'll be right back."

Mama put on her warm coat and went out to help the man. Lily and Joseph ran to the living room and knelt on the couch in front of the windows. They saw Mama and the man walk inside the barn. When they came back out, the man was carrying Papa's big red chain saw. Lily wondered what he needed with Papa's saw. Lily and Joseph weren't allowed to touch it.

Mama and the stranger disappeared behind the barn. Lily and Joseph kept watching out the window. Dannie was happily building towers on the floor with his wooden blocks. Lily heard the chain saw start with a roar. She couldn't think of anything behind the barn that needed cutting.

And then she had a dreadful thought.

Maybe . . . the stranger was cutting off Mama's legs! Lily could imagine the entire scene in her mind. Poor Mama! She wouldn't be able to walk or cook or do anything she was used to doing. It was all too terrible to think about. Lily turned to Joseph and said in a thin, scared whisper, "That man is chopping Mama's legs off!"

Joseph looked at her with big eyes. He started to cry. Big, loud, gasping wails. Dannie's mouth opened wide and he started to bawl. The three of them sat on the floor, held each other, and cried at the top of their lungs.

All of a sudden, Mama was standing in front of them. "Whatever is wrong?" Her eyes scanned all three of them to see if someone had bumped a head or scraped a knee.

Why, Mama's legs were still there! They weren't cut off at all! Lily was so glad to see Mama, still in one piece. But then she felt a little sheepish.

Joseph wasn't feeling at all sheepish. "Lily said that man was cutting your legs off."

Lily frowned at him. Little boys needed to learn not to tattle.

Mama looked exasperated. "There was a long branch on the big ash tree behind the barn. The man had to cut it so he could back his trailer up to the barn door." She crouched down to Lily's level. "A healthy imagination is a good thing if you use it for the right things, Lily. But it is never a good idea to use it to worry about things that might not happen. Worrying is a big waste of time."

Lily wiped away her tears. She would try harder not to think of worrisome thoughts again. But she still thought Joseph should learn not to tattle.

Mandy Mast's Visit

On a sunny Saturday, Nate Mast stopped by Singing Tree Farm with Mandy at his side. He needed to buy another draft horse at a horse auction and would be gone all day. Would Mama mind if Mandy stayed to play with Lily today?

Of course, Mama said yes. Normally, Lily liked having friends come for the day, but Mandy was a continual worry. It seemed that every time Mandy came over, Lily ended up doing something that made Papa and Mama sad. And usually, Lily ended up getting sent to her room to think about the choices she had made with Mandy. And Joseph would cry and Dannie would cry and then Lily would cry—mostly because she was sent to her room.

The problem was that Mandy thought of things to do that Mama had never told Lily not to do until *after* she helped Mandy do it. Lily hoped that Mandy wouldn't get any new ideas this time. She didn't want to get into trouble. She didn't like to make her parents sad. And she definitely didn't like to get sent to her room.

Lily thought back to Mandy's last visit. She had helped Lily gather the eggs in the chicken coop. Mandy showed Lily how she could hold the little pail filled with eggs and swing her arm around in a wide circle without any eggs falling out of the pail. But when Lily tried it, she didn't swing her arm fast enough. Every egg in the pail fell to the ground and splattered on the floor. Mama was not at all happy about wasted eggs. At least the hens were happy. They enjoyed pecking them until they had cleaned up the whole mess.

Lily would not swing the egg pail today. She worried that Mandy would trick her into doing something else, just as

138

bad. This time, Lily would try extra hard to make sure not to do anything that she knew she shouldn't. *Think, think, think*, she reminded herself.

After Mandy's father left, Mama sent Lily and Mandy out to the chicken coop to gather eggs. She warned them not to break any eggs this time. Lily promised they would be very careful. They gathered the eggs and brought them safely in the house. They had not cracked a single one this time. Not one.

As Lily and Mandy went back outside to play, Joseph and Dannie wanted to join them. Mama asked Lily to keep an eye on Dannie. Everyone was having fun until Mandy grew bored and wanted to play on the swing. Lily stayed with Dannie until Mandy called out for her to come push the swing.

"I'm supposed to watch Dannie," Lily said. She was pleased with herself. She hadn't jumped up to push Mandy on the swing when she knew that Mama wanted her to watch over Dannie.

Mandy jumped off the swing and ran to the sandbox. "We can all play with Dannie," she said.

Lily was shocked! Mandy was thinking of someone else. She was actually being nice.

"Come with me, Dannie," Mandy said. She held out her hand to him and he grabbed it. She started walking away and looked back over her shoulder at Lily. "Let's pretend to be hikers in the wilderness. I'll be the leader and you and Joseph can follow me."

Mandy led the way across the yard, holding onto Dannie's little hand. Lily and Joseph followed behind. Mandy stopped under a tree, pretending to rest for a while from their long hard hike. Then she started walking again. Mandy pretended she was a hiking guide and chattered as they walked. Every little hill turned into a mountain. Dandelions were special food that they gathered into their aprons to pretend to eat when they stopped at their camp.

Lily bent down to pluck a few more bright yellow dandelion blossoms from their stems. She was enjoying Mandy's game and admired her imagination. She could have never thought up such a fun thing to do.

Suddenly, a piercing yell filled the air. Lily ran over and saw that Mandy had led Dannie right over a big thistle. He had stepped on it with his little bare feet and was crying up a storm.

"That was not a very kind thing to do, Mandy," Lily said. "You should not have done that."

"I know," Mandy said. "But I just couldn't help it!" Then she started to giggle.

Lily quickly scooped Dannie up into her arms and carried him to the house. Mama came outside to see why Dannie was crying. She had heard Dannie's wail. Mama sat Dannie on a kitchen chair and removed all the little prickles that were stuck in his feet like sharp needles. Lily wiped tears from his round cheeks. Joseph brought him a cookie.

When Mama finished helping Dannie, she turned to Lily. "I asked you to watch over him, Lily. You need to be more careful."

Mandy stood at the door with a sly smile at the corner of her mouth. Lily was so cross with Mandy that she wanted to slap her. She didn't do it, but she wanted to. And she was mad at herself too. Mandy had done it again! She had gotten Lily into trouble *again*.

Lily's Birthday

*L*ily woke up early. Today was her seventh birthday! She had been looking forward to it for a very long time and now it was finally here. She jumped out of bed and hurried to get dressed and go downstairs. She knew Mama would be making a special birthday breakfast. Mama's breakfast was the start of a very special day and she wanted to enjoy every minute of it.

When Mama heard Lily's light footsteps on the stairs, she turned around. "Good morning, Lily!" she said cheerfully. She gave Lily a hug. "And happy birthday!"

Lily's face broke into an ear-to-ear smile. "What are you making for breakfast?"

"I'm frying bacon right now," Mama said. She turned her attention back to the stove. The bacon was hissing and sputtering and crackling in the heavy cast iron frying pan. "We'll have eggs and fried cornmeal mush and tomato gravy."

She glanced at Lily. "And for a special treat I bought a box of cornflakes for your birthday when we were in town last week."

Lily was excited to hear about the cornflakes. Bacon was nice, but cornflakes were much more special. They almost never had cold cereal. And best of all, she would not have to eat porridge today! She did *not* like porridge.

Mama handed Lily the plates to set the table. On top of the stack was the special birthday plate: it had red roses on the bottom and a narrow bright blue rim. Lily put it carefully at her place at the table. Food always tasted extra delicious on that special plate.

The kitchen door opened and in walked Papa. He held out his arms to Lily and scooped her up. "There's my birthday girl," he said swinging her high in the air. As he set her back down on the floor, he said, "You're getting to be so big. I won't be able to swing you much longer."

How sad! Lily liked birthdays, but she also wanted to stay small enough for Papa to swing her in the air. It felt as if she were flying.

At breakfast, Mama said that Grandpa and Grandma Miller, Aunt Susie, and Uncle Elmer, Aunt Mary, Hannah, and Levi would be joining the family for supper. "We'll wait to give gifts until after supper tonight," Mama said. "For now, it's time to get ready for school."

Lily would have rather stayed home today. It was the first time she wouldn't be at home all day on her birthday. She couldn't have a special birthday lunch with the special birthday plate if she stayed at school.

Mama packed Lily's lunch box as she went upstairs to change her clothes. When she came back down, Joseph acted as if he had a big secret. It made Lily mad. She wondered if

Mama had told him some fun things they planned to do while she was stuck in school with crabby Teacher Katie. Not fair!

Lily sat on a chair next to the table. "Can I stay home from school today?"

Mama looked surprised. "Certainly not. You're not sick. You wouldn't want to miss out on any of the things the first graders are learning today. Get your lunch box. We need to hurry or you'll be late."

Lily picked up her lunch box and followed Mama outside. The ride to school didn't seem to take very long as Joseph chattered happily all the way. He was going to help Mama bake a birthday cake for Lily and they would let Dannie lick the spoons. Not fair!

At the school yard, Hannah ran to meet Lily as soon as she hopped off the buggy. "Happy Birthday!" Hannah said. She grabbed Lily's hand and pulled her into the schoolhouse. "The big girls made something pretty for you. Let's go see!"

Lily cheered up with that news and ran into the schoolhouse. Her desk was piled high with cards and gifts. Most of the children in school had made a birthday card for her, but the big girls had all made something a little extra. One of them had crocheted a bookmark with delicate thread. Another had made a pretty star from old, used wooden matchsticks and glued glitter on it. Someone else had made a tiny heart-shaped pin cushion. Before Lily could open the cards, Teacher Katie rang the bell. It was time to start school.

After the students had sung their usual three hymns, they sang "Happy Birthday" to Lily. She felt awkward. What should she do? Should she join in or just sit and listen? It was embarrassing to have everyone look at her. So many eyes watching her! After the song ended, she said, "Thank you," but it came out in a squeaky little voice.

At noon, Lily opened her lunch box. Next to her egg sandwich and dish of peaches, Mama had tucked in a Snickers candy bar. So *this* was Joseph's secret! Lily opened it and took several bites. It was delicious. She folded the wrapper over it again and put it back into her lunch box. She would try to make that candy bar last for a long time. A Snickers bar was her second favorite candy, right behind Smarties.

When it was time for school to dismiss, Mama was waiting outside with Jim and the buggy. Dannie sat on Mama's lap and Joseph sat beside her. Lily hurried to gather the cards and little gifts from her desk. Hannah helped her carry them to the buggy. "My mama said I could go home with you tonight since we are all coming to your house anyway."

"Oh good!" Lily said. This day kept getting better and better!

By the time they returned to Singing Tree Farm, Grandpa and Grandma Miller were already there. Aunt Susie sat on the couch with a doll. Lily and Hannah brought their dolls and went to join her. This was Lily's happiest moment: to play dolls with her cousin and her aunt.

Lily noticed a small pile of gifts sitting on Mama's sewing machine. She tried not to glance at them too often, but she couldn't help herself. She couldn't stop thinking about those gifts.

Not much later, Uncle Elmer, Aunt Mary, and Levi arrived. Levi and Joseph ran out to the barn to play while Aunt Mary set Davy on the floor next to Dannie. She gave them some toys to play with so she could help Mama make supper.

Supper was ready to eat by the time Papa arrived home from work. Aunt Mary poured water into the glasses while Grandma helped Mama dish out the hot food. Lily looked over each dish. Mama had made all of Lily's favorite foods.

Crispy fried chicken—and she knew she would get a nice big drumstick today without even having to ask—mounds of mashed potatoes with melted butter dribbled over the top and sprinkled with chopped parsley, noodles with melted store-bought cheese, bits of chicken meat topped with crisply fried buttery pieces of bread crumbs, and green beans fried with crushed crackers. On the countertop were three cherry and two vanilla crumb pies. Best of all, there was a chocolate layer cake smothered with creamy white frosting. Mama had placed seven pretty pink roses around the top, each with a twisty green vine and several leaves. In the center were the words: *Happy Birthday Lily*.

When it was time to cut the cake, Lily thought it was a shame to cut it. It looked too pretty. She watched as Mama sliced thick pieces of chocolate cake for each person. When Lily was handed her piece, she was too full to eat another bite.

"Can we save my piece for tomorrow, Mama?" she asked.

"I think that's a good idea," Mama said. She put Lily's slice of cake into a plastic container to keep it nice and fresh until she was ready to eat it.

Finally, it was time to open her gifts. Mama and Papa gave her a pretty new purple dress and a cute white tie-on apron just like Mama wore when she cooked or baked. In another box were brand-new shoes. Black and shiny, with long laces. The shoes Lily wore now made her toes pinch tight. Lily tried them on right away, and Mama helped her tie the shoelaces. Then she put on the apron. She felt very grown-up.

Lily's next gift was from Uncle Elmer and Aunt Mary. They gave her a cute puzzle of a puppy holding a red ball in his mouth and a coloring book. Her last gift was from Grandpa and Grandma Miller. Grandma had made a new dress and bonnet for her doll, Sally, and a pretty blanket to wrap her in. Grandpa gave Lily two special books from his book cabinet. She had often admired those very books. Lily stroked the glossy covers carefully and looked at some of the illustrations. They looked even prettier now that the books belonged to her.

Lily thanked everyone for the special gifts. She sat on Papa's big rocking chair in the living room. The room, lit by flickering firelight, was warm and cozy, filled with the people Lily loved most. This had been the best birthday of all. She was seven years old, and she was sure there was no other little girl anywhere as happy as she.

A Lesson to Remember

Joseph burst through the kitchen door to find Mama. "A baby bird fell from its nest!" he said, panting. "Can you help me put it back in?"

Mama wiped her hands on her apron and followed Joseph outside. Lily trotted behind her. She wanted to see a baby bird too. She hoped it would be a baby cardinal or maybe a baby goldfinch. Those were the prettiest birds. Those would be the baby birds Lily would want to see.

Joseph was under a tree, kneeling on the ground. Mama crouched down beside him to examine the baby bird. Lily leaned over Mama's shoulder. What a disappointment! This was a very ugly bird. It was brown with little speckles on its chest. It didn't look like any bird she had ever seen before.

"It's a baby robin," Mama said softly. "Joseph, I'm afraid we can't put it back into its nest. If the mama bird smells a

147

human scent on this baby or any of the other little birds in the nest, she won't take care of them."

Joseph started to cry. "But he'll die! He needs someone to take care of him."

Mama thought for a little bit. "There's a little box in the kitchen. We could make a nest for it in the box and try to feed it until it's big enough to fly." She stood. "But it will need a lot of care. You will have to be the bird's mother. You'll have to dig for worms so it has something to eat."

Lily knew that Joseph would not mind digging for worms. He was always digging for worms or trying to catch insects in a net. Sure enough, he ran to the kitchen to get the box. Mama gently lifted the little bird and set it inside. It opened and closed its mouth and made funny little chirping noises.

"Let's name him Chirp," Joseph said.

"That sounds like a good name," Mama said. "It looks as if Chirp is hungry. I think you had better go dig some worms for it."

Mama carried the box into the house while Joseph ran to the sandbox to get his little shovel, then he rushed off to Mama's garden to dig for worms. Not much later, he came into the house with three big squirming earthworms in his hands. Mama showed him how to pinch the worms into little pieces to feed to Chirp.

Earthworms made Lily squirm. Watching them be fed, in pieces, to Chirp was too much. She started to gag. Joseph's bird was ugly and he ate gross things. It was too much for a little girl to bear. She ran upstairs to play with Sally.

But Joseph was a good bird mother. Day after day, he sat next to Chirp's box to talk to him and feed him when he was hungry—which was often. Joseph didn't even want to play with Lily or Dannie. All he wanted to do was to take care of

Chirp. Lily wished Chirp would hurry up and grow. Joseph was not much fun anymore.

Finally, one morning, Chirp started to stretch his wings. Mama peered in the box. "I think it's time we move his box outdoors so he doesn't take his first flight in the house."

Lily sat next to Joseph on the porch steps. She wanted to watch Chirp fly for the first time. Joseph held the little bird in his hands. Chirp flapped and flapped his little wings. He gave a little jump and fluttered down to the ground. It reminded Lily of the time when Joseph tried to fly off the chicken coop and ended up with a broken arm. *Flap, flap, jump, crash*. Lily thought that Chirp couldn't fly much better than Joseph.

Joseph bent down to pick Chirp up. The little bird seemed to want to try to fly again. This time it fluttered a little farther before it landed on the ground. Joseph brought some worms to feed it. Feeding Chirp was still gross to Lily, but at least Chirp stayed on the grass to eat his worms. He ran and fluttered along the ground to try to test his wings.

Even for a bird, flying looked like hard work.

A few days later, Chirp was able to dig and scratch for his own worms and bugs. He was starting to take longer flights too.

And then came the day when Chirp went missing. Joseph cried and cried until Mama pointed to a branch in the big cedar tree. There sat a robin that looked just like Chirp.

"This is what we wanted for Chirp, Joseph," Mama said. "He is able to take care of himself now. He can join his family and be a real bird. He was never meant to be a pet."

Joseph felt sad, but Lily was glad. She wanted to have Joseph play with her and Dannie like he did before Chirp fell out of his nest. She looked up in the tree. It was high time that Chirp find his own playmates. Birds were too much work.

Early on Sunday morning, Lily hurried to get dressed for church. She pulled her black socks up to her knees and took her new shoes out of the box. She sniffed the brand-new leather smell and ran a finger along the shiny black top. They were the most beautiful shoes Lily ever had. Carefully, she tied her shoelaces to the rhyme Mama had just taught her:

> Bunny ears, bunny ears,
> playing by a tree.
> Criss-crossed the tree,
> trying to catch me.
> Bunny ears, Bunny ears,
> jumped into the hole,
> popped out the other side
> beautiful and bold.

Lily pulled the two bunny ears tight to make a knot. Done! She jumped off of her bed, wiggled her toes, and smiled. Wait until Mandy Mast saw these new shoes. Her smile faded as she thought what Mama would say if she knew what Lily was thinking. Mama was always reminding Lily to guard against vanity. Still, they were wonderful new shoes. And Mandy was always showing off her new things to Lily.

Lily heard her father's deep voice calling for her. She ran downstairs, grabbed her bonnet off the wall peg, and hurried outside to the waiting buggy. Church was going to be at Isaac's home. Isaac's farm had a big pond where the children liked to play. It was a beautiful spring day after a long, cold, gray winter.

After lunch, Lily, Hannah, and Mandy ran down to the pond. The boys were on one end of the pond—as far from the girls as they could be. They stood by the shoreline, throwing their pocketknives on the ground. The girls were gathered on the opposite end of the pond. They liked to pretend they were fishing. When the water was warm, they would even try to catch minnows in their hands. Not today, though. The water was too cold. Hannah started a game to see who could best skim a rock along the water's surface. It took a special twist of the wrist to make the rock jump on top of the water. Levi had taught Hannah how to do it just right, so she tried to teach the other girls. Lily caught on quickly. Two skips of the rock. Three skips, then four! This was fun.

Mandy said she didn't like the game, but Lily knew it was because she wasn't very good at it. "Let's kick the rocks, instead," Mandy said. "Whoever kicks the farthest, wins." She glanced down at Lily's new shoes. "Your shoelaces are untied, Lily. I'll tie them for you."

Mandy bent down to help Lily tie her shoes. Lily felt her heart soften toward Mandy, just a little. Lily wasn't very good at tying her shoelaces yet and had to keep stopping to retie them. It was nice of Mandy to help her.

Mandy told everyone to look for big rocks. She lined up the rocks along the water's edge and had the girls stand about ten feet away. "When I say 'go,' everyone run and kick their rock!" She put her hands on her hips, like the handles on a sugar bowl. "I'll watch and see which rock goes the farthest."

All of the little girls lined up behind their rocks. This was very exciting.

"Go!" Mandy shouted.

Each girl ran to the water's edge and kicked their rock as hard as they could. Lily's rock went flying in the air, *up, up, up!* But so did her new shoe. The shoelace had come undone. Lily was horrified! Her new shoe dropped into the middle of the deep pond with a loud *kerplop!* before it was swallowed

up by the water. A quiet hush fell over the girls, then Lily started to cry. Hannah ran to find a big stick to see if she could dredge the pond, but even Lily knew that would be hopeless. The shoe was at the bottom of Isaac's cold pond. She had to go tell her parents what she had done. Lily wiped away her tears and turned to hop up the hill to find Mama. She might have just imagined it, as she hopped along on one shoe, sniffling and whimpering, but from behind her she thought she heard Mandy's giggle.

❧❧

Every now and then, Lily was invited to spend an afternoon at Grandma and Grandpa Miller's, all by herself. She loved those special times with her grandparents. She would help Grandma bake or play dolls with Aunt Susie or work with Grandpa in his harness shop.

On this spring day, Lily was helping Grandma pick asparagus from the garden. She thought spears of asparagus looked odd as they grew, like tall trees sprouting from the straw. After the basket was filled with green spears, Grandma and Lily went back to the house. Grandma stopped at the flower bed to admire the daffodils bobbing in the gentle breeze. In front of the daffodils was a line of pretty little white bell-shaped flowers.

Lily crouched down to smell them. They had a sweet scent. "What kind of flowers are these?"

"They're called lily of the valley." Grandma picked a flower to sniff.

Lily was happy that she shared a name with such sweet little flowers. She admired how each dainty, tiny bell had perfect little scallops around the edges.

Grandma plucked four sprays of lilies and handed them to Lily. "Let's take these into the house. I have something to show you."

In the kitchen, Grandma opened a cupboard door and pulled out four little glass bottles. She told Lily to fill them with water.

Lily carried them to the washbasin. She carefully filled each bottle with water and set them on the counter. Grandma had her head in another cupboard, hunting for something.

"I'm sure I still have some," she muttered. With a satisfied sigh, she pulled out a box of little bottles of food coloring.

Grandma opened the bottle of red coloring and handed it to Lily. She showed Lily how to squeeze a few drops into the bottle. Lily watched the red drops swirl through the bottle and change the water into red. Grandma had her do the same with the blue and green coloring, but she left the fourth bottle with clear water.

"Now add one spray of flower to each bottle," Grandma said.

Lily tucked one flower spray into each bottle and stood back to admire them. She liked the bottle with the red water best. It looked pretty with the white lilies.

"See how nice and white all those flowers are now, Lily," she said. "Soon, the bottle with red water will turn the lilies pink. The blue water will turn those flowers blue, and the green water will turn those flowers green. The water in the bottles is just like the friends you choose. They will affect you, Lily, whether you want them to or not."

Lily stared at the flowers, amazed.

"Can you guess what color the lilies will turn that are in the clear water?"

Lily bit her lip. "White?"

"Yes."

"Will they stay white?"

"Yes, they will. They are like little girls who choose their friends wisely. They don't have to worry about changing who they are no matter how much time they spend with them. But those other lilies are just like friends that you don't choose wisely. Right now they are all white, but by the time your mother comes to take you home, they will start changing colors. They will never be the same again unless you remove it from the bottle and put it in clear water."

Grandma carefully packed the lilies in their bottles of colored water into a box so they wouldn't spill on the way home. She set them beside the front door so Lily wouldn't forget to take them with her.

When Mama arrived to take Lily home, she walked carefully to the buggy with her box of flowers, making sure that none of the water in the bottles spilled. On the way home, she told Mama all about the flowers.

"Looks like Grandma was sharing the importance of choosing your friends," Mama said. "I remember when she showed me the flowers in colored water when I was a little girl."

Lily tried to think of Mama as a little girl. What would she have looked like? Or acted like? Would she have liked to play dolls? It was hard to imagine.

At home, Lily carried the box into her bedroom and set the jars on her dresser. Already the colored water was starting to change the colors of the lilies. Even though Grandma and Mama were too kind to say, she knew who they were thinking of: Mandy Mast.

CHAPTER

22

An Unwanted Schoolhouse Visitor

$\mathcal{L}$ily sat at her school desk, working in her spelling book. She heard the soft crunchy sound of gravel churning as a car came to a stop in front of the schoolhouse. All of the children turned around in their chairs to see out the window. Who had come to visit their schoolhouse?

A loud knock sounded on the door. Teacher Katie went to the door to open it. Lily leaned over in her seat and caught a glimpse of an English man. He had a thin brown satchel tucked under his arm. Lily could hear Teacher Katie talk to the man in the coatroom. Then she heard the rattle of a folding chair as it was removed from the closet—the sound that meant the man would be coming inside to stay for a while. She quickly turned around and got busy working in her book again before Teacher Katie returned.

Teacher Katie placed the folding chair at the back of the

room. She walked to the front and stood next to her desk. "Mr. Wilt is the superintendent of schools," she said. "He came to visit our school and will be staying the rest of the day. I want you all to continue your work as usual."

Lily peeked over at Mr. Wilt. His name didn't suit him at all. He didn't look wilted. He was very big, with a large double chin resting on his broad chest. The top of his head was bald, with a horseshoe of wispy, wiry gray hair from ear to ear. Under his nose was a moustache that looked like the bristles of a little broom. Mr. Wilt tried to cross his arms over his chest, but they were too short to reach all the way across.

Lily turned back to her spelling book but became distracted by the sound of heavy footsteps in the aisle. Teacher Katie was at the blackboard, explaining an assignment to the third grade class. Lily peeked and saw Mr. Wilt walking around the desks. He was watching the children do their lessons.

Lily tried to stay focused on her own work. Teacher Katie instructed the first grade to work on a page in their *Learning Through Sounds* book. Lily had to cut out pictures and glue them beside the letter that started with the same sound. She liked this easy work. She cut each little picture out carefully and placed them in a neat pile next to her book.

Suddenly, Mr. Wilt loomed over her desk. He pointed one of his stubby fingers at a picture of a buggy. "Where does this picture go?" he asked.

Lily pointed to the B. Mr. Wilt gave a short nod of his head and moved along to Hannah's desk to ask what she was doing. Mr. Wilt must not have realized that visitors were supposed to sit at the back of the room and remain perfectly quiet. Lily wished Mr. Wilt would go home.

All day long, Mr. Wilt looked over the students' shoulders to see what they were doing. All day long, Teacher Katie kept her mouth pinched together. Her wooly eyebrows were knit deeper together than Lily had ever seen them. Everyone was happy when the day ended and Mr. Wilt drove away in his big car.

Several weeks later, Mr. Wilt arrived at the schoolhouse. He didn't knock at the door. He walked right in. In his arms was a big box. He marched right up to Teacher Katie and emptied the box on her desk. Lily tried to stretch her neck to see what was on the desk. It looked like flashcards and books and a big folded piece of paper.

Mr. Wilt said that he was there to test the children to make sure they had been prepared for their grade level. He told Teacher Katie to sit at the back of the room. Lily thought Teacher Katie looked as if she might explode—her face turned as red as a ripe tomato and her hands were clenched in tight fists—but she did as he said. She walked to the back of the room and sat down.

Mr. Wilt looked at the students. "First grade, please come forward." Lily and Hannah and two other little first grade girls rose from their desks and walked up to stand in front of the teacher desk. Mr. Wilt held up some flashcards and asked if the girls could tell him if the pictures on the cards rhymed or not. Easy! Lily and the others took turns answering yes or no. Then they were excused and went back to their desks.

Next, Mr. Wilt picked up a different set of cards and asked the second grade to come forward. He tested each grade. No one had trouble answering his questions. Not even cousin Levi. Lily was relieved that Levi hardly even stuttered when Mr. Wilt called on him.

Next Mr. Wilt picked up a big chart and tacked it to the frame of the blackboard. "Who knows what this is?" he asked.

Lily looked carefully at the chart. There were pictures of monkeys and odd-looking half-animal, half-people. At the end of the chart were real people. She didn't know what the chart was supposed to be. Neither did anyone else.

"This chart shows how evolution works," Mr. Wilt said.

Lily didn't know what evolution was, but it sure made Teacher Katie mad. She jumped to her feet, outraged. "We do not teach evolution in our school!" she said.

Mr. Wilt dismissed her with a flick of his hand. "This is required education for the state of New York. It's important that every child learns the facts." He turned his attention to the children. "This is how man evolved over time." He pointed to the picture of the little monkey. "Man began looking like this, and over millions and millions of years, he has turned into a human being." He pointed to the picture of the man.

Lily stared at him in amazement. She had *never* been a monkey! She knew that God made people and God made monkeys. When God had given them baby Dannie, he had started out tiny and ugly, but everything about him had been a person. Not a monkey! Lily wished Mr. Wilt would go home.

That evening, Lily told Papa and Mama about Mr. Wilt's chart. Their faces grew very serious as Lily told them that Mr. Wilt said they had all started out as monkeys.

Papa listened carefully to everything Lily said. "I think it's time we had a meeting with the rest of the parents to see what they think we should do about Mr. Wilt dropping into school whenever he feels like and teaching our children theories we don't believe in."

"Something needs to be done," Mama said. "This is one of the reasons we don't want our children going to public schools." Her gentle face looked troubled.

Lily went upstairs to get ready for bed. She wondered how the parents could get Mr. Wilt to stop dropping by Pleasant Hill School. She thought of one idea that might work.

Whenever they heard the sound of Mr. Wilt's big car roll into the driveway, they should lock the door to the schoolhouse. That would work. That would keep him out.

&x&

Lily cringed whenever the second graders were lined up in front of the blackboard for their reading class. Levi had a stutter, and when he had to read aloud, his stutter was very apparent. Every time the second grade had their reading, Teacher Katie would get upset with Levi. She would hit him with the ruler and make him go stand in a corner. Levi's stutter had grown worse and worse since Teacher Katie became their teacher.

Today, it was Levi's turn to read in front of the class. "One d-d-d-day, M-m-m-mother w-w-w-w-ent—"

"Stop reading right now, Levi!" Teacher Katie said. "Since you are too much of a baby to read correctly, you can go sit at your desk while the rest of the class finishes the story."

Levi hung his head, cheeks flaming, as he walked back to

his seat. Teacher Katie grabbed the trash can and followed behind him. As Levi sat down, she turned the trash can upside down on his head. Crumbled paper and shavings from pencil sharpeners fell on his lap and down to the floor. "You can sit with this trash can on your head for the rest of the day," Teacher Katie said. "It will give you time to think about how to be a better reader so we don't have to have a big baby in this schoolroom."

It wasn't fair! Lily wanted to shout out but didn't dare. It was wrong that Teacher Katie was mean to Levi. He couldn't help his stutter.

At home that evening, Lily didn't talk very much. She couldn't get the image of Levi, sitting with the trash can on his head, out of her mind.

"Is something troubling you, Lily?" Mama said.

"Yes," Lily said. "But I don't want to tattle." Not like Joseph did. Little boys tattled all the time.

"There is a difference between sharing your problems and tattling just to get someone in trouble," Mama said. "If something is troubling you, maybe I can think of a way to fix your problem."

So Lily told Mama about how mean Teacher Katie was to cousin Levi. "She yells at him every time he stutters when they have reading class. And today, she dumped a trash can on his head and made him sit with the trash can for the rest of the day."

For a very long time, Mama didn't say anything. Lily could tell that she wasn't happy to hear of what was going on at school. Finally, she took a deep breath. "We will have to pray for Teacher Katie."

After Lily went to bed that evening, she could hear Papa and Mama talking in the kitchen. When she heard her name mentioned, she sat up in bed and strained to listen. They were saying something about school and Teacher Katie.

The next morning, Mama took Lily to school, just like she usually did. But this time, she tied Jim to a tree and went into the schoolhouse with her. In a very cheerful voice, she told Teacher Katie, "I will be visiting school this forenoon."

Teacher Katie set out two folding chairs in the back for Mama and Joseph and baby Dannie to sit on. Lily was happy that Mama was there. Teacher Katie was much kinder. All forenoon she didn't yell or hit anyone. Not one single time. When Teacher Katie announced it was time to eat lunch, Mama got up to go home. Lily said goodbye to her and Joseph and Dannie and watched them drive away.

That afternoon, Teacher Katie acted more cross than ever before. It seemed to Lily she had stuffed down all her crossness until Mama was no longer there. Then it popped out, like Dannie's jack-in-the-box toy.

Every day, one parent or another came to school to visit. Lily was always glad when she heard a buggy drive into the school yard and someone knock on the door. It meant someone was there to make sure Teacher Katie would not yell at them for at least part of the day.

On the last day of school, all the families came and made a big bonfire to roast hot dogs. Mothers packed picnic lunches to eat as everyone sat around the fire. Papa helped Lily roast a hot dog over some red embers. Afterward, they toasted marshmallows. Lily liked the crunchy brown outside of the marshmallows and the sweet gooey centers. She gave Dannie a toasted marshmallow. She laughed when she saw how big his eyes became when he bit into the marshmallow. He had never tasted one!

As everyone cleaned up to get ready to go home, the school

board gave Teacher Katie a check. "Thank you for teaching our children," the school board men said to her. "But we will not be needing you next year."

Lily stood quietly beside Mama and watched as everyone lined up to shake hands with Teacher Katie before she left to go to her home. Inside, Lily wanted to clap and shout for joy! Summer was here, no more school, and no more Teacher Katie!

23

Mama's New Business

$\mathcal{E}$verywhere Lily looked in the kitchen there was something delicious to eat. All day long, Mama had been baking cookies, breads, and pecan tarts. Mama pulled another sheet of oatmeal raisin cookies out of the oven and lifted them carefully onto a rack on the counter to cool. Tomorrow, she told Lily, she would get up extra early to make cinnamon rolls. "And then, we're off to town to sell all of these good treats."

Lily woke up to the sweet smell of cinnamon floating up the stairs. She hurried downstairs and found Papa had already hitched Jim to the buggy. He had fitted shelves in the back of the buggy and filled them with Mama's bread and cookies. Lily helped carry pans of cinnamon rolls outside. Papa stood on a stepladder and hung signs on the sides of the buggy: FRESH BAKED GOODS.

Mama helped Lily into the buggy and they were ready to

leave. Mama didn't let Jim trot down the driveway. It would be too bumpy. As soon as they reached the smooth asphalt road, then Mama let Jim break into a trot. When they reached the town, Mama turned onto a side street. All of the pretty houses had neatly trimmed yards and lawn ornaments in the gardens. Mama found a tree to tie Jim. She held Lily's hand and they walked up to knock on a door.

An older lady opened the door.

Mama smiled at her. "Good morning. I'm selling freshly baked bread and cookies and some other baked goods."

The lady followed Mama and Lily out to the buggy. Her eyes went wide as she saw the delicious treats Mama had baked. "Everything looks so good, but I think I'll only buy a loaf of bread today." She handed Mama some money for the bread.

"We'll be back again next Saturday," Mama said. After the lady went back to her house, Mama grinned at Lily. "Our first customer!" They walked to another house and knocked on the door. This lady said she didn't need anything so they walked down the sidewalk to the next house.

A man opened the door. Lily stared in amazement. The man's skin was chocolate brown. She had never seen anyone with such dark skin. Mama didn't seem at all shocked. Cheerfully, just like at the other houses, she told the man she was selling baked goods.

The man was interested. A little girl peeked around the man. Her skin was just as chocolatey brown as her father's. She had two long shiny black braids with bright pink beads at the end. She looked curiously at Lily. "I'm Larry Smith and this is my daughter, Trisha," the man said. "Would you mind if she comes out to see your horse?"

Mama smiled at Trisha. "I think Jim would like to meet you."

They crossed the street and Trisha reached up to pet Jim's nose. He blew softly through his nostrils into her hand. She quickly drew her hand back and stepped back.

"Jim won't hurt you," Lily said. "He likes children."

Cautiously, Trisha touched Jim's nose and he nickered at her. "His nose feels so soft. Almost like velvet." She smiled at Lily.

Lily smiled back. She liked Trisha.

Larry Smith bought one of every baked good in the buggy. Mama told him they would return next week. "We'll be watching for the horse and buggy, won't we, Trisha?" he said. They smiled and waved as Mama drove the buggy past their house to another street.

"Why is their skin so dark?" Lily whispered to Mama.

"That's the way God made them, Lily," Mama said. "He made people in many different colors, but inside everyone is the same. God loves everyone, whether they are big or small, black or white. The color of skin makes no difference at all to God."

Lily sat and thought about Mama's words. "So people are like God's coloring book, aren't they? He makes hair, eyes, and skin different colors."

Mama laughed. "I guess you could say that." They spent the rest of the morning going door to door, until the shelves in the back of the buggy were empty. Mama had sold everything!

Soon, Saturdays became Lily's favorite day of the week. The best part of the day was when Trisha would come out of her house with her father or mother. They always bought items from Mama, and Lily and Trisha could have a few minutes to visit. Trisha liked to stroke Jim's velvet nose.

One morning, Trisha's parents lingered. "Our babysitter is going on vacation for two weeks," Larry Smith said to Mama.

"We haven't found anyone to watch Trisha while we're at work. We wondered if you might consider taking care of her."

"I'll have to talk to my husband," Mama said, "but I can't see a reason why it couldn't work out."

Larry Smith scribbled his phone number on a piece of paper and handed it to Mama. "We'd really appreciate it if you could let us know your decision by tonight."

Lily was excited to think that Trisha might be staying with them for a while. She was sure that Papa wouldn't mind and he didn't. He didn't mind a bit. Later that day, Papa called Larry Smith and told him Mama and Lily would be happy to have Trisha come stay with them. He gave him directions to Singing Tree Farm.

On Monday morning, a tan station wagon drove up the driveway. Trisha hopped out and walked around in a circle with an amazed look on her face. Lily ran outside to meet her while Mama talked to Trisha's father. After he left to go to work, Trisha followed Lily into the house. Lily had made so many plans for Trisha's visit, but now that she was here, she couldn't think of anything to say or do. Her mind was blank!

Mama sensed the girls' awkwardness. She handed a little pail to Lily. "Take Trisha and go gather eggs for me."

Trisha and Lily crossed the yard to the chicken coop. Lily showed Trisha how to check all the nests for eggs and to reach under the hens to see if they were hiding any eggs. After all the nests were checked, Lily handed the pail to Trisha. She unhinged the ramp to the coop to let the chickens out. The chickens scurried down the ramp to peck at the grass and dirt. Another chicken sat down to make a dust bath. She flapped her wings to settle deeper into the dust. Trisha laughed at the silly hen. Lily laughed too. The awkwardness disappeared. It would be fun to have Trisha to play and work with all day.

Mama came outside to join them. "We need to take some milk to Grandpa Miller's. Run inside and wash up while I get the buggy ready."

Trisha's face lit up. "I get to go on a buggy ride!"

As the girls washed their hands from handling the chickens, Lily wondered what could possibly seem exciting about a buggy ride. As they climbed into the back seat of the buggy, Lily noticed that Mama had brought along a loaf of bread and a few freshly baked cookies. "Are those for Grandma?" Lily said.

"No, I thought we would stop at Harold Young's house and give them to him," Mama said. "I'll let you take them up to his porch while I watch Jim."

As they drove into Harold Young's driveway, Lily admired the gravel on his driveway—the little rocks were smooth and white and looked like miniature marshmallows. Mama reined Jim to a stop. Lily hopped out of the buggy and Mama leaned out the window to hand her the bread and cookies.

"Can I help carry them to the house?" Trisha said.

"Of course," Mama said.

Together, Lily and Trisha walked up to the house. Lily carried the bread and Trisha carried the cookies. A big brown dog barked furiously, scaring them. Lily was glad the dog was tied to his doghouse. Harold Young opened the door before they reached the porch. Lily's heart was thumping so loudly she was sure Trisha could hear it. She handed the loaf of bread to him. "Mama made this for you."

Harold Young took it from her.

Trisha held out the cookies but Harold Young shook his head. "I'm not taking anything from a colored girl." He shut the door firmly.

How mean! How cruel. Harold Young was hateful. A tear

ran down Trisha's cheek. Lily felt so bad. She took Trisha's hand in hers to comfort her. "He's a crabby old man, Trisha. He pointed a shotgun at my papa once. Don't pay any attention to him."

As they climbed into the buggy, Mama knew something was wrong. Lily told her what Harold Young had said to Trisha. "Oh Trisha, I'm so sorry," Mama said. "Some people are so concerned about the color of skin that they forget what color their heart is. Dark skin is beautiful to God, but dark hearts make Him sad."

One afternoon, Papa blew into the kitchen like a warm breeze. His eyes were twinkling bright. "Come see what I brought home from the sale barn today."

Lily had been standing on a chair to help Mama wash dishes. She hopped right down.

Papa held up the palm of his hand. "You can finish the dishes first, Lily. My surprise can wait." He winked at her. "And waiting will give me a chance to eat some of Mama's good chocolate chip cookies."

Lily picked up the towel and got back on the chair to dry the dishes, but all she could think about was Papa's surprise. Soon the last dish was dried and placed into the cupboard. Lily followed Papa out to the chicken coop. Strutting around the chicken yard was a big brown rooster. He had a proud red comb and a long red dangly beard hanging at his throat. His tail had red and greenish feathers. Lily thought he was the most beautiful rooster she had ever seen.

Mama was thrilled. "I had just been thinking how nice it would be to have a rooster. Daniel, you must have read my mind."

Papa grinned. "No farm is complete without a rooster." He pointed to the barn. "I've got something else too."

Inside the barn was a wide-eyed calf, standing in a pen. "A baby cow!" Lily said.

"No, you don't call it a baby cow," Papa said with a laugh. "It's a calf. Actually it's a young steer. I thought we could put him out to pasture and fatten him up until winter."

The calf lifted his head and let out a loud, strange sound. It didn't sound like Jenny's soft moos. Lily had never heard such a strange sound from an animal. She clasped her hands over her ears. "I think we should call him Bellow!"

Papa burst out laughing. "Bellow, it is! I can't think of a better name."

☙❧

Trisha's father dropped her off early in the morning. Lily had plans to spend every minute doing something they both liked. First on the list today was to show Trisha the new rooster and Bellow, the new calf.

The two girls ran out to the barn to see the calf, but Papa had already put Bellow out to pasture in the fenced-off woods. They climbed over the fence, and walked along a creek bank looking for a place to cross. Lily still couldn't see any sign of Bellow, even in the middle of the woods.

Trisha pointed to a tree. "Do you see that squirrel?"

Lily looked up and saw a squirrel dart into a hole high in the tree. "I wonder if it has babies in that hole."

"I could climb up and look," Trisha said. She started to climb the tree.

Lily watched as Trisha climbed higher and higher. Lily had never seen such a brave little girl! Trisha kept climbing, but just as she reached the squirrel's hole, she paused and

looked down. "I don't want to climb higher!" she said. She started to make her way down the tree, slowly and carefully, but then she stopped. The next tree branch was too far below her. "I'm stuck!" Her voice held an edge of panic.

Lily wasn't sure how to help her. If she climbed up the tree, they might both get stuck. They might never get down! They might never be heard from again. How awful! "Hold still, Trisha! Don't move! I'll run and get Mama." If anything happened to Trisha, it would be Lily's fault for taking her so far from the house. She ran back along the creek bank, climbed over the fence, and into the barnyard. She didn't stop running until she burst into the kitchen, panting for air.

Standing at the stove with Dannie on her hip, Mama spun around. She looked behind Lily. "Where's Trisha?"

"She's . . . ," Lily gasped, "stuck up in a tree . . . ," she took a deep breath, "out in the pasture."

Mama sighed. "Papa and Joseph aren't home. Just how am I supposed to climb that tree to help her down?"

Lily couldn't quite imagine Mama trying to climb a tree. "Maybe you could use our big ladder."

"You will have to carry Dannie while I carry the ladder." Mama handed Dannie to Lily and went outside to get the ladder.

Lily hoisted Dannie to her hip. He wouldn't be able to walk in the woods very far.

Mama pushed the big ladder under the fence, climbed through it, and lifted Dannie over while Lily climbed through. It took a long time to walk to the tree. Dannie was over a year old, and heavy. He was turning into a big little boy. Lily lifted him, then let him walk a little, then lifted him again. Lily thought she couldn't carry him one more step, but Mama looked tired as she carried the ladder.

When they reached the tree, Mama set up the ladder and Trisha scampered down. "I'm sorry, Mrs. Lapp," she said as she hopped off the bottom rung of the ladder.

"I'm glad you're safe and sound, Trisha," Mama said. "But I think it would be a good idea if you girls play around the house and barnyard instead of wandering off alone."

Lily and Trisha nodded. On the way back to the house, Trisha and Lily took turns carrying Dannie. But Mama still had to manage the ladder by herself. And they never did find Bellow.

❧✦❧

Lily took her favorite tan-colored dress out of her closet. It was a little worn out and getting too short, but Lily still loved it. Down the back ran a row of bright red buttons. She wished she could see the buttons while she wore the dress, but just knowing they were there always made her feel a little prettier.

Today was the last day that Trisha would be staying at their house. Lily had everything planned. After they gathered eggs, they would play hide-and-seek in the barn. She would ask Trisha to show her how to make a chain of daisies, and then they would spend the rest of the morning in the sandbox, and help Mama whenever she needed them.

When Trisha's father drove up the driveway, Lily ran out to meet her. She had two empty peanut butter pails to gather eggs. Inside the chicken coop, the hens ignored the girls as they approached the nests to check for eggs. The rooster pecked at the grain in the feeder while the hens scratched at the straw and dirt on the floor or drank from the water pan.

Lily reached into one nest and grabbed a handful of eggs. She placed the eggs carefully in the little pail. Suddenly the rooster flew onto her back! He squawked and flapped his wings. Lily fell to the floor and the rooster kept pecking at her and beating his wings. Trisha tried to shoo the rooster away, but he didn't pay her any mind. Finally, Trisha darted out of the chicken coop and ran to get Mama.

Lily tried to get away, but the rooster kept flying at her and knocking her down. Mama dashed into the chicken coop and scooped Lily into her arms. Out on the grass, she dried Lily's tears. "I don't think it's a good idea to wear this dress when you gather the eggs. The rooster wanted to get those red buttons. He must have thought they were red berries. That is why he knocked you down."

Lily looked down at her dress. It was covered with dirt and smudges from the floor of the chicken coop. Mama sent her upstairs to change into another dress. Up in her bedroom, she took off her dress and looked at the buttons. The rooster had pecked them so hard that he had made scratch marks all over them. The red buttons were ruined. She would never again feel pretty and special whenever she wore that dress. Stupid, stupid rooster.

Off to Kentucky

*L*ily could hardly keep still in her excitement. It seemed like a Saturday even though Lily knew it was just Wednesday. She had had her bath earlier that evening and Mama had washed and braided her hair. Tomorrow was going to be an exciting day. The entire family was going, by bus, to visit Grandpa and Grandma Lapp in Kentucky. Lily was happy that her grandmother would get to see Dannie. She would be surprised at how big he had grown. He could walk now. He toddled around the big kitchen with short steps, and he was starting to talk too.

The suitcase was propped open on the couch in the living room. Lily tucked a few pretty, flowery handkerchiefs into the red satin pocket inside of the big black suitcase Mama was packing. Mama carefully placed Papa's Sunday coat on top of everything else and closed the lid. Lily helped her fasten the clasps. Mama set it on the floor next to the door beside a smaller suitcase and her satchel. Done!

Papa was polishing shoes: Papa's, Mama's, Lily's, and Joseph's. Each one ended up shiny black. Joseph sat on the floor with his eyes fixed on Papa. Papa set the pairs of shoes on a piece of newspaper to dry. He stretched his arms high above his head and gave a huge pretend yawn. "Time for bed. We need to wake up extra early tomorrow morning to catch that bus."

Lily was much too excited to sleep. She decided she would stay awake all night so they wouldn't miss the bus. She counted the low-pitched bells of the grandfather clock down below. One, two, three, four, five, six, seven, eight . . .

The next thing Lily knew, Papa was calling her name. Everything was pitch dark. Then her eyes flew open. Today was the day they were going to go see Grandpa and Grandma Lapp! She hopped out of bed and quickly got her dress that Mama had hung on her bedpost last evening. She wiggled into it and then ran to find Mama to button her.

After everyone was dressed in Sunday clothes, they sat in the kitchen to wait until the driver arrived to take them to the bus station. Papa wore his Sunday vest over his light green shirt. His straw hat rested on the table so he could quickly snatch it up as soon as the driver turned into the lane.

Lily watched the second hand on the clock tick slowly around and around the clock. She wished the driver would hurry up and get here. She was ready to go. *Hurry, hurry, hurry,* she thought.

Papa jumped up. "I think I hear his car." He reached for his hat and plopped it on his head, then pushed the chair under the table. Through the window, Lily saw two bright lights coming up the driveway. She quickly got her heavy black bonnet and waited for Mama to tie the ribbons under her chin. She wished she didn't have to wear the bonnet. It was so hot. Mama was busy filling a jug with cold water. She set it beside a brown paper bag filled with sandwiches for their lunch on the bus. Then she turned to help Lily tie her bonnet.

When the driver pulled up to the house, Papa opened the door and carried the suitcases out to the car. He came back to help Mama carry the rest of the things. He looked around the house to make sure all the curtains were closed tight. The last thing he did was turn down the oil lamp and blow it out. It was time to go.

At the bus station, Papa paid the driver and got the luggage out of the car. They found a funny wire-looking bench to sit on in the station while they waited for the bus to come. Dannie slept on Papa's lap, but Lily had too much to look at to even think of sleep. A tall, thin man stood in front of a large metal and glass box and pushed a few buttons. The man bent down, reached into a little door, and took out a candy bar.

What a wonderful invention! She leaned over and whispered to Mama, "Can I get one too?"

Mama shook her head. "You can't just get free candy bars, Lily. The man put some money into the machine before it gave him the candy. We'll be fine with the sandwiches I packed."

Lily wished she had some money. She wanted to see what kind of candy that machine might give to her.

A loud voice boomed from a box in the ceiling to announce that the bus had arrived. Papa and Mama quickly herded Lily and Joseph into line. Papa's hands were full, so he had Joseph hold one of the suitcases. Lily held on to Mama's skirt as they made their way to the bus. The driver took their tickets and let them climb into the bus to find seats. Lily wondered where all the other people on the bus were going. She hoped they weren't all going to Grandpa Lapp's house. It was big, but not big enough for everyone on the bus.

Lily settled into her seat and closed her eyes. It was still dark outside and she felt a little sleepy. But she would *not* sleep! She had never been on a bus before and she wanted to enjoy every moment. She would not sleep. She would not . . . sleep. She . . . would . . . not . . .

Mama gently shook Lily's shoulder. "Wake up, wake up. It's time to get off the bus."

Lily popped her head up to look out the window. The sun shone brightly. She scrambled to her feet and followed Mama down the aisle. This bus station was even bigger than the last one. There were people everywhere, walking fast, talking fast, coming and going. They had a short wait until the next bus arrived to take them to Kentucky. Lily scooted closer to Mama on the bench. She liked watching everything around her. They ate their sandwiches and drank some of the water from the water jug. It wasn't very cold any longer. Lily wished Papa would go to one of those wonderful machines and get a cold drink or a snack like the other people were doing.

When the next bus came, Papa quickly guided them to stand in line for the bus driver. Lily held on to Mama's skirt. She was afraid that someone might bump her and she would get lost in the crowd. Maybe the bus would leave and she would be forgotten. She might never see her family again. Oh, what a dreadful thought!

As they stood in line for the bus, Papa took Dannie out of Mama's arms. He looked around him. "Where is Joseph?"

Mama's eyes went wide. She looked behind her. "He was right here! He was holding a suitcase!" Her face looked tight and pale.

Lily started to cry. They couldn't go and leave Joseph alone in this big scary place. He was just a little boy! He would never find his way home. Papa told Mama to get on the bus while he went into the station to look for Joseph. Mama watched Papa go. Suddenly, Lily saw Joseph! He was already in the bus and waved to them from a window. She pulled on Mama's sleeve and pointed to Joseph. Lily watched as Joseph climbed down the steps of the bus and ran to them.

"Why didn't you come?" Joseph said. "I was waiting for you!"

Papa saw Joseph run to Mama. He hurried to join them. "We have to stay in line, Joseph, and stay together." Papa and Mama exchanged a look of relief. "Next time, keep hold of the suitcase. We don't want to lose our little boy."

Lily was relieved when they were sitting on the bus, all together. The next time they would get off, Grandpa and Grandma Lapp would be waiting to meet them.

It was nearly dinnertime when the bus pulled into the station in Kentucky. From the window, Lily saw her grandparents. *Hurry, hurry, hurry!* she wanted to tell the people in the aisle. *My grandmother is waiting for me!* But the line moved so slowly.

Finally, Lily jumped down the bottom step of the bus and into Grandma Lapp's arms. "My, my! How you've grown!" Grandma Lapp stepped back to look Lily over. She patted her head. "You must be getting to be a good helper for your mama."

"She is a very good helper," Mama said. "I don't know what I'd do without her."

Lily felt so pleased!

"I guess that means you won't want to leave her with us when you go home," Grandpa said, eyes twinkling, but Lily knew he was only teasing. He liked to tease. He led them to a big white van that was waiting to take them to their house.

The farm at Grandma and Grandpa Lapp's looked just the way Lily remembered. They lived in a cute little white house with a porch. It was connected to a big farmhouse where Uncle Ira and Aunt Tillie lived with their eight children. Lily looked forward to playing with her cousins while they were there.

Grandma and Mama began to make supper while Papa and Joseph went out to the barn to help Grandpa feed the horses. Lily wished she could help make supper or at least set the table with Grandma's pretty dishes. She wanted to show Grandma what a big helper she was, but Dannie was acting bashful. He was clinging to Mama, so she asked Lily to play with him while they cooked.

Grandpa and Papa came back inside and sat in the living room to visit until supper was ready. Lily asked Joseph to play with Dannie and went to the kitchen to see if Grandma had something for her to do to help get supper ready. She was getting hungry.

Grandma handed Lily a big yellow flashlight. "You can go down to the basement and fetch a jar of peaches."

Oh. Lily had hoped she could stay in the kitchen with Grandma and Mama. Grandma's basement was dark and spooky and had a funny musty smell. Cautiously, she tiptoed down the stairs. There were no windows. The light from her flashlight wasn't very bright. Lily was sure the batteries were almost dead. She hoped the flashlight wouldn't go out completely before she found the peaches and made it safely back upstairs to the sunny kitchen.

She shined the flashlight over the shelves. Peaches! She grabbed the jar just as something cold and funny and wet and alive touched her bare foot. She flashed the light on her toes and gasped in fright. A big ugly toad hopped away. She dropped the jar of peaches and it shattered. Lily raced up the stairs and into the kitchen.

Grandma had heard the crash and met her at the door. "What's wrong? What happened? Couldn't you find the peaches?"

"I found the peaches," Lily said. She felt embarrassed. "I dropped the jar when a toad hopped on my foot."

Mama put a hand on Lily's shoulder. "Do you have something I can use to clean up her mess?"

"There's an old broom and dustpan beside the staircase," Grandma said. "And you might want to keep your eyes open for frogs while you're down there. They seem to like our basement, though I sure can't figure out where they get in."

This visit wasn't going well. She had wanted to show Grandma what a good helper she was but had only made more work when she dropped the peach jar. She had wanted Grandma to see how big and grown-up Dannie was getting, but Dannie was acting shy. He buried his head into Mama's lap so no one could see him. During dinner, he didn't even want to taste Grandma's good food. Lily looked down at her plate. She wasn't very hungry either.

25

Aunt Tillie
and the Pow-Wow Doctor

The next morning was warm and sunny. After breakfast, Lily and Joseph ran outside to play with their cousins. There was a swing tied to the limb of a tall oak tree and they took turns pushing each other on the swing. Lily noticed a big sandbox with a blue shingled roof that looked like a wishing well. Dannie loved to play in sandboxes! She ran inside to get him, but he refused to leave Mama's side.

Aunt Tillie, gaunt and long-necked as a sandhill crane, frowned as she observed Dannie's reluctance. "There must be something wrong with that boy," she said. "There is a good Pow-Wow doctor in our church district. I'm sure she would be able to cure him. I'll ask Ira to fetch her."

A troubled look crossed Mama's face. "No. Dannie is just a little shy. Once he gets used to everyone he'll come out of his shell and chatter away and play with everyone." She stroked Dannie's hair off of his forehead. More firmly, she added, "Besides, we don't want anything to do with a Pow-Wow doctor."

"Well, why ever not?" Aunt Tillie looked the very picture of astonishment. "It's one of the best ways to cure folks. It's cheap, it works, and the Pow-Wow doctor chants Bible verses. It's the biggest favor you could do for your children."

Again, Mama said no, as politely as she could. Aunt Tillie didn't look happy. She could be a little bossy. As Lily went back out to play with her cousins, she wondered about the Pow-Wow doctor. She had never met a Pow-Wow doctor before and, by the way Mama sounded, wasn't sure she ever wanted to.

✺

A little later that morning, Grandpa had a surprise. He had hired a driver so Lily's mother could visit some of their friends in the community. Aunt Tillie and Grandma wanted to come too, so they all piled into the van. Lily wished she could have stayed at the farmhouse to play with her cousins. Instead, she was stuck in a hot van, stopping at people's houses so the women could chat for half an hour. Then it would start all over again as they went to visit someone else.

It was an altogether boring morning until they stopped at an Amish store. Now Lily was glad she had come along. There were so many pretty things to see in the shop. Grandma pressed some money into her hand to go buy something for herself. Lily walked up and down the aisles, looking every-thing over. Should she buy a new coloring book? Or a toy? So many choices!

As Lily turned the corner, her breath caught. All along the shelves were the most beautiful oil lamps. Never in her

183

life had she seen such beautiful lamps. Big pink ones with frilly-looking shades that covered the glass chimney. Blue and green ones, tall ones, short ones, some with flowers and some were plain. How could she possibly choose one? Then she saw the perfect lamp. It was white with dainty little pink flowers painted on the bowl. The chimney was a milky white and all along the top were little scallops.

Lily found Grandma in the fabric section. She tugged on her sleeve and whispered, "I think I found what I would like to buy."

Grandma followed her to the aisle with the lamps. Lily pointed to the little white one. Grandma got it down carefully and handed it to her. "This is a fine choice, Lily. It will be something that you can use for many years." She bent over. "And it's very pretty too."

Slowly and carefully, Lily carried the lamp to the counter. She handed money to the cashier, who counted out the money and gave change back to Lily. She tried to give the change to Grandma.

"You keep it, Lily," Grandma said.

Lily put the change into her pocket. The day had flip-flopped, from boring to happy. She had a new oil lamp, and some change in her pocket too.

After they had finished shopping, Aunt Tillie announced that it was time to head home. She had invited a friend over for lunch.

As the van turned into the driveway to the farmhouse, Lily could see a horse and buggy tied to the hitching rail. Aunt Tillie's friend was already at the house. As soon as the van came to a stop, Aunt Tillie hurried to the house. Mama and Grandma and Lily carried their purchases into the little house. Then they walked over to the big house to help Aunt Tillie with lunch and meet her friend.

In the living room sat Aunt Tillie's friend, an older woman, at least forty. Lily thought it was strange that this woman didn't help prepare lunch in the kitchen with the others. Instead, she sat on a rocking chair and watched the children play. She pulled a bag of candy out of her pocket and offered it to the children. Everyone lined up to get a piece. Lily ran to get Dannie from Mama and take him to get a piece of candy. Candy was a rare treat and she didn't want him to miss out, but Dannie refused to accept candy from the woman. Lily took two pieces and gave him one. She was helping Dannie open the wrapper when the woman scooped him up in her arms.

Dannie squirmed and wiggled to try to get off the woman's lap, but she held on to him firmly. She reached into her pocket and pulled out a piece of red cloth. Then she rolled up Dannie's pant legs and started rubbing the cloth all over his legs. She muttered words that Lily couldn't understand.

Lily hurried to the kitchen to find Mama. "That woman is doing weird things to Dannie in the living room," she whispered in her ear.

Mama dropped the lettuce into the bowl, wiped her hands on her apron, and marched into the living room. She didn't even stop to see what was going on but snatched Dannie off the woman's lap. The woman didn't seem at all bothered by Mama's abruptness. In fact, she seemed pleased with herself.

But Mama was upset. She went straight to Aunt Tillie in the kitchen with Dannie in her arms. "I thought we had made it clear we don't want anything to do with a Pow-Wow doctor!"

Lily shivered. She had never heard Mama talk to anyone in such a cross voice. Not even Joseph when he was in trouble.

Aunt Tillie stood there still as stone. "Dannie needed help

and you weren't helping him. So I asked Lizzie to come Pow-Wow for him. And I'm not sorry that I did."

Grandma blew a puff of air out of her mouth. "Oh, Tillie," she said quietly, but she knew not to say more. Aunt Tillie wasn't one to confront.

Everything felt odd after that, stiff and uncomfortable. The Pow-Wow doctor decided not to stay to eat with them. After she left, Mama and Tillie and Grandma worked quietly in the kitchen. Lily's stomach twisted into a knot.

Lunch was finally ready. As everyone gathered at the table and bowed their heads for a silent prayer, a loud "POP!" sound blew out of the stove. Aunt Tillie rose from the table and sailed to the kitchen. She opened the stove's ash drawer and pulled out the red cloth that the Pow-Wow doctor had rubbed on Dannie's leg. It was wrapped around an egg. The pop they had heard was the sound of the egg breaking open.

Aunt Tillie looked triumphant. "Dannie is cured!"

Lily was all eyes, shifting around to see until Mama laid a calming hand on her.

Papa was puzzled. "What do you mean, Dannie is cured? There was nothing wrong with him in the first place."

Aunt Tillie hooked her hands on her hips. "You can't tell me that there is nothing wrong with a child who wants to hide instead of eating, and doesn't want to play with other children." She folded her arms against her chest. "So I asked Lizzie to come Pow-Wow for him."

Papa jumped up from his chair. "You did what?!" He was livid!

Aunt Tillie lifted her chin. "I asked Lizzie to come Pow-Wow for him."

"Oh, Tillie," Uncle Ira said quietly. "You shouldn't have done that. You knew they don't like Pow-Wowing."

"You had no right getting someone to practice Pow-Wowing on our son." Papa picked Dannie up from his chair. He glanced at Mama. "Rachel, we should go."

Lily and Joseph bolted from their chairs and followed Mama and Papa over to Grandpa and Grandma's house. A moment later, Lily's grandparents came into the house.

Papa sat at the kitchen table and steepled his fingers together, as if in prayer. He was quiet for a long moment. "To ask someone to heal you in ways other than using medicine or prayer is wrong," he said. "We believe Pow-Wowing is a form of witchcraft. It's filled with superstitions and mumbo-jumbo. It's not something any Christian should practice or allow to be practiced."

Grandma and Grandpa apologized that Aunt Tillie had gone against Mama and Papa's wishes. Lily was so happy that the upset was over. It felt like a dark thunderstorm had swept through the farm, and now the sun was shining again.

CHAPTER

26

Buggy in the Ditch

One morning, a week after Lily and her family had returned to Singing Tree Farm from Kentucky, the sky was dark gray and the air smelled of rain. Mama needed to go to town to buy groceries and several bags of feed for the animals. Usually, she took Lily, Joseph, and Dannie with her in the buggy. Not today, though. Mama worried they would get soaked from rain if they went with her, walking from grocery store to feed store. So, instead, she planned to drop them off at Grandma and Grandpa Miller's.

Lily and Joseph kneeled on the back seat of the buggy to look out the window as Mama drove Jim down a favorite shortcut—a winding field lane that led to Grandpa Miller's farm. Mama liked to take the field lane so she could avoid driving the buggy on the busy road or drive up the steep driveway with the deep ditch beside it. Lily liked staying at Grandpa Miller's. There was always something fun to do there. She could help Grandma in her kitchen. She could watch Grandpa work in his harness shop. Best of all, she could play with Aunt Susie.

Grandma was happy to see their faces when she opened the door. "Come in, come in," she said, holding the door wide open.

Mama stayed on the porch to talk to Grandma while Lily darted inside to find Aunt Susie. She found her aunt in the kitchen, coloring with a yellow crayon in one of her coloring books.

When she saw Lily, she jumped up from the table. "Do you want to play dolls?"

"Oh yes!" Lily was hoping Aunt Susie would want to play dolls, Lily's favorite game.

Lily followed Aunt Susie into her bedroom. Together they picked out the dolls they wanted to play with and carefully chose the dresses for the dolls to wear. Lily always chose a certain red dress. It was the prettiest one. She wished her own sweet Sally could have a red dress like that. They packed their little diaper bags with cute toys for their dolls and wrapped each doll in a blanket. Now they were ready to play! They sat on the living room sofa to pretend they were in church while they played with their dolls.

Joseph and Dannie were playing with wooden blocks and animals on the floor beside the big green toy box, with its lid propped open. Dannie kept hunting for more toys inside the green toy box. He liked digging toys out of the toy box more than he liked to play with them. Toys were littered around the box. Grandma rocked slowly on her rocking chair as she sewed tiny neat buttonholes in Grandpa's new shirt.

It felt nice and cozy inside the house. Everyone was having a good time. Rain started gently, tapping the windows with drops. Soon, the gentle drops turned to a steady downpour. Lily was glad she didn't have to worry about getting wet from walking around town. She hoped that Mama could stay dry under the big black umbrella.

Thud! Thump! And then came a muffled *wail*. Dannie had been leaning over the edge of the green toy box and tumbled inside. The lid fell shut on him. Grandma jumped up and opened the lid to the toy box. She scooped Dannie up and held him on her lap while he whimpered and whined. Aunt Susie hurried over to stroke his head and soothe him. It upset her to see a child cry. Dannie soon forgot about his scare and wiggled off Grandma's lap to play with Joseph.

Grandpa came in from the harness shop and sat in the living room on his big creaky rocking chair. "Well, well," he said, pretending to be surprised by the sight of Lily and Joseph and Dannie. "Who do we have here today?"

Lily laid her doll on the sofa and ran to Grandpa. He reached into his vest and then brought out his hand, tightly closed. Lily and Joseph tried to pry his fingers open to find the hidden treat. Sometimes it was raisins, other times peanuts, or their favorite—little papaya mints. Today, his hand held a few toasted pumpkin seeds. They ate them slowly to make them last as long as they could.

As soon as Grandpa had come in from the harness shop, Grandma went to the kitchen to prepare lunch. "Lunch is ready, if anyone is hungry."

Grandpa scratched his head. "I can't imagine that these little children might be hungry, can you, Susie?"

"Oh, but Papa, I think they are," Susie said. "It's lunchtime." She didn't know he was teasing.

They ran to the table to find their chairs. Grandma helped Dannie sit in a wooden highchair. Lily thought it looked hard and uncomfortable compared to the nice one they had at home with the soft cushions Mama had made for it. Just as they began to pass the sandwiches around the table, Mama drove up in the buggy. Grandma quickly set another plate at the table so Mama could join them. Lily liked listening to Grandpa, Grandma, and Mama visit while they ate. Sometimes, they would tell stories about Mama and Aunt Susie as little girls. But not today. Jim was standing patiently by the barn, dripping wet. Mama ate quickly. She wanted to get poor Jim out of the rain.

"Don't worry about the dishes," Grandma said. "Susie likes washing dishes and we can take care of them after you leave. I'm sure Jim would like to get home out of the rain."

Grandpa helped them out to the buggy. Lily and Joseph and Dannie sat on the front seat beside Mama this time because the back of the buggy was filled with bags of feed and groceries. Grandpa handed Jim's reins to Mama. "Rachel, I think you had better drive on the road instead of taking the field lane. The lane is too muddy and the buggy is heavy with that load of feed bags in the back."

Mama clucked "giddyup" to Jim. He started down the driveway in the rain. Lily liked to watch the raindrops hit the storm front of the buggy and run down in little trickles. Inside, the buggy was nice and dry except for the two little holes where Jim's reins entered the buggy. Water ran down the reins and dripped on the floor under those two little holes. It was raining *that* hard.

At the end of Grandpa's driveway, Mama pulled on the reins. "Whoa," she told Jim.

Several cars and a big milk truck were zooming past. The milk truck splashed a big shower of water all over them. Jim did not like to get splashed with water. Mama held firmly on the reins as more cars zoomed by and splashed water on them. Jim started backing up a little.

"Whoa, Jim, easy, boy!" Mama said.

Jim backed a little more. Another big truck passed and showered them with a huge splash of water. Jim backed up a little more. *Bump!* The back wheel of the buggy dropped off the edge of the driveway into the deep ditch beside it.

"Whoa, Jim!" Mama said. She pulled on the reins to make him stop, but he kept backing up a little more.

Lily could feel the buggy start to tip. Slowly, slowly, the buggy leaned farther into the ditch. *Crash!* The buggy tipped over on its side. Lily landed on top of Mama. Dannie sprawled on top of Joseph. Jim lay on the ground. He lifted his big head and looked back at the buggy as if to say, "How did *that* happen?"

Lily, Joseph, and Dannie started to cry. Cars stopped beside the road and people jumped out to see if they could help. A man with a long gray ponytail opened the storm front and lifted Lily and Joseph out.

"Run back to the house, Lily, and tell Grandpa we need help," Mama said. She and Dannie were still trapped inside the buggy.

Lily held Joseph's hand as they ran back up the driveway. Lily tried to run as fast as she could, but her legs still felt wobbly from the scare. She wondered how they would ever get Jim and the buggy out of the ditch.

Grandpa saw Lily and Joseph run up the driveway and met them on the porch. "What's happened?"

"Our buggy!" Lily said, panting for breath. "Jim backed the buggy into the ditch and Mama needs help."

Grandpa plucked his hat and coat from the hook inside the door and hurried to help Mama.

Grandma helped them out of their wet coats and told them to sit next to the stove to dry. Aunt Susie was at the sink, washing the dishes. She dried her hands and fussed over Joseph and Lily to make sure they were both okay. It troubled her whenever anyone was sad or hurt or scared.

Lily held out her arms to show Aunt Susie. "Not even a scratch," she said, wanting to reassure Aunt Susie. "Mama made a nice soft landing to fall on."

Lily stood by the window to watch Grandpa unhitch Jim from the buggy. Jim scrambled to his feet and stood quietly to wait for Mama to tell him what to do. Lily thought Jim looked sorry. So very sorry. She knew he would never do anything to hurt them on purpose. He was a good horse.

Mama passed Dannie to Grandpa through the buggy door, then climbed out. When Grandpa was satisfied she wasn't

193

hurt, he handed Dannie to her and turned his attention to righting the buggy. Mama held the corner of her shawl over Dannie's head to try to keep the rain off him. The two of them watched Grandpa and the man with the long gray ponytail set the buggy back on its wheels. Lily was surprised to see that the buggy still looked fine. The little side windows weren't even broken. Grandpa hitched Jim to the buggy again. He drove the buggy up to the house, with Mama and Dannie in it. Then he helped Lily and Joseph out to the buggy, covering them with his big black umbrella.

Jim trotted slowly and carefully all the way home, as if he was carrying a buggy filled with delicate china teacups. Lily couldn't wait until Papa came home to tell him about their day. It had been exciting! And no one had been hurt. Not even Jim. She knew Papa would want to hear all about it.

Great-Grandma's Big Cane

*M*ama had hurried extra fast through the morning work. Lily tried to keep up behind her. She knew today was a special day. She helped Mama gather a bouquet of daisies and black-eyed Susans and put them into a little vase. Mama tied a pretty pink ribbon around the top of the vase.

"Lily, I think we're ready to go," Mama said. She looked Lily up and down and frowned. "On second thought, we will be just as soon as you wash your face and hands." As Lily bolted up the stairs, Mama added, "And don't forget your bonnet."

"Face and bonnet," Lily repeated.

Lily ran to the washbasin to splash cold water on her face and hands, then dried them on the fluffy blue towel. She glanced into the mirror to make sure there was nothing on her face that would make Mama spit on the corner of her handkerchief and wipe it off. She did *not* like that. Satisfied that she could pass Mama's inspection, she ran back downstairs, took her heavy black bonnet off the wall hook, and stood quietly while Mama tied the ribbons under her chin. If only she could wear a straw hat like Joseph did instead of the hot bonnet. It held her head in a tight grasp and made her feel as if she were in a tunnel.

Today, they were going to Grandpa Miller's to see a special visitor. Mama's grandmother was visiting! Mama couldn't wait to see her. Lily tried to imagine how old Great-Grandma must be since she must be older than Grandma. And Grandma Miller was old. Almost fifty. Grandpa called her his little antique and she would swat him, playfully, when he said it. It always made Lily laugh.

When they arrived at the farm, Grandpa came out of his harness shop to unhitch Jim and put him in the barn. He took Jim out of the buggy shafts whenever the visiting would last a long time. Lily saw Uncle Elmer's buggy next to the barn. She knew that Aunt Mary and Hannah must have come to see Great-Grandma too. What a happy day!

Mama knocked on the door. Lily could hear voices inside and then Grandma's quick footsteps as she came to the door. When Grandma opened the door, Lily caught sight of Hannah in the kitchen.

Hannah jumped up and ran to Lily, whispering furiously to her.

Lily couldn't understand what Hannah had said. This awful bonnet! She couldn't even hear right. She yanked the ties and pulled it right off. "What did you say?"

"Great-Grandma is sitting in there," Hannah whispered, pointing to the living room. "She's scary! She has a big cane and she keeps poking it at people."

Lily did not want to get poked by a cane! She wasn't sure she

196

wanted to go into the house, but Mama held the door open. "Come in, Lily. I want you to say hello to Great-Grandma before you and Hannah run off to play."

Lily followed Mama into the house but tried to hide behind her. She could see Great-Grandma sitting on the rocking chair. Her hair was snow white and her leathery face was lined with deep wrinkles. Her hands looked bony and wrinkled and covered with blue veins. Most concerning to Lily was the wooden cane held across her lap.

Mama went up to shake hands with Great-Grandma. She set the vase of flowers they had brought along beside the rocking chair so Great-Grandma could see them. Lily was surprised how happy and pleased Mama's voice sounded. Great-Grandma seemed glad to see Mama too. Lily decided that Hannah had been playing a joke on her. Great-Grandma wasn't scary. Not scary at all!

Just then, Great-Grandma lifted her cane and looped the crooked end around Lily's neck. She pulled it forward. "And who is this little girl?"

"I'm Lily." Lily's voice surprised her. It wobbled, barely above a whisper.

"You'll have to speak louder so I can understand you," Great-Grandma said. She tugged the cane closer to her. Lily stumbled forward.

"My name is Lily," she said, relieved that this time her voice was clear and Great-Grandma seemed to hear her.

"So you are Lily. I hope you are as sweet as the flower." Great-Grandma leaned forward in her rocking chair and peered at Lily over her wire-rimmed spectacles. "Tell me. Do you know how to gather seeds for summer geraniums?"

What an odd question! Lily nodded her head. "Yes. I help Mama gather seeds every fall."

Great-Grandma smiled. Satisfied, she released the cane from around Lily's neck and settled back into her rocking chair. "Summer geraniums have been a part of our family for generations. Every year we plant them in our garden and enjoy their pretty pinks all summer. We harvest the seeds in fall to save and plant next year. Those seeds come from the only pretty things my grandmother had and her mother before her. They've been handed down from mother to daughter, generation after generation. Who knows how long our family has been raising those flowers?" She shook a boney finger at Lily. "And you are part of this family of women. When you are old enough to have a garden, I expect you to plant a row of summer geraniums every year."

Mama gave Lily permission to go play with Hannah and Aunt Susie. As Lily turned to leave, she decided that Great-Grandma was definitely scary, but not quite as scary as Hannah led her to believe. But Lily wished Great-Grandma would use her cane only for walking. She did not like having it hooked around her neck like she was a little lamb.

Mama and Aunt Mary helped Grandma cook a nice big lunch. After they had eaten, Great-Grandma said to Grandma, "I would like to go outside to see your summer geraniums."

"Are you sure you want to walk in the garden?" Grandma said. "The path is very uneven to walk on."

Great-Grandma sat up tall in her chair. "I may be old and I may shuffle when I walk. But I'm not so old that I can't be the judge about what I'm able to do."

Grandma and Mama exchanged a look. Even Aunt Susie looked surprised at Great-Grandma's huffy tone of voice. But they all went out to the garden. Slowly. Ever so slowly. As slow as a caterpillar. Lily thought she had never seen anyone walk as slowly as Great-Grandma did, shuffling along. Once they

reached the garden, Great-Grandma walked along the row of summer geraniums. Lily wondered what she was thinking. Was she remembering herself as a little girl, or thinking about her own mama and grandma? After all, these flowers were just like the ones she had gathered seeds from as a child—in fact, those flowers were the great-grandmothers of these very geraniums! Lily looked up and observed her mother's face, her grandmother's and great-grandmother's, her aunts', her cousins'. These geraniums were just like the women in her family—all ages, all shapes and sizes, all belonging together. Same thing.

Great-Grandma moved along the rows, admiring the pretty blossoms and pointing out a few fat bumblebees that flew lazily from blossom to blossom. One bee started to buzz around her. Great-Grandma waved her cane at it. There went that cane again! *Watch out, bumblebee,* Lily wanted to say, *or you'll find yourself with a cane around your tiny fuzzy neck!*

Suddenly, Great-Grandma crumpled to the ground in a heap.

Mama and Aunt Mary tried to help Great-Grandma to her feet, but she couldn't get up. Her eyes were open, but she was listless. "Run and get Grandpa, Lily," Mama said. Her voice sounded filled with worry.

Lily ran to the harness shop to fetch Grandpa. As she opened the door, Grandpa looked up from the sewing machine where he had been mending a harness. "Great-Grandma fell in the garden and can't get up!" Lily said.

Grandpa bolted to the garden. Lily ran after him. She had never seen Grandpa run that fast before and could hardly keep up. He knelt beside Great-Grandma. Her mouth looked funny and twisted and her eyes didn't look right. "I think something more happened than just a tumble. I'll go call an ambulance."

Mama sat in the garden and held Great-Grandma's head in her lap. Grandma and Aunt Mary crouched down to talk to Great-Grandma even though it didn't seem as if she could hear them. Her cane lay on the ground next to her. Lily wished that Great-Grandma would sit up and wave it around—even if it meant that Lily would be hooked around the neck. That would be better than having her lay here in the garden like this.

The wail of the ambulance's siren came closer and closer. Grandpa came running back from the neighbor's house just as the ambulance flew up the driveway. The ambulance stopped near the edge of the garden. Two men in blue uniforms jumped out and hurried over to see what was wrong with Great-Grandma. One man checked her pulse as the other pulled a stretcher out of the ambulance. Together, they carefully lifted Great-Grandma onto the stretcher and rolled it into the back of the ambulance. Grandma asked if she could go along. They motioned for her to quickly climb in. Then they shut the doors of the ambulance. The two men climbed in the front cab and the ambulance hurried back down the driveway, siren wailing.

Everyone stood there, listening to the siren's sound as it drove down the street. It had all happened so fast. One minute, Great-Grandma was looking at summer geraniums. The next moment, she was being taken away in an ambulance. It was too much to take in. Aunt Susie started to cry. Mama put an arm around her sister.

"It will be okay, Susie," she said, patting her shoulder. "Let's go back to the house and help do the dishes. I'll wash them if you'll dry them."

Aunt Susie wiped her tears and smiled. She liked to wash dishes. Having everyone help would be even more fun.

Grandpa decided he should go to the hospital. "Rachel, would you mind taking Susie home with you?"

"We'll be happy to have her stay with us as long as necessary," Mama said.

Lily was glad. It would be fun to have Aunt Susie stay with them.

Later that evening, Lily was getting ready for bed when Grandpa stopped by Singing Tree Farm. "Great-Grandma had a stroke," he said. "She will have to stay in the hospital for a while. I guess Susie and I will have to do the best we can while Grandma stays with her."

Lily was happy to hear that Great-Grandma would be all right, but she was sorry Aunt Susie was leaving. She understood that Grandpa needed her. As they said goodbye at the door,

Mama said, "If you need any help with cooking or doing laundry or anything, anything at all, just let me know."

"I think we'll be fine," Grandpa said. "Susie is a good helper." His eyes twinkled as he added, "But if you ever feel like baking a cherry pie, I won't turn it down."

Everyone chuckled. Cherry pie was Grandpa's favorite. Everybody knew that. It felt good to laugh a little. It had been a long, hard, and sad day, but laughter made everything feel a little better.

CHAPTER

28

Lily and Mama

$\mathcal{E}$arly on Saturday morning, Mama hurried everyone along at breakfast. "It's time to get ready," Mama said, as Lily and Joseph finished their last spoonfuls of porridge. "Papa will soon be driving up to the house with Jim and the buggy."

Lily ran to her room to change into a fresh everyday dress and apron while Mama helped Joseph and Dannie change their shirts. They were back downstairs just as Papa drove up to the front porch. Lily climbed into the back of the buggy and knelt on the seat beside Joseph, peeking out the back window. They were going to Isaac's house today to help load a big truck with all the family's belongings. Lily had been sad to learn that Isaac and his five younger brothers were moving away. The schoolhouse would seem empty without them.

This summer, three other families had moved away. Ten more children, besides Isaac and his brothers, wouldn't be going to school this fall. Lily wondered what school would be like with so few children. What would they do at recess? What games could they play without Isaac? He was the one who always invented new games. The only children left in the district were her cousins, Levi and Hannah, Mandy Mast, and Joseph and Lily. Poor Joseph. He had been so excited to start school. Lily had been looking forward to having him in school. She wanted him to see how much fun school could be, but a school made up of only five children—one of whom was Mandy Mast—didn't seem like fun at all. And the school board still hadn't found a teacher. That was the biggest problem of all.

Two nights later, Lily had just finished cleaning her plate of the last spoonfuls of potatoes and gravy and then sat waiting, patiently, as Joseph and Dannie finished up. Mama was feeding Dannie from his little bowl. Papa sat back in his chair and told Mama about his day. He was building a shed for an older man who liked to tell stories while Papa worked.

As soon as Dannie ate his last bite of food, everyone bowed their heads to pray a silent thank-you to God for all they had eaten. They thanked God before a meal, and they thanked God after a meal. Before and after. Twice.

Afterward, Lily quickly gathered dishes from the table and carried them to the kitchen sink. Monday nights meant that Lily didn't have to dry dishes for Mama like she usually did. Monday nights meant that Lily and Joseph headed downstairs to the basement and filled the big iron kettle with water. Papa fastened the green garden hose to the faucet in the basement and turned it on, full blast. Lily held the hose so that the arc of water landed inside the big kettle. It would have to be filled all the way to the top with gallons and gallons of water.

After Mama had washed the dinner dishes and put them away, she came down to the basement with the clothes hamper. She carefully sorted all the dirty clothes into piles. Once sorted, she put each pile into its own big five-gallon bucket. After Lily and Joseph had finished filling the kettle, Mama took the hose and filled each bucket to the brim with water. The clothes would soak overnight. Tomorrow, Mama and Lily would do the laundry.

Early the next morning, Papa opened the little door in the bottom of the iron kettle and stuffed an armload of wood inside. With a match, he lit the wood on fire and closed the door. The fire would heat the water while the family was upstairs, eating breakfast.

After breakfast, Papa checked the water in the kettle and found it bubbling hot. He picked up an empty five-gallon pail and carefully dipped it into the boiling water. He poured the hot water into the washing machine until it was almost filled to the top. He checked the gas supply in the little motor attached under the machine. He made sure the exhaust pipe, snaking from the motor to a specially designed hole in the wall, was snug and secure. Satisfied, he went back upstairs to the kitchen.

"Everything is all set for the laundry, Rachel." He peered out the window. The sun was just rising. There wasn't a cloud in the sky. "Looks like a beautiful day. It won't take much time at all for clothes to dry."

Mama handed Papa his lunch box and gave him a special smile, one she had just for Papa. "Thank you, Daniel."

Papa whistled as he walked down the steps, on his way to work. Papa was always whistling.

Mama gathered up the pot holders and tea towels she had used for breakfast and handed them to Lily and Joseph. "Run down to the basement and put these into the pail with towels."

Joseph and Lily carried the towels downstairs. Mama followed behind them with Dannie in her arms. She placed him into a large cardboard box, partially filled with sand and toys. Papa had created an indoor sandbox for Dannie to play in while Lily and Joseph helped Mama do the laundry.

Mama pulled the starter rope on the little gas motor. She lifted up the heavy pail filled with soaking clothes and started feeding them, one by one, through the wringer. Water ran from the wringer down on a little tilted tray and back into the pail. She started with white clothes. The last load of the day would be Papa's dirty work trousers. By the time they got to Papa's trousers, the water had turned from crystal clear to muddy-colored.

Lily and Joseph liked watching the agitator turn back and forth, back and forth. Steam rose from the washing machine. When Mama was satisfied that the clothes were clean, she added a little bit of bluing to make the rinse water nice and blue. With a big wooden stick she carefully lifted the clothes from the hot water and fed them through the wringer.

"Careful," Mama cautioned.

Lily and Joseph stood back so they wouldn't get splattered with hot water. Then they pushed the clothes down into the cold water as deep as they could. Every piece had to be rinsed by itself. Mama lifted a big towel as high as she could, then plunged it back down into the water. She plunged it three times before she fed it into the wringer.

Lily liked to help Mama with the rinsing. Mama let her do the smaller pieces. Up and down. Up and down. A little river of water was squeezed out of each piece of clothing as it went through the wringer. The one thing Lily didn't like washing was bread bags. Mama reused store-bought plastic bread bags for her home-baked bread. The butter Mama spread on top of her own loaves made the bags greasy, so they had to be washed, like everything else. Mama didn't want them going through the wringer—she was certain they would tear. But if Mama happened to turn her back, Lily would feed a bag through the wringer. They didn't tear. They never had.

Lily reached into the water to get another piece of clothing. She swished her hand around and felt one of the plastic bread bags. An idea popped into her head. If the bread bag were filled with water, the little river of water that squeezed out of it in the wringer would be like a waterfall! Mama was checking on Dannie in the sandbox and bent over to tie one of his shoelaces. Her back was turned. Lily quickly fed the bread bag through the wringer.

Mama stood up and turned her attention back to the washer. She saw what Lily was up to. She darted over to stop the wringer but—too late!—the bread bag burst, showering Mama with cold water.

"Oh, Lily!" Mama said, dripping from head to toe with water. "You should know never to put bread bags through the wringer. I was trying to save the ones I had left. Now I'll have to buy a loaf of bread the next time we go to town."

Lily felt a little guilty, but not too much. She preferred store-bought bread to home-baked bread. But she *was* sorry Mama had gotten soaked. "I'm sorry, Mama," she said truthfully.

Mama dried herself off. Finally, after all the clothes and towels and sheets had been rinsed, Mama tied her clothespin bag around her waist. Lily carried Dannie and followed behind Mama and Joseph. They handed pieces of clothing to Mama to hang on the clothesline. Mama sang happily as she hung up her clean clothes.

Now came the fun part. Mama carefully drained the washing machine into several big pails and carried them out the basement door that led to the edge of the garden. Lily and Joseph dipped tin cups into the soapy water and poured the water over the cabbage, cauliflower, and broccoli plants. Three cups for each plant. Mama said the soapy water helped to keep bugs and worms away. "Shoo, bugs!" Lily would say as she gave each plant some soapy water.

Mama dumped the rest of the water on the basement floor. She scrubbed it with her broom until it was nice and clean and all of the water was swept down the drain.

It had taken all morning to do the laundry. Lily was hungry.

Mama fixed a few sandwiches and chocolate milk for everyone. It was time for Dannie to take his nap. Then, Mama and Joseph and Lily went outside to see if the first batch of hung clothes were already dry. Mama piled fresh, clean-smelling clothes onto Lily and Joseph's wide-open arms. Lily ran into the house and piled the clothes on the table. She waited for Joseph—in case he needed help with his pile of clothes—before she ran back outside for another armload.

When the last of the dry clothes were piled on the table, Mama came inside to fold them. As she folded, she sang a little song she had made up for laundry days.

> Thank you, Lord, for this nice day.
> Bless us as we put away
> All the garments clean and bright
> That were dried by wind and light.

Lily and Joseph sang the song with Mama until the last pieces of clothing were folded and put away. Lily loved laundry day, especially on warm sunny days. She loved helping Mama. She loved plunging the clothes in the rinser. She loved the smell of fresh, sun-dried clothes in the house. Next week, she would skip slipping a bread bag through the wringer. She definitely would skip that part.

But Lily *was* looking forward to eating a slice of store-bought bread, lathered with sweet creamy butter and dripping with Mama's homemade plum jam.

School without a Schoolhouse

Late on a hot August afternoon, the mailman came and left a big parcel on the porch. Lily and Joseph were shocked. They never got any mail. Lily watched as Mama opened the box with a knife. She pulled out glossy new books, with pages for writing and arithmetic. Schoolbooks!

Mama handed Lily the books. "Papa and I have decided we will have school at home until the school board finds a teacher."

Lily stroked the covers of the shiny new books. She was glad that she could keep learning even if she and Joseph couldn't go to a real school.

Papa and Mama moved the furniture out of the spare bedroom and put it into the attic. Papa carried two little school desks upstairs and put them in the room. He built a frame around a piece of blackboard and hung it on one of the walls. Mama moved the little brown table from the living room into the room. The spare bedroom didn't look like a bedroom anymore. It looked like a little schoolhouse.

Lily clapped her hands. This was going to be fun!

Mama set a strict new routine. As soon as the breakfast dishes were washed, they went upstairs to have school. Lily liked having Mama for a teacher. She didn't lose her temper like Teacher Katie. She was much nicer than Teacher Katie. As soon as Lily and Joseph finished their workbooks, Mama let them go outside to play or help her in the kitchen or keep Dannie out of mischief. Mama was working hard to keep up with selling baked goods out of the buggy while also teaching school to Lily and Joseph.

But there were some things Lily didn't like about having school at home. Mama never had time to read Lily a story anymore, or sit on the porch to listen to birdsong. And Lily hardly ever saw her friends. She did miss her friends.

❧❦

One night, Lily lay in bed and listened to the barks and howls from a pack of wild dogs that had been roaming around the farms. It was a scary sound. She worried that wild dogs might eat little girls and little boys. Usually, the wild dogs roamed at night, stealing chickens that didn't make it into the coop to roost at night. Once in a while, Lily would spot a few dogs running through the fields in the day. They were ugly and mean. Papa said the wild dogs were worse than wolves because they weren't afraid of fire or light. They weren't afraid to get too close to people.

Tonight, the wild dogs sounded close by, as near as Jim and Jenny's pasture. Though it was a hot night, the sound made Lily shiver. Lily hoped that Jim and Jenny were both safe. Stormy didn't like having those wild dogs get too close. She barked at them, loud and long. Lily was glad Stormy was trying to keep the wild dogs away.

211

At breakfast the next morning, Papa spread butter on a piece of toast, deep in thought. "Those stray dogs got the rooster last night."

The rooster? Their proud, strutting rooster? Lily was sad, though she hadn't forgiven the rooster for pecking at her red buttons. She stayed clear of that rooster, but she never wished him to be killed by wild dogs.

"It seems as if those dogs are getting bolder and bolder," Mama said.

Papa nodded. "They worry me more than coyotes. They're more vicious and dangerous."

"At least we don't see them much during the day," Mama said. "But I am getting tired of having them around during the night. The barking woke Dannie up so much last night that he'll be cranky today."

Oh no! That was sad news to hear. Whenever Dannie was cranky, Mama would ask Lily and Joseph to play with him to keep him happy. It was hard work to make a cranky little boy happy.

Mama wanted to work in the garden after breakfast. The last of her sweet corn was ripe, ready to be gathered for canning. She spread a blanket under one of the cedar trees in front of the house and asked Lily and Joseph to play with Dannie. She sat Dannie on the blanket and gave him a few toys to play with. She handed Lily a pretty picture book to read to Dannie and Joseph.

Dannie wasn't interested in the toys. He wanted to be with Mama and cried when Lily told him to stay on the blanket. Lily opened the book that Mama had given to her. It was filled with colorful pictures.

"Let's play picture hide-and-seek," Lily said. "I see a pink tulip. Can you find it?"

Dannie looked and looked at the picture, but Joseph spotted the tulip first, so it was his turn to choose something to find.

"Can you find a brown horse?" Joseph said.

Lily pointed out the horse right away. It was the main thing to see on that page. She didn't even have to look for it. She wished that Joseph would pick something that was a little harder to find.

Lily's turn. She asked Joseph to find a little mouse. It was taking him a long time to find it. Suddenly, Lily heard Stormy barking behind the barn. Then she heard the bark of another dog. Stormy came bounding around the corner of the barn chasing a big, ugly, spotted yellow dog. A wild dog!

Where was Dannie?

While Lily and Joseph had been looking for things in the book, Dannie had toddled off. Lily saw him heading toward the garden. The dogs were hurtling right at him! The wild dog was in the lead, with Stormy right behind, snapping at its heels. Joseph hid behind the tree. Lily jumped to her feet and ran to scoop Dannie into her arms while the dogs raced around them, circling and circling. Her heart was pounding. She didn't know what to do!

Mama came running toward them and snapped her big blue apron at the wild dog. It looked like a wolf—curling its lips, baring its teeth, snarling, growling viciously, but Mama didn't back down. "Shoo, shoo! Get away from here!"

The wild dog didn't like getting whacked by Mama's apron. He howled, tucked his tail between his legs, and ran back to the woods. Mama grabbed Dannie out of Lily's arms and hugged him close to her. She was trembling.

"Lily, you were very brave to grab Dannie before the wild dog could snatch him! Weren't you scared?"

"I was! I was scared," Lily said. "But Joseph was scareder."

"I wasn't any such thing!" Joseph said, but Lily knew that wasn't so. He was still behind the tree.

Stormy flopped down on the blanket, her long pink tongue dangling out of her mouth. Lily went over to pat Stormy and tell her how wonderful she was. She thought Stormy looked pleased with herself.

"I'm glad we have such a good dog," Mama said. "No telling what all those strays might do if it weren't for her."

Lily was glad Stormy was their dog. But she was even more glad that Mama had a big apron and knew how to snap it at snarling wild dogs.

30

Off to Town

On a hot afternoon in September, Trisha and her father, Larry Smith, stopped by Singing Tree Farm to buy a dozen eggs from Mama's chickens. After Trisha's father had paid for the eggs, he leaned against his car to chat with Papa for a while.

"Trisha's school is having their annual parade next weekend," Larry Smith said. "I was wondering if you might consider giving people rides with your horse and buggy. You could charge them a dollar a ride. I think you'll have a pretty long line of people wanting rides."

Papa took his straw hat off and raked his hand through his hair, mulling that over. "As long as it's on Saturday instead of Sunday, I think we could probably do that." He put his hat back on. "Just let me know what time I should be there."

Larry Smith's face broke into a broad smile. "I'll talk to the parade organizers and let you know. Thanks, Daniel."

He opened the car door. "Hop in, Trisha. We're ready to go home."

Lily gave Trisha a goodbye hug. She stood next to Papa and waved and waved, until the car disappeared down the road. "Can I go to town with you, Papa?"

"We'll have to see what Mama wants to do. It all depends if she wants to come. If she does, then we'll all go. But if not, she'll need your help with the boys. You'll need to stay and I'll have to go by myself."

Lily ran to the house to find Mama. "I want to see a parade and Papa said I can only go if you go. Please, Mama, please go! Say yes!"

Mama looked at Papa curiously as he came into the kitchen. He walked over to the sink to wash his hands.

"What parade?" Mama said. "Where and when?"

Papa wiped his hands with a dish towel and explained what Larry Smith wanted him to do. "I thought you and the children might like to pack a picnic lunch and sit on one of those benches beside the street. You could watch the parade while I give people rides in the buggy. I was thinking of using the open buggy. It's lighter, so Jim won't get as tired from having to give so many rides."

"That sounds interesting," Mama said. But she didn't say she was going. She didn't say she was staying at home, either.

Lily wished Mama would give her answer right away, but she knew she should not ask again. One time was enough. Lily knew that from past experience. Mama would tell her after she had made a decision.

On Saturday morning, Papa woke up extra early to brush Jim until his coat shone. Every little hair was perfectly in place. The night before, Papa washed and polished the little open buggy so it would be ready to go.

And here was the best part: Mama had decided to go along! Lily was so excited. She watched Mama pack a basket filled with delicious food. Mama had made little buns of bread stuffed with cold chicken and homemade cheese. Lily had helped her bake little pecan tarts. She placed them carefully into the bottom of the basket. Mama carefully wrapped Papa's favorite, Apple Schnitz Pie, into a soft clean towel. She filled two water jugs to the very top with fresh water. Lily carried the water jugs to the buggy while Mama carried Dannie and the picnic basket.

They were ready for the parade!

The open buggy was small. It had only one seat. Papa had fastened a board against the dashboard for Lily and Joseph to sit on while they were driving. Dannie sat in Mama's lap. After everyone was settled in, Papa flicked Jim's reins and they were on their way.

Lily loved to ride in the open buggy. There was so much more to see than when they used the top buggy. She and Joseph counted eleven lambs, standing close by their ewe mothers, in a pasture. They saw a Cooper's hawk soaring in the sky. A doe and her fawn peeked shyly at them through the trees.

Jim trotted briskly all the way to town, as if he knew what an important job he had for the day. Papa pulled up to the town square and helped Mama and Dannie out of the buggy. He lifted Lily and Joseph and set them down. Papa jumped back into the buggy and drove off to meet Trisha's father. Mama led the way to a bench under a big shady maple tree. She tucked the picnic basket beneath the bench, then they all sat down to wait for the parade to begin.

Soon, Papa and Jim drove by with someone in the buggy. Lily loved how Jim lifted his feet so proudly as he walked along. Papa said he did that because Jim's father had been a Hackney horse. Lily was sure no other horse in the world was as handsome and high stepping as Jim.

Papa and Jim drove customers back and forth, back and forth. Soon, Lily grew bored. Mama said she had to stay on the bench or sit in the grass next to it. There was nothing to see or do except watch Papa give people rides in the buggy.

More and more people started arriving at the town square. Some brought funny-looking chairs to sit on while others walked around or stood chatting with their friends. Lily heard a funny, far-off noise. *Boom, boom, boom boom boom*. The booms got louder and louder and closer and closer. *BOOM, BOOM, boom boom boom*. Lily looked all around her, but she couldn't see what was making the booms.

And then Lily saw what was making the booms, far down the street. Rows and rows of young people in peculiar uniforms with odd hats, marching toward her. A row of them held something round against their tummies. They pounded on it with sticks.

"What are they doing, Mama?" Lily asked.

"The parade has started," Mama said. "Those are drums that they're beating."

Lily didn't like the sound of beating drums. She thought about covering her ears with her hands. She glanced at Joseph to see if he was cringing with the loud booms. To her surprise, Joseph was pounding his little fists on his knees the same way the drummers were beating their drums. He was fascinated.

The row behind the drummers was a group of girls in bright blue one-piece bathing suits and white cowboy boots. They twirled sticks up in the air, caught them, then tossed them up again. Lily wondered how they could keep walking and twirling like that without growing dizzy and stumbling. Or hitting each other with a stick. She was sure she would hurt someone if she tried to walk while tossing a stick in the air.

The parade continued on. The twirling stick girls were followed by another group, then another. Lily could hardly hear anything because of the drumbeats: *BOOM, BOOM, boom boom boom.*

After the parade ended, Mama pulled out the picnic basket so they could eat lunch. Lily was ready to go home. The parade wasn't what she had expected it to be. It was too loud. Too loud. She did not like it at all.

But Joseph loved it. He turned the empty picnic basket upside down and pretended it was a drum. He beat out the same rhythm as the drummers. *BOOM, BOOM, boom boom boom.*

Finally, finally! Papa and Jim finished giving buggy rides. As Mama saw him drive up to the square, she said, "Okay, children. It's time to go." Lily helped gather up Dannie's little toys while Mama packed up the lunch.

Lily didn't talk much on the way home. Her ears were still ringing from the loud drummers. But Joseph couldn't stop talking about the parade all the way home.

"Papa, I think I want a drum," he said.

Papa and Mama exchanged a glance. "We can't get a drum for you," Papa said. "But if Mama doesn't mind, you could use one of her mixing bowls and some wooden spoons."

Joseph was thrilled.

Lily had a bad feeling about this.

Day after day, Joseph pounded on his mixing bowl drum with his wooden spoon drumsticks. *BOOM, BOOM, boom boom boom.*

By the end of the week, Lily was sorry they had ever gone to that parade. She wished she had never begged Mama to go to the parade. She wished she had never heard of parades or ever seen marching drummers. She wondered if Mama and Papa had the same thought, but they never said a word.

CHAPTER

31

Another Business for Mama

One night in late September, Lily was so hot that she couldn't sleep. She crept downstairs and sat on the bottom step when she heard Mama and Papa talking.

"I have to find something else to do besides baking," Mama said. "It's simply too much work to do all that baking and try to have school too."

"I could see about finding some extra work," Papa said.

"You're already working such long hours, Daniel," Mama said. "I'm sure I can find some way to get everything done and to help make ends meet. Maybe even save some money too. It would be nice to have a nest egg."

Lily slipped up the stairs and went to bed, worried. That night, she dreamed about baking cinnamon rolls and putting them in a bird's nest.

The next day, Mama went to town and came home happy and excited, filled with plans. "I stopped at a quilt shop," she

221

told Papa as she handed Jim's reins to him. "The owner was putting up a sign in the window. She is looking for people to do quilting for her. She gave me some pieces of fabric to show her how my quilting looks. She liked my work." Mama looked pleased but embarrassed by the praise, all at the same time. "Next week, she said she would send over my first quilt. She said she would pay thirty-five cents for every yard of thread I use."

As Papa and Mama continued to talk about the quilt shop, Lily tried to figure out how much money Mama would be making. She knew it would take three yards of thread to make a dollar. She wondered how many yards of thread went into one quilt. Probably dozens and dozens. Maybe millions. Mama was going to be rich!

❧❧

Papa made Mama a large wooden frame to hold the quilt. Mama set it up in the living room, on top of four chairs. She started with the fabric for the backing. Mama carefully opened the fabric and pinned it securely to the frame. It reminded Lily of a big trampoline. Mama opened a large roll of soft, fluffy batting and rolled it out to smooth every wrinkle. On top of that, she laid the quilt top from the shop owner.

Lily's eyes grew wide as she saw the quilt top unfold. It was so beautiful! Shades of pink and cream, with little flowers on the fabric. Lily thought she had never seen such a pretty quilt top.

Walking slowly around the quilt, Mama pinned the three layers together. At last, the time had come to start quilting. She measured out a yard of thread from a spool, snipped it, threaded her needle, and started to stitch. Tiny, even little stitches, so small that Lily could hardly see them.

Lily watched for a while. Soon, she grew bored. Joseph had set up his toy farm under the quilt. Lily decided to get her doll, Sally, and Sally's cradle to play with him.

It didn't take long for a new routine to take shape. After Lily and Joseph had finished with their schoolwork, Mama would sit at the quilt to sew as much as she could while Dannie napped, and before Papa came home from his carpentry work. Then, it was time to make supper.

Lily thought there was nothing in the world as boring as quilting. Sometimes, Mama would tell them stories about the olden days, when she was a girl. But she would only tell one or two stories because she had to concentrate on the quilt, she said. So Lily would go back to playing with her puzzles and her doll, or help watch Dannie. Every now and then,

223

Joseph would play dolls with her, but only if she would first play farm with him.

One rainy afternoon, Lily had already put all her puzzles together. She didn't feel like coloring or playing farm with Joseph. "Do you want to play church?" she said, peeking under the quilt at Joseph and Dannie. Church was their third favorite game to play together.

Joseph jumped up and climbed up on Papa's big rocking chair. Dannie toddled behind him so Joseph helped him up. Lily ran to get her doll, Sally, and Sally's diaper bag and join him. The rocking chair was their buggy. Joseph pretended to drive the horse. Together, they rocked as hard as they could. When Joseph called out "Whoa!" Lily hopped off and took Dannie with her to go upstairs to her room. She sat Dannie on the bed, propped Sally next to him, then hopped up. The three sat on the bed like pigeons on a telephone wire, waiting for the preacher to arrive.

One minute later, Joseph came into the bedroom, serious and solemn. He stood in the center of the room, pretending to be Preacher Ed, one of the ministers in their church. Joseph could sound just like Preacher Ed, husky voiced and leather-lunged, slamming his fists against each other to make his points, shaking his chin to make his pretend beard wiggle.

"And another thing!" Preacher Joseph shouted, pointing a long boney finger at the church members. "Oversleeping is a sin!" *Wham!* He slapped one fist against the other. "Stealing cookies is a sin!" *Wham! Wham!* "Wishing you had your friends' toys is a sin!" *Wham! Wham! Wham!*

Lily startled to giggle, and Joseph couldn't keep a straight face. Soon they were both laughing so hard they couldn't talk. Dannie laughed along with them, even though he was too young to understand what was so funny. Pretend church was so much more fun than real church, where Lily didn't even dare to smile. And Preacher Joseph was much, much funnier than Preacher Ed.

"Let's play again," Lily said. "This time, I have a new idea." She jumped off the bed and yanked the bottom drawer of her dresser open. "We can use this for a bench." She sat in the drawer.

"You be the preacher," Joseph said. "I'm tired of always being the preacher."

He climbed in the dresser drawer. Dannie slipped off the bed and joined them. As Dannie tried to climb in to the drawer, the dresser tipped forward. The oil lamp and pretty candy bowls that were on top of the dresser slipped off and crashed to the floor. Lily quickly jumped out of the drawer and away from the dresser, but Joseph and Dannie weren't as quick. The dresser pinned Joseph and Dannie to the floor. A horrified silence followed.

They were dead! Joseph and Dannie had been killed! Lily was sure of it. She let out a piercing scream. Mama came running up the stairs to see what had happened. Lily was hysterical. All she could do was to point to the dresser. Mama lifted the dresser up. Joseph and Dannie looked up, a little stunned. Lily was so relieved. They weren't dead after all! As soon as Mama was convinced Joseph and Dannie were all right—no broken bones or cuts or bruises—the shock of near-death wore off. Joseph started to yell in terrible, yowling screams. Dannie chimed in at the top of his lungs. Mama made them sit on the bed while she cleaned up the mess.

Lily looked at all the broken glass littering the floor. The candy bowls and the lamp chimney were shattered to smithereens. Mama swept the glass pieces and splinters into the dustpan. When she was finished, she told them to come downstairs to play where she could keep an eye on them. All afternoon, Mama's face was pinched and tight, as if she seemed mad. Or sad. Lily couldn't tell which.

Maybe both.

Papa's News

*P*apa came home with news one evening that Great-Grandma was released from the hospital. She was staying at Grandpa Miller's until she felt strong again. As soon as they finished supper, Papa hitched Jim to the buggy while Lily and Joseph helped Mama wash and put away the dishes. They all wanted to see Great-Grandma. Lily wondered if she was strong enough to wave her cane. If she did, Lily wanted to be sure to stay out of reach.

When they arrived at Grandpa Miller's house, Lily was surprised to discover that Grandma's sewing room had been converted into a bedroom for Great-Grandma. The bed she lay in looked like it belonged in the hospital. It had rails at the side and a handle at the foot so Great-Grandma could be propped up or lay flat.

Lily glanced around the room but couldn't see Great-Grandma's cane anywhere. She was glad that she didn't have to worry about having it hook around her neck. When Great-Grandma tried to talk to Mama, her words sounded slurred. Lily noticed that Great-Grandma's mouth looked twisted and unsmiling. Grandma whispered to Lily that Great-Grandma could no longer move anything on the right side of her body. Lily felt sorry for her. She was so old, and now she couldn't move. Lily never wanted to get old.

Papa and Grandpa came into the room to see Great-Grandma. Grandma hurried and brought in some more chairs so that each person had a place to sit. Lily hoped that Great-Grandma liked having all of these visitors, even if she couldn't talk.

Mama turned to Lily and said, "Why don't you and Joseph go play with Aunt Susie?"

Papa ushered them out and closed the door behind them. Lily thought that was strange. She and Joseph were always allowed to be with the grown-ups, as long as they didn't interrupt. And why was Dannie allowed to stay? Not fair!

Lily and Joseph found Aunt Susie in the living room. She was coloring a book with her new box of crayons. They all lay on their tummies on the floor and shared the crayons and the coloring book. It was easier to color that way.

The murmur of the grown-ups' voices in the next room was like the sound of buzzing bees. Lily couldn't stop thinking about it. She sat up. "What do you think they are talking about?"

Aunt Susie put her finger over her lips. "Sh-h-h. Follow me."

Lily and Joseph tiptoed behind Aunt Susie. Very carefully they pressed their ears against the door to Great-Grandma's new bedroom. Lily could hear Papa's deep voice say, "I hate to think about leaving everything after we worked so hard to get our little farm built up."

"I don't see any other choice," Grandpa said. "There are already five other families planning to move. I'm sure it's just a matter of time before more of them leave."

"But where would we go?" Mama said.

Grandpa cleared his throat. "I've heard of a nice little Amish community in Pennsylvania that sounds like a good place to raise a family."

Pennsylvania? Where was that? It sounded far, far away from Pleasant Hill.

Lily drew away from the door. She didn't want to move away from Singing Tree Farm. Surely, Mama would say they shouldn't move. Their little farm finally had a garden, and a barn, and animals. What about Jenny and Chubby? And what about Jim? Papa wouldn't leave Jim. Surely not! Papa would put a stop to this talk!

"Lily, what is Grandpa talking about?" Joseph asked. "What's Pennsylvania?"

Lily shrugged. She had to know more. She pressed her ear to the door when she heard Papa start to talk. "The children are young enough that they could adjust quickly and make new friends."

Lily hadn't even thought about leaving her friends! What about Hannah and Levi? And Trisha? Oh, this was a terrible idea. *Say no, Mama! Tell Papa you want to stay at Singing Tree Farm!*

But Mama didn't say anything.

"We can always build up another farm," Papa said. "It's not the farm that makes a home. It's the people who live there."

Lily could hear Mama and Grandma and Grandpa murmuring. It sounded as if they were all agreeing with Papa. This was terrible news.

Lily and Joseph and Aunt Susie went back to the coloring

books in the living room. Lily and Joseph didn't feel like coloring anymore. Aunt Susie didn't look very happy, either.

"I'll come help you pack your toys before you move," she said.

The very thought brought Lily near tears. She didn't want to move away. She loved her home and having her grandparents nearby, and her Aunt Susie. Her eyes welled with tears.

On the way home from Grandpa Miller's, Lily and Joseph were quiet. So were Mama and Papa. Jackrabbits stood on their hind legs along the road, with their tall, twitching ears. As the buggy rolled nearby, they bounded away. Lily thought their tails looked like little white cotton balls. Usually, the sight made Joseph and Lily laugh, but not today. They were too sad about leaving Singing Tree Farm.

Finally, Joseph couldn't stand it any longer. "Papa, we don't want to move!"

Papa glanced at Joseph in the back of the buggy. "What makes you say that?"

"Lily and Aunt Susie put their ears against the door," Joseph said. He wiggled over to the far edge of the buggy seat, away from Lily, trying to make himself smaller.

Lily poked Joseph in the ribs. Little boys should learn not to tattle.

"Ow!" Joseph said. "I didn't do nothing!"

"You didn't do *anything*," Mama corrected. She turned around in the buggy to look at Lily and Joseph. "Nothing has been decided. But we are concerned about not having a school for you children."

"We like having school at home, Mama," Lily said. "We don't mind not having a teacher. We're learning just fine. Even Joseph. He can just about read, if you don't mind that he points at each word."

Joseph tried to jab Lily with the bony part of his elbow, but she leaned out of the way and he hurt his elbow on the back of the bench. She didn't feel sorry for him. It served him right for tattling on her about eavesdropping.

"It might be fine for now, Lily," Papa said, "but we want you and Joseph—and someday, Dannie—to go to school with other children."

Lily opened her mouth to object, but Papa cut her off. "Nothing is decided for now. Moving is just something to consider." He looked back at them with a very serious look on his face. "And we definitely don't want you children to eavesdrop on conversations that aren't meant for you to hear."

It was amazing how small Joseph could make himself. It was almost like there was nobody there. Lily wished she could do that.

CHAPTER

33

Pumpkins!

Trisha and Lily stood in front of Jim, stroking his velvety nose, as Mama showed Trisha's father the baked goods she had made to sell. Every week, Trisha's father chose a loaf of bread and a different kind of pie.

He handed Mama some cash and turned to the girls. "How would the two of you like to go to the pumpkin patch on Monday?"

Trisha jumped up and down. "Oh, yes!" she said, grasping Lily's hands. "We would like that!"

Mama tucked the money safely into her money box. She smiled when she saw Trisha's excitement. Lily couldn't imagine what would be so wonderful about going to a pumpkin patch. To her, it sounded like a big garden filled with pumpkins. Boring!

"Daniel and I were planning to take our spring wagon to get a load of pumpkins after he gets home from work,"

Mama said. "We can stop by so Trisha could ride along with us or we can meet at the pumpkin patch."

"Please, Daddy! Please can I ride with them?" Trisha asked.

Larry Smith shrugged a shoulder. "Sure. As long as they don't mind and have plenty of room."

Mama smiled. "We'll see you late Monday afternoon." She untied Jim's rope from the tree and climbed in the buggy to drive down the street to their next customer.

"Mama, why do you need the wagon to bring home a pumpkin?" Lily said.

"We'll be getting a lot of pumpkins on Monday," Mama said. "And then I can bake pumpkin pie, pumpkin rolls with cream cheese filling, and pumpkin bread. We can eat some and sell the rest."

Lily's eye grew wide. She thought of all the good things Mama would be making with those pumpkins. She thought of how spicy and cinnamony the house would smell! And then she wondered what Trisha's family would do with all their pumpkins. They didn't bake. They always bought Mama's baked goods to feed their family.

On Monday, as soon as Papa came home from work, he hitched Jim to the spring wagon. It had one seat in the front and a long wooden wagon bed with low sides. There was no roof. Papa helped Mama climb up over the front wheel and sit on the seat, then lifted Dannie up to her. He placed several blankets on the wagon bed for Joseph and Lily to sit on, and added another blanket so Trisha would have something to sit on after they picked her up.

The autumn air was crisp and cold as they drove along. Now and then, Lily smelled a farmer's burning leaves in the air. Joseph's nose looked red and chilled; Lily knew hers probably looked the same.

233

As Papa pulled Jim to a stop in front of Trisha's house, she ran out to greet them. She had been watching for them in the window. Her father walked out behind her and hoisted her into the back of the spring wagon. Lily showed her how to stay nice and warm while curling up inside a blanket nest.

It was a short drive to the pumpkin patch. Lily was surprised by its size. It was much bigger than a garden. There were pumpkins as far as she could see. Big ones, little ones, fat ones, tall ones. Their vibrant orange color made the field look like a patchwork quilt. She saw many other people walking around the patch, trying to choose pumpkins. They only chose one or two. Lily felt sorry for them. Those poor people wouldn't be getting very many pumpkin pies and other good baked things with only one or two pumpkins. She was glad that Papa and Mama were getting a big load of pumpkins.

Papa tied Jim to a tree while he and Mama gathered pump-

kins. Trisha's father drove in a car behind the wagon. Trisha helped her father try to find the pumpkins they liked best.

It took an hour, but finally the spring wagon was piled up with pumpkins. There was no room for Lily and Joseph to sit in the back to ride home so Papa folded the blankets and put them under the seat.

"Where will we sit?" Lily asked.

"You and Joseph will have to stand in front of Mama and me and hold on to the dashboard," Papa said.

Lily quickly climbed up on the wagon seat to reach her favorite standing spot, on the edge, before Joseph could claim it. The middle was the best place for him anyway, she thought. That was the best place for a small boy.

While Papa paid for the pumpkins, Lily waved goodbye to Trisha and her father. Poor Trisha. How sad. They left with only two medium-sized pumpkins.

At home, Papa and Mama carried the pumpkins into the basement so they would be easy to get to when Mama was ready to bake.

The next morning, Mama cut the pumpkins open with a big sharp knife and scooped out the seeds. She cut the pumpkins into chunks, put them into a big pot, poured water over them, and set them on the stove. After the pumpkin chunks had boiled for a long time, she carefully drained the pot of hot water. She scooped all the soft pumpkin flesh out of their shells and into a large bowl. She cut and cooked pumpkins until the big bowl was towered high with soft, boiled pumpkin chunks.

Then came the fun part. Mama got the Victoria strainer out of the cupboard and fastened it together. She clamped it to the table and placed the large funnel on top and a big bowl under it. She spooned the pumpkin chunks into the funnel and started to crank the handle. A thick orange mush squeezed out of the strainer, slid down the special tray, and plopped into the bowl. When the last of the pumpkin chunks had made their way through the strainer, the big bowl was filled to the very top. The pureed pumpkin was now ready to be used for Mama's baking.

Mama's pumpkin pies were the best, the very best. Mama mixed everything together for the pie filling in only one bowl. After it had been baked, there was a layer of good, sweet pumpkin filling on the bottom and a fluffy, foamy pumpkin layer on top. Lily could not understand how that happened in the oven. She wanted to peek inside to see when it turned into two layers of pumpkin, but Mama said no.

Mama was busy with something else. She had baked very thin pumpkin cakes. She spread cream cheese filling on top and rolled them up to make a pretty log with a white swirl in the middle. Lily wanted to help, but Mama said that they had to look perfect to sell.

"I'm sorry, Lily," she said. "When you're older, then you can help." She handed Lily a few scraps of pie dough and a little rolling pin. "Why don't you make a nice little pumpkin pie for Papa?"

Lily carefully rolled out the pie dough and placed it into a little pie pan. Mama spooned some pie filling into it and popped it into the oven. Lily couldn't wait to give Papa a pumpkin pie that she had made all by herself. He would be so happy.

On Saturday morning, Lily went with Mama to peddle all the good pumpkin baked goods she had made. The whole buggy smelled like pumpkin, cinnamon, and nutmeg. Lily thought it would be nice to stop now and then to sample some of those things that smelled so good, but Mama kept right on going.

Trisha's neighborhood was always the first stop. The people who lived on Trisha's street seemed to be on the lookout for Mama's buggy today. They hurried out of their houses, eager to see what she had baked. Lily was sure it was because they could smell the sweet spices floating from the back of the buggy.

By the time Mama tied Jim to a tree, Trisha was already at the buggy. "Mrs. Lapp, can I show our pumpkins to Lily?" Trisha asked.

Lily had been wondering what Trisha had made with the pumpkins her father had bought at the pumpkin patch. Mama gave Lily permission and she ran with Trisha to the house. As Lily neared the front porch, she stopped abruptly. The two beautiful pumpkins they had picked at the pumpkin patch were ugly and scary. Someone had cut a big ugly mouth with jagged crooked teeth and triangle-shaped eyes into them. One had a big grin, but it still looked like an ugly jeer to Lily. The other one was worse—a big glaring frown on it. It reminded her of Teacher Katie's scowls.

Trisha was so happy and excited about these ugly pumpkins. She looked at Lily and her smile faded. "Don't you like them?"

Lily wasn't sure how to answer. She didn't want to hurt Trisha's feelings, but these pumpkins were hideous. Awful! Why would anybody do such a thing to a nice pumpkin? She stood quietly looking at them. "Weren't they hard to cut?" It didn't look easy when Mama was cutting the pumpkins into chunks.

"Daddy likes carving pumpkins," Trisha said. She seemed disappointed by Lily's lack of enthusiasm.

Lily heard Mama call her name, so she turned to go back to the buggy. Trisha followed behind to stroke Jim's nose, but Trisha's parents had their arms filled with baked goods and were ready to go back inside. Trisha was only able to give Jim a quick pat.

Lily told Mama about those ugly pumpkins as they drove down the street to another neighborhood. "Why would Trisha's papa cut scary faces into their pumpkins and then set them on their porch for everyone to see?"

"They're called jack-o-lanterns," Mama said. "A lot of people like to carve pumpkins for Halloween. The children dress up in costumes and go from door to door, saying 'trick or treat,' and collect candy from their neighbors. The Amish don't celebrate Halloween."

"Why not?" Lily thought Halloween sounded like fun. She liked dressing up and she loved candy.

"We want to glorify God in everything we do and we don't feel celebrating Halloween does that. But English people weren't raised the same way. They think it's only a fun tradition. What is okay for them would be wrong for us, but we must never think it is wrong for them."

Lily thought about Halloween and Trisha's pumpkins for the rest of the morning. She was glad they didn't have those scary-looking pumpkins on their porch. She didn't like those pumpkins. But she did like candy. Collecting candy from neighbors would be very nice. Candy, Lily thought, was always a good thing.

The Sewing Machine

On a cold and rainy morning in late October, Mama set Lily to work on a science lesson. Yesterday, Mama had Lily gather all the different leaves she could find in the yard. Mama taught Lily how to identify the trees from the leaves. Lily's task was to label each leaf and write some information about each tree. Lily had just spread all of the leaves on her desk when a knock came on the front door.

"Keep working until I get back," Mama said, pointing to Lily and Joseph.

Lily wished she could go downstairs and see who had come by for a visit. Instead, she was fastening a large oak leaf to her book. She tried to think of something she knew about oak trees. THEY HAVE ACORNS, she wrote in her careful handwriting. She finished that sentence and couldn't think of anything else about oak trees. She knew how to spell many words, some of them important. Words like DOLLHOUSE and RED DRESS and PUMPKIN COOKIES. But she didn't know any other words about oak trees. She tiptoed to the door to see if she could hear who Mama's visitor was, but she heard Mama come up the stairs so she scurried back to her desk.

Mama raised an eyebrow at Lily when she came back to the room they used for school. How did Mama seem to know everything? It was a mystery.

"Helen Young was at the door," Mama said. "She wondered if Jenny might have extra milk to spare. She'd like to buy a quart of fresh milk from us three times a week. Lily, I told her I would send you over tomorrow with a quart."

"I could take her some now," Lily offered, trying to sound helpful. She had run out of oak tree knowledge after ACORNS and would rather go play.

"I set out all our milk to sour this morning or I would have given her some," Mama said. Every week, Mama would let some of Jenny's milk sour to make all kinds of delicious-tasting butter, yogurts, and a variety of cheeses: cottage cheese, cheese curds, hard cheese to slice, and Lily's favorite, "smear kase." It spread like peanut butter or honey, and was used in the winter on top of fresh bread. "Tomorrow, you can take some milk to Helen Young. For now, back to the oak tree project."

As Lily wrote another sentence about oak trees—SQUIRRELS LIKE TO EAT ACORNS—she looked forward to taking the milk to Helen Young's. She liked Helen Young, but she did hope Harold Young wouldn't be at home. She still thought he was frightful. Always scowling! And she hadn't forgotten that shotgun he had pointed at Papa. That was hard to forget.

The next day, after school, Mama poured some fresh sweet

240

milk into a clean quart jar. She wrapped it into a towel and placed it in a little box. "Set the box in our little red wagon," she said. "That way you won't spill a single drop."

Lily and Joseph held the handle of the wagon and pulled it down the driveway and up the road to the Youngs' house. Lily was happy to hear the roaring sound of Harold Young's tractor, far off in his field.

Helen Young met them at the door. "Why, it's my milk delivery!" she said. "Come in, come in. You must be hungry after walking over here. Let me get you some cookies."

Lily and Joseph stepped into the warm and friendly kitchen. Lily had never been in an English person's kitchen. It was fascinating! Frilly white curtains, embroidered with strawberries, framed the window. A big white refrigerator purred noisily next to the kitchen counter. On the front of the refrigerator were magnets that held pictures of children and other people. The room was bright too. Lights were on even though it was a sunny day. Several pictures hung on the walls. Artificial vines with strawberries and strawberry blossoms twined and twisted together and draped above the pictures. A big soft rug was under the table and chairs. Lily wondered how Helen Young kept the kitchen looking so clean. At home, one of Lily's jobs was to sweep the crumbs around the table after every meal. How did Helen Young sweep the rug? Maybe Harold and Helen Young didn't get crumbs on the floor when they ate. Maybe they were tidier eaters than Joseph and Dannie.

Helen put the quart of milk into the refrigerator. Lily was amazed to see a light inside the refrigerator. What a good idea! It was so much easier to see what was inside. On the counter sat a big white cookie jar. It had strawberries on it too. Lily thought Helen Young must love strawberries best of all. Everywhere Lily looked, she saw strawberries.

Helen took some cookies out of the cookie jar and handed them to Lily and Joseph. Lily had never seen such a tiny cookie. It fit into the palm of her hand. She could get the whole cookie inside her mouth with just one bite, though she knew that would be rude. It would take four or five of these cookies to make one of Mama's.

Now Lily realized why all the English people made a fuss over Mama's baked goods. They must eat only tiny cookies. What a wonderful surprise it must be for them to discover Mama's big cookies!

Lily nibbled her cookie slowly. When it was finished, she motioned to Joseph that they should leave. On the way home, Lily spotted a bunch of goldenrod flowers growing beside the road. She stopped to pick them for Mama. Mama liked every kind of flower and would be happy to get their bouquet.

Every other day, Joseph and Lily took a quart of fresh milk to the Youngs'. Harold Young was never at the house. He always seemed to be out in his fields, which made Lily happy. Each time, Helen Young would invite them inside for a treat. Helen Young always had a gift for them—often tiny cookies or miniature bars, but other times, she had stickers or some unusual rocks. Lily looked forward to seeing what surprise Helen Young had for them. One time, she gave them a box of new crayons. Taking milk to Helen Young felt like a little bit of Christmas to Lily. Papa and Mama always said it was better to give than to receive, but Lily thought it was much more fun to receive.

※

One day, Helen Young didn't have anything waiting on the table for Lily and Joseph, like she usually did when they brought milk to her. Instead, she put the milk into the refrigerator and asked them to come into the living room.

Lily and Joseph followed her. Lily hadn't gone into the living room before. She tried not to stare, but it was decorated even prettier than the strawberries in the kitchen. A big soft sofa and matching chairs with plump pillows scattered on them. Helen Young walked over to a black sewing machine. The word Singer was written in gold lettering on the top of it.

"This used to be my grandmother's sewing machine," Helen Young said. She placed a hand on the top of the machine. "It's a treadle machine. She used to pump the treadle with her foot while she sewed clothes." She looked at the machine. "I never use it. It only stitches straight lines. It just collects dust." She looked up at Lily. "If you think your parents wouldn't mind, I'd like to give it to you."

Lily's eyes went wide. A sewing machine of her very own? Oh, what a wonderful surprise! She hoped Papa and Mama would say yes. They simply *had* to say yes. She had to have this beautiful black machine!

Helen Young smiled. "I'll write a note to take to your parents." She burst into a laugh. "Lily, if your eyes get any wider, you'll need a bigger face." She sat at the kitchen table and wrote a note, then handed it to Lily.

Lily walked slowly and calmly out of the house. As soon as they were out of sight of the Youngs' house, she started to run. Joseph pulled the wagon along, trying to keep up with her as it bounced and clattered behind him. Today, Lily didn't stop to find pretty flowers or leaves to take home for Mama. All that Lily could think of was to get that note to Mama as soon as she could. They ran until they were too tired to run any longer and then walked the rest of the way.

"You put the wagon away this time, Joseph," Lily said as she bolted up the porch steps. She let the door bang shut behind her and ran to give the note to Mama.

But Mama wouldn't take the note from Lily. "Go open the door and close it nicely," she said, eyebrow raised.

Lily knew they weren't allowed to let the doors bang. She hurried back to open and close the door quietly. Then, she handed Mama the note. Mama read it and tucked it into her pocket. She didn't say a word.

But Lily couldn't leave it at that. She simply had to know! "Mama, will you let me have the sewing machine?"

"I'll talk to Papa about it first." Mama turned her attention to her quilting.

Lily sat by the window. Gray clouds hung heavy in the sky. She wished it would start raining so Papa would come home early. He couldn't do carpentry work in the rain. *Rain, rain, rain*, Lily wished, squeezing her eyes shut. But when she opened her eyes, the ground was dry.

The afternoon dragged on. Finally, Mama put away her thread and needles and started getting supper ready. Lily watched for Papa by the front window. When she saw him, she ran outside to meet him and tell him about the special note in Mama's pocket.

Papa looked a little curious as Mama handed it to him. Lily watched anxiously as he read it.

A big smile spread over Papa's face. "I think I can go pick it up tonight just as soon as we're done with the chores."

Lily jumped up and down. She would be getting her very own sewing machine! Mama could teach her how to sew! She already knew what she wanted to make. A red dress for her doll, Sally.

The next morning, Lily brought Sally downstairs and sat in front of her new sewing machine. Her feet couldn't quite touch the treadle. If she stood, she could push her foot to make the needle move up and down. A little awkward for

her, but she could manage. After all, she had an important job to do today! "Mama, I'm ready."

Mama popped her head out of the kitchen. "For what?"

"To sew Sally clothes!"

Mama looked at Lily as if she were trying not to laugh. She wiped her hands on a rag and came into the living room. "Lily, when you are learning something new, you have to start at the beginning."

"I know," Lily said. "So I thought we could make Sally a red dress."

Mama shook her head. "We're going to start with a nine-patch square for a quilt for Sally."

A nine-patch square? For a dumb little quilt? Lily was so disappointed. Quilting was boring. Mama pulled out some

245

extra fabric, some scissors, and a little square template. "Before you start to use the sewing machine, you need to cut your patches, nice and straight."

When Mama went back into the kitchen, Lily whispered to Sally, "I'm sorry, Sally. Soon, I will make you a red dress." She looked at the stack of fabric, the scissors, the square template. Boring!

Christmas

The skies were bleak and gray. Day after day, Lily wished it would just go ahead and snow. It was cold, so cold, but it hadn't snowed much that winter. Every now and then they would get a dusting, but Papa said there was hardly enough snow to track a cat. The wind would sweep that little bit of snow in funny wavy patterns across the frozen barnyard. It would gather in tiny drifts beside the barn or under the trees. Everything looked brown and drab during the long winter without pretty white snow to cover it like powdered sugar.

Each evening, Lily would press her nose against the cold windowpane and hope that the ground would be nice and white when she woke up. Each morning, she was disappointed. Christmas was coming, but without snow Lily worried it would not seem like Christmas at all.

Mama and Papa didn't seem to mind that there was no

snow. Papa went whistling off to work every morning while Mama worked in the kitchen, humming and singing Christmas carols.

Today, Mama was making Christmas treats. Rice crispy candy, chocolate-coated pretzels, and—Lily's favorite—chocolate-covered peanut butter balls. When Mama was finished dipping the pretzels and peanut butter balls into the melted chocolate, she handed Lily a bag of raisins. "Dump these into the leftover chocolate and stir them. Then put little spoonfuls on the sheet of waxed paper."

Lily loved to help Mama make Christmas goodies. It was fun to drop the chocolate-covered raisins into little mounds on the waxed paper. She hoped these would be Papa's favorite Christmas treat.

As Lily worked, she wondered what she might get for Christmas. She could never guess but knew it would be something she liked. Christmas was always filled with wonderful surprises.

As she thought of presents, she had an idea. She wanted to give something to Papa and Mama too. But what? She didn't have any money to spend. She would have to think of something to make.

Later that day, Lily dug through Mama's bag of fabric scraps to see if she could find anything she liked. She didn't know how to sew anything except dumb nine-patch squares, but at least she could make a pretty nine-patch pot holder for Mama. She set to work carefully cutting patches from the fabric. Purple and green on one side, lavender and blue for the other. She sewed the patches together on her sewing machine. First one side, then the other side. Then she put the sides together and sewed a seam around all of the edges—but she left a little hole so she could turn it inside out, just like she had seen Mama do.

After she had turned the pot holder inside out, she studied the hole. What should she do with it? She didn't like to sew by hand, so she sewed it shut with the sewing machine. It didn't look very neat. There were loose threads sticking out from the hole. She had planned for the pot holder to be a nice big square, but it wasn't much of a square. More like a triangle. Lily didn't know how to fix it. It was the best she could do. She would have to give it to Mama the way it was. She hid it in her dresser drawer so Mama wouldn't see it before Christmas.

Now, what to make for Papa? She tried to think of the kinds of things Papa liked. She dug through the fabric scraps again and found a long narrow piece of fabric—as long as an apron belt. An idea popped into her head. She would make a tool belt for Papa! She sewed little strips of colorful fabric together and then used them to make pockets. Papa could put nails and his tape measure into the pockets.

Mama walked through the living room and stopped by Lily at the sewing machine. "What are you making?"

Lily looked up at her. "Something for Papa for Christmas. But I want to keep it a secret."

Mama smiled, conspiratorially. "I won't tell him."

Lily went back to sewing the tool belt. Next, she had to sew the pockets to the strip of fabric that would become the belt for Papa to tie around his waist.

After she finished, she held it up to admire it. It looked very colorful. Almost like a rainbow! She was sure Papa would love this pretty tool belt. She jumped up from the sewing machine and hid the tool belt in the dresser, next to the pot holder she had made for Mama.

Christmas morning finally arrived but still no snow. Lily was so disappointed. Delicious smells wafted up the stairs.

She knew that Mama was already working on their special Christmas breakfast. Lily couldn't get dressed fast enough. She flew down the stairs to help. Mama pointed to the special Sunday china in the cupboard. Lily set the table with the china, as carefully as she could, and then placed an orange beside everyone's plate. Her mouth watered at the thought of eating a juicy orange. Christmas was the only time they had oranges.

Papa came in from milking Jenny in the barn and washed his hands at the kitchen sink. Mama broke eggs into the frying pan and started scrambling them with a flick of her wrist—*swish, swish, swish*. Lily filled the glasses on the table with water while Papa helped Mama dish up the food. There were plump sausages, crispy bacon, strips of Mama's homemade French toast, fried potatoes, fried cornmeal mush, and cheese sauce to spoon over the scrambled eggs. There was even real store-bought bread that Mama fried in butter on both sides until it was golden brown. Beside each water glass was a mug of steaming hot chocolate with little marshmallows floating on top. Lily was sure that Christmas breakfast was the best meal of the year. The very best.

Too soon, breakfast was over. Lily helped clear everything away. There were so very many extra things that needed to be cleared away and washed.

This part of Christmas breakfast was not fun. Not fun at all.

After the last dish was washed, dried, and put away, Papa looked at Lily, Joseph, and Dannie with a twinkle in his eyes. "It's time to go upstairs and wait for Mama and me to get your gifts ready."

Lily held Dannie's hand as they climbed the stairs. Joseph ran ahead and hopped on Lily's bed. After Dannie had climbed on the bed and sat beside Joseph, Lily opened her favorite storybook and started reading to them. She would read a page, then strain to listen for Papa calling, then read another page, then strain to listen. She had just finished the second story when she finally heard Papa call to them.

"You can come downstairs now."

Lily quickly put her books away and grabbed her gifts out of her dresser drawer. She hurried downstairs to join Joseph and Dannie. She didn't want them to start opening presents without her!

At their places at the kitchen table were funny, lumpy-looking piles covered with Mama's prettiest towels. Lily peeped under the corner of her towel and then gently pulled it away. Underneath was a beautiful red Etch-a-Sketch, a plate filled with candy and nuts, and a book. Joseph and Dannie each had a toy barn, plus a plate of candy and nuts.

Papa showed Lily how to use the Etch-a-Sketch. He turned the knobs and made funny wiggly pictures. Joseph and Dannie were excited about their barns. They opened up the barn doors and found all kinds of surprises inside. Miniature animals, a small buggy, a yellow tractor, and four little people. They had never had a toy tractor. They immediately set up their farm sets and began to play.

In her excitement, Lily had completely forgotten about her gifts for Mama and Papa. She handed Mama the pot holder.

Mama *oohed* and *aahed*, admiring the pretty colors. "What a good idea to make it into a triangle shape," she told Lily. "It's much easier to hold on to."

Lily was so pleased. Then Lily gave the tool belt to Papa. He tied it around his waist, grinning from ear to ear. Lily was afraid he might think it would be silly looking. It was too colorful.

Papa removed it and folded it carefully. "I will have to find a place to keep this nice," he said. "I don't want such a pretty tool belt to get dirty."

Lily was so happy that Papa and Mama both liked her gifts. Papa sat on the floor to help Joseph and Dannie play with their farm sets for a little while. Lily started reading her new book.

She had not read very far when Papa noticed the time.

"The morning has flown!" he said, rising to his feet. "It's time we get ready to go to Grandpa Miller's. Grandma is preparing a big Christmas dinner."

Lily was sad to close her book. She would have to wait until they got home before she could find out what happened next. Joseph and Dannie were reluctant to leave their farm sets too, but Grandpa and Grandma Miller were expecting them. They went upstairs to change their clothes and get ready to leave.

When they arrived at Grandpa Miller's, Lily was happy to see Uncle Elmer's buggy—that meant Hannah was already here! Lily ran inside to find her playing with Aunt Susie. They told each other what they had received for Christmas that morning. Aunt Susie was excited about her own new coloring book and crayons and a little bonnet for her doll. Lily was happy for her aunt. She knew that dolls and coloring books were Aunt Susie's favorite things.

After Christmas dinner was over, the entire family gathered in the living room outside of Great-Grandma's bedroom door to sing Christmas carols to her. The beautiful music cheered Great-Grandma up and she looked happy, but Lily still kept one eye on that cane by her bed. Great-Grandma was getting stronger and Lily did not want to get anywhere near that cane.

While everyone was singing the last song, Grandma motioned to Hannah and Lily to come into the kitchen with her. She handed them bowls of Christmas treats to hand to the grown-ups. After everyone had a treat, Grandma gave Hannah and Lily their own plate, filled with goodies. Lily sat beside Hannah and nibbled at everything. It seemed she had been eating all day. She really wasn't hungry any longer.

As the sun was dropping low in the sky, behind the pine trees, it was time to go home. Even on Christmas, Jenny needed milking and all of the animals wanted their dinner. Grandma stood beside the door to say goodbye to everyone. As they went out the door, she handed each child a cute little horse and buggy. The buggy was made out of a big marsh-

mallow with Lifesaver candies for wheels. A little gummy bear sat on top of an animal cracker horse. It was fastened to toothpick shafts with a piece of thread. Joseph and Dannie couldn't wait. They ate their horse and buggy right away, but Lily thought it was much too cute to eat fast. Little boys needed to learn to wait.

Back at home, Mama popped a popper full of popcorn. The family sat around the kitchen stove to eat it while she read a story aloud. The room was filled with flickering light from the oil lamp. And warmth and love.

Even without the snow, it was a wonderful Christmas.

The Househunting Trip

One cold morning in January, Papa woke Lily early. "Wake up, sleepyhead!" He patted her head. "We have a big day ahead."

Quickly, they all ate breakfast, wasting no time in talk, and Mama and Lily washed and dried the dishes. Any minute, a big red van was due to arrive at Singing Tree Farm. In the van would be Grandma and Grandpa Miller and Aunt Susie. They were all going to visit an Amish community in Pennsylvania. They wanted to visit the church and school and look at farms to buy. Grandma Miller's sister came to care for Great-Grandma while they were househunting.

Lily liked to travel. She was getting used to the idea of a move, even though she still wished Mama and Papa might change their mind and stay at Singing Tree Farm. She didn't think they needed school at all. But if they had to move, Lily hoped there would be a lot of children in this new community.

Mostly, she hoped there would be a nice teacher in the school, and not a cross teacher like Katie Zook.

By the time the sun was up, the van had arrived and the adventure had begun. Lily sat by the window to see the sights, but the van whizzed along too fast. She couldn't see the things she usually liked to see from the buggy. She couldn't see little birds flit from branch to branch in the trees beside the road. Why, the van was going so fast that Lily could hardly see the branches!

Lily's tummy was growling by the time they arrived in Pennsylvania, at the farm of Papa and Mama's friend, Jonas Raber. Jonas and his wife, Alice, bustled out of the big house to welcome them. They had been expecting them. Alice had made a big pot of chicken noodle soup for lunch, along with bread, butter, and jam, and peaches and cookies for dessert. The soup was simmering gently on the back of the woodstove where it wouldn't burn. The big kitchen table was set with spoons and napkins.

Alice set the soup kettle on the table and poured water into glasses. Everyone, including the driver of the van, sat at the table. After a silent prayer, Alice ladled soup into bowls as the men talked about farms and properties that were for sale. They talked about how many families lived in the community and what people did for a living. The soup was delicious, but Lily quickly grew bored listening to grown-ups talk about grown-up things.

Alice noticed Lily's boredom. "I'm guessing you are almost the same age as my little girl. My Beth is seven. How old are you?"

"I'm seven too!" Lily's whole day brightened. That meant there was at least one other little girl in Pennsylvania.

Alice smiled. "Beth and Reuben are both in school right

now. I'm sure they wouldn't mind if you and Joseph played with their toys until they come home."

Lily perked up. Pennsylvania had her half interested. She tried to imagine what Beth would look like. Would she resemble her mother or her father? Lily stole a glance at Jonas. He was a strange-looking man. His hair and beard were like dry straw, and his snaggled teeth jutted out in all directions. Lily wasn't even sure how he could chew food. She hoped Beth looked like her mother. Alice was very friendly looking. She hoped Beth would be a nice little girl who liked to play with dolls. Dolls were so important.

As soon as lunch was over, Alice showed Lily and Joseph to the toy box. Lily could hardly believe her eyes. On top of the toys was a real doll! This doll had bright blue eyes and a tiny red mouth that was parted just enough to show a tiny tooth. She was dressed in Amish clothes. Perfect, she was perfect. Lily gathered the doll gently in her arms.

Joseph was busy with blocks and toy animals and tractors. He tried to coax Dannie to come play, but he was acting shy around strangers again and refused to leave Papa's lap.

The afternoon flew by. All of a sudden, a little girl appeared and stood by the toy box. "I'm Beth," she said. "I see you like my Sally too."

Lily jumped to her feet. Would Beth be angry with her for playing with her doll? She held the doll out to Beth. Beth's face broke into a big smile. She didn't take the doll back.

"My doll is named Sally too," Lily said. "But she's only a rag doll. She isn't as pretty as your doll."

"I have a rag doll!" Beth said. "I'll go get her." She ran upstairs to her room and came down with a limp rag doll. She sat next to Lily and started playing with it.

"Here." Lily held out the pretty doll. "You play with Sally."

"You can play with her while you're here," Beth said.

Beth was such a nice girl! If Papa and Mama decided to move to Pennsylvania, Lily would have a very good friend. Lily stole peeks at Beth while they played dolls. Beth was pretty. She had very light blonde hair, so light it was almost white. Her eyes were bright blue and she had cute little dimples in her cheeks.

"Where is your brother?" Lily asked.

"Reuben is out in the barn feeding the calves and helping with the chores," Beth said. "He said he would do my chores tonight so I can stay in the house to play with you."

Reuben sounded as nice as Beth. Lily had always wanted an older brother like Reuben. If everyone else in Pennsylvania were as nice as Beth and Reuben, it might not be quite so terrible to leave Pleasant Hill.

The next morning, both families piled into the big van. The plan was to drop Reuben and Beth at school, stay for a brief visit, then look at nearby farms for sale.

The first thing Beth did at school was to put her lunch box on a shelf. Then she pulled Lily over to meet her friends. Lily was sorry to see there were only two other little girls. All the other lower grade children were boys. Lily thought she had never seen so many boys in one place. That was a huge disappointment. Huge.

The teacher came to the back of the classroom to shake hands with the visitors and welcome them to school. When she approached Lily, she said, "I am Teacher Rhoda. What is your name?"

"I'm Lily."

Teacher Rhoda smiled kindly at her. "Welcome to Greendale

School, Lily. Today, you can sit and watch everything. I hope you enjoy your visit."

"I will," Lily said. She liked Teacher Rhoda. She reminded Lily of Teacher Ellen, kind and sweet.

Lily looked around the schoolroom. The walls were covered with pictures that the children had created. Teacher Rhoda liked art. Any teacher who liked art must be a good teacher.

As Teacher Rhoda rang the bell, the students hurried to their desks. After roll call, Teacher Rhoda read a chapter from the Bible. The scholars stood to recite the Lord's Prayer together. After they had sung three songs, Teacher Rhoda assigned arithmetic to everyone. Carefully and patiently, she explained the math problem to the scholars. She didn't even get cross when a boy had to ask her for help.

Too soon, Papa rose to his feet. It was time to go. Lily was sorry they couldn't stay longer. She would have liked to stay longer at this school. It looked like fun!

Jonas Raber sat in the front seat of the van to give the driver directions. They stopped at a farm and looked over the house and barn. Papa and Grandpa walked the property lines with the owner. The women and Lily, Joseph, and Dannie stayed in the warm van to wait for them. It was too cold to trudge through the snow to see property lines.

After that farm, they went to another, then another. Lily was tired of househunting. She was ready to go back to Jonas and Alice's house. Alice had packed some pretzels for snacks, but they hadn't expected to be gone so long. Lily was hungry, and Beth would probably be coming home from school soon. Lily didn't want to miss a moment of playing dolls with Beth.

"There is one more property to look at," Jonas said. "It's

only fifteen acres. You might just like it, though, if you wanted to do something other than farming for an income."

Papa looked intrigued. He liked carpentry more than he liked to farm. "I'd like to see it."

The van stopped in front of an ugly olive green house. It had dirty yellowish gables. This house would not do. It would not do at all. Lily was sure Papa would not like this ugly house.

They all spilled out of the van and walked up to the front porch of the olive green house. Jonas knocked on the door. An older lady opened the door and invited them inside.

Lily followed Mama into the kitchen. The countertop was bright orange—so bright that Lily had to blink her eyes fast, like she was looking at the sun. Upstairs were two small bedrooms, a tiny bathroom, and a little corner that was half-room and half-hallway. Papa went to look at the attic and basement, but Dannie was getting cranky so everyone else went out to the van to wait.

Papa came out to the van. He said he wanted to walk the property lines and look through the barn. Lily thought that was a waste of time. The house was too small. It was painted an ugly color on the outside. The kitchen had bright orange counters. No, Lily decided, she would not want to live at that house. No, no, no.

Papa came back to the van with a broad smile on his face. "I think we found the place we've been looking for." He sounded very happy. "What do you think, Rachel?"

It seemed a long time before Mama said gently, "Well, Daniel, I think we could be happy here."

Oh, this was terrible news.

Papa hopped in the van. "Let's sleep on it overnight. If we still feel like it's the right place, we can make an offer tomorrow."

But what about Lily? What if she didn't think it was the right place? No one ever asked her what she thought about this ugly olive green house with the orange countertops.

Except for meeting Beth and her doll, and maybe school, Pennsylvania was a huge disappointment to Lily. Huge.

CHAPTER

37

Packing Up

The ugly olive green house with the orange countertops in Pennsylvania now belonged to Lily's family. On the long ride in the van back to New York, Papa and Mama talked and talked with Grandpa and Grandma Miller. By the time they reached home, Grandpa and Grandma Miller decided to move too. That meant Aunt Susie would come too! And just a few days later, three of Mama's brothers and their families said they would come too. So now, everyone was coming. Even Hannah and Levi! As soon as their farms sold, they would join the Lapps in Pennsylvania.

Lily was relieved. It made the move so much nicer to think there would be cousins and aunts and uncles there, instead of only strangers. And there was Beth. She had one friend in Pennsylvania. She had Beth.

The date of the big move was set for early February. Next came the packing. Grandpa Miller scheduled an auction to be held at his farm, so Mama was going through everything in the house to see what things could be sold. The ugly olive green house was much, much smaller than the one they lived in now. Papa and Mama decided to sell extra furniture and belongings at the auction.

Lily helped Mama clear out some dressers. They packed into boxes all that had been in the dresser drawers. Mama mixed a pail filled with warm water with a splash of lemon oil. Lily's job was to carefully wash every inch of an empty dresser drawer until there were no smudges or fingerprints anywhere. Mama wanted it to be gleaming.

"I'm all done with this dresser, Mama," Lily said.

Mama came over to look at it. "You did a good job. Now you can clean out your nightstand and wash it."

Cleaning out the nightstand made Lily sad. She had liked having it beside her bed. She kept her books in it and Sally's doll clothes.

When Papa came home from work, Lily showed him the full boxes and the gleaming empty dressers. Joseph had played with Dannie so Mama and Lily could work faster. They accomplished quite a bit for one day and Papa was pleased.

Papa smiled at everyone. "I'm glad you all help Mama so well while I am gone." He turned to Mama. "Do you have anything planned for tonight?"

"Nothing that can't wait," said Mama. "Did you have something in mind?"

"I thought we could all go outside and spend some time with Chubby before we sell him at the auction," Papa said.

Sell Chubby? How awful! They couldn't sell Chubby. Chubby was part of their family.

"That would be nice," Mama said. "I'll miss that little

horse. He's so sweet and gentle and the children have enjoyed him so much."

Lily's eyes filled with tears. "Please don't sell Chubby, Papa. We can take him to Pennsylvania too. There will be a barn there."

"I'm afraid we can't take him, Lily," Papa said. "We are going to take Jim and Jenny, but there won't be room for Chubby. He will make some other little children very happy."

It wasn't fair! Chubby liked living with them. He liked sharing a pasture with Jim. He liked taking Lily and Joseph on rides. And now they were selling him like he was nothing more than an old dresser. Lily knew not to beg and she tried not to cry, but she dreaded saying goodbye to Chubby.

After dinner, the family bundled up and went outside for a final ride with Chubby. The darkness was velvety soft and quiet. All over the huge sky, the stars were twinkling merrily. Even though the moon was bright, Mama brought the kerosene lantern along so they could see. There wasn't much snow left on the ground—only little heaps here and there. Papa said the snow would be gone soon. The days were growing longer.

Lily and Joseph took turns holding the reins with Papa as they drove around and around the barnyard. Chubby shook his head and pranced, as if he was proud to take his family on a ride in the moonlight. He didn't know that this was the last ride they would take together. Never again.

After the ride, they all helped bed Chubby down for the night. Papa added extra sweet straw, and Joseph and Lily fluffed it up for Chubby. It was way past Lily's normal bedtime when she climbed into bed that night. She wished the ride with Chubby in the moonlight had never ended.

Grandpa's Auction

On Saturday, the morning of the auction, Papa and Mama woke early. They were in a hurry to get to Grandpa Miller's. The skies were gray and a few snow flurries drifted lazily through the air. Earlier that week, Papa had taken all of the furniture and belongings that they wanted to sell over to Grandpa Miller's. Nothing was left to do for the move except to go watch the auction. Mama would help Grandma Miller and Aunt Mary make good things to eat and sell them to the people who came to the auction.

Papa hitched Jim to the buggy and handed the reins to Mama. He would be driving Chubby and the cart to Grandpa's. As they trotted down the lane, Lily peered out the back window and watched Papa and Chubby follow behind them. Chubby's legs were short. He couldn't keep up with Jim. It wasn't long before they had fallen so far behind that Lily couldn't see them anymore.

As Mama drove up to the house, Grandpa Miller met them and helped unhitch Jim from the buggy shafts. "Grandma is already busy in the harness shop," he said.

Mama carried Dannie on her hip. Lily and Joseph followed Mama as they walked to the shop. Lily wondered what Grandma Miller would be working on. She had never seen her make a harness. She thought only Grandpa Miller could make harnesses.

When they entered the harness shop, Lily had to blink her eyes. It didn't look like Grandpa's shop any longer. In fact, there was no sign of harnesses at all! It didn't even have the leather and saddle soap smell that infused the room. Instead, it smelled like Grandma's kitchen.

There was a long table set out in the middle of the shop. On it, Grandma Miller was frying big, delicious-looking doughnuts in a big fryer behind the table. As soon as the doughnuts came out of the big pot of hot oil, Aunt Susie sprinkled them with powdered sugar.

Mama put Dannie down and slipped out of her coat. "What needs to be done?"

"There is bread that needs to be sliced for the hot sandwiches we'll be making," Grandma Miller said. She pointed to the broiler. "And that needs to be lit to start cooking the hot dogs."

Mama got right to work. Lily, Joseph, and Dannie watched them work, hoping they might get to taste a sugared doughnut or two. Soon, Aunt Mary and cousin Hannah arrived, so Joseph took Dannie by the hand and they went outside to find Levi. Hannah sat next to Lily in a corner. She had brought her doll along. Of course, Lily had brought Sally.

Soon, the shop filled up with people. Many had come early to look at the things that would be selling at the auction. One whiff of Grandma's delicious-smelling doughnuts lured people into the harness shop to buy a doughnut and a cup of coffee or hot chocolate. Happy and satisfied, the people went back to the auction site.

More and more people arrived until there was a long line stretching out the door and into the barnyard. Grandma kept frying doughnuts as fast as she could while Mama and Aunt Mary scurried around, waiting on customers and collecting money.

Before noon, Papa came into the shop and motioned for Lily to come. She laid her doll on the chair and ran over to him to see what he wanted. "I hitched Chubby to his cart and thought you might like to have one last ride with him before he gets sold."

Lily was still sad that Chubby was going to be sold. She certainly didn't want to miss her last ride with him. She hurried to find her coat and join Papa. They walked past the

crowds of people, gathered for the auction. Lily had never seen so many people in one place.

The auctioneer spoke in a loud, peculiar chant. It made Lily's head hurt as she tried to understand what he was saying. He spoke so fast that his words slurred together. She couldn't understand a single bit. Not a single word.

Some men stood on a hay wagon. They lifted Grandpa Miller's chairs up high so that everyone could see them.

"Why are they doing that, Papa?" Lily asked.

"So people can see what the auctioneer is selling," Papa said.

Lily thought that was a good idea. If people couldn't understand the auctioneer, at least they could see what he was trying to sell.

Lily followed Papa out to the barn. She looked at all of Grandpa's big workhorses. Someone had braided their manes and tails. They looked silly.

Papa noticed that Lily was staring at them. "The auctioneer asked some of his helpers to braid their manes and tails to make them look prettier. It helps fetch a higher price if they look pretty."

Lily didn't think they looked prettier. She thought that the mighty horses looked embarrassed. And it made her sad to learn that Grandpa Miller was selling his beautiful horses. "Why is Grandpa selling his horses?" she asked.

"Grandpa wants to retire from farming," Papa said. "He is selling all of his animals except Tony, the buggy horse."

Lily didn't think it would be possible to feel even sadder, but now she did. Moving wasn't fun at all. Too much was changing.

In the barn, Chubby was hitched up to his cart and ready to go. Lily sat on the seat next to Papa. Papa handed her the reins and said, "Here, you can drive him for one last time."

Lily drove Chubby slowly down the lane in Grandpa

Miller's fields, away from all the noise of the auction. She could have driven all afternoon. Too soon, Papa said it was time to turn around and go back.

As Papa unhitched Chubby, he glanced at her. "Do you want to watch the auctioneer sell Chubby?"

Lily shook her head. "No. I don't want to see him go away."

Papa didn't press her. He understood that she was feeling sad. He reached into his pocket, pulled out his wallet, and handed her a dollar. "Go buy yourself something good to eat at Grandma's food stand."

A whole dollar! "Oh, thank you!" Lily hardly ever held that much money in her hands. She turned and ran back to the shop and got in the long line of customers. When she reached the front of the line, Mama pretended she didn't recognize her and asked her what she could get for her. She acted as if Lily was a customer and not her little girl!

Lily played along. She told Mama she would like to order a hot dog, a doughnut, and a hot chocolate. When Mama gave the food to her, Lily handed her the dollar. She felt so grown-up! Then she went to find cousin Hannah to share her treats.

By the time the sun was setting, the auction was over. People were loading up the things they had bought to take to their homes. Lily was tired and ready to go home. She watched wagons roll away, filled with furniture from her home. She saw her special nightstand go into someone's buggy. Someone had bought Chubby and the cart. Lily knew she would never see Chubby again. Auctions weren't much fun when people were buying your favorite belongings.

After helping Grandma and Grandpa Miller clean up the harness shop, the whole family went home with Jim in the buggy. Lily was very glad that Papa had given her one last ride with Chubby. She would remember it always.

CHAPTER

39

Moving Day

*C*hurch didn't feel right to Lily. Grandpa Miller wasn't on the front bench like he usually was. He didn't announce the songs like he usually did. He didn't ask someone to lead the songs like he usually did. Aunt Susie wasn't there to play with after church. Right after the auction, Grandpa and Grandma Miller had loaded a truck with all their belongings and moved to Pennsylvania.

All that Lily could think about was moving. She could not sit still. She wanted to go, and she did not want to go.

Tomorrow, a big truck would come to Singing Tree Farm. They would start loading their belongings and make the move. Pennsylvania sounded much nicer now that she knew Grandpa and Grandma Miller already lived there and would be waiting to welcome them. On Saturday, Mama had taken Lily to say goodbye to Trisha. Trisha promised to write to Lily every week. Lily thought that was a nice idea, but she knew that it was hard to remember to write letters. After all, she had only written Teacher Ellen once.

Early Monday morning, Lily sat by the living room window and watched a big truck back up slowly and carefully to the front porch. The driver hopped out of the cab to talk to Papa, then he unhitched the trailer and drove away.

Lily grabbed her coat and ran outside. Papa was opening the trailer doors. "Can I see the inside of the trailer?" she said.

"Go and get Joseph and Dannie," Papa said. "They might like to see the inside too. I'll help you up so you can play inside."

Lily ran back inside to find her brothers. They were both playing with their farm sets. When Lily explained that Papa had said they could play in the big trailer, they jumped up and ran to get their coats. Lily helped Dannie close his coat and slip his little hands into mittens.

Papa hoisted each child, one by one, into the trailer. Lily liked the hollow echo as they walked up and down the long trailer. It sounded even better when they ran. But it wasn't long before they grew tired of that game. There wasn't much to do or see inside an empty trailer.

Papa helped each one hop out. "Mama probably needs your help to get the last of our things packed, Lily," he said. "You should go inside and help her."

Lily went back to the house, while Joseph and Dannie followed Papa out to the barn. Mama handed Lily a box and told her to pack all her toys. Even Sally. Lily did not like stuffing Sally in a box. She knew she was only a rag doll, but it still felt as if she were suffocating her.

Mama helped Lily tape the box of toys shut. She handed Lily the marker to write LILY'S TOYS on the top, and then set it next to the door. Many other boxes were piled up. They were waiting for Papa to load them onto the trailer tomorrow morning.

That evening, as Lily got ready for bed, she looked around her room. It looked so bare. It looked sad and unfriendly. There was nothing on top of her dresser. If she looked in the drawers, they would be empty. Her closet was empty. Everything looked too empty. She climbed into her bed and squeezed her eyes shut so she wouldn't have to see it. She did not like moving. She did not like it at all.

Morning arrived, and with it came their friends and neighbors. Everyone came who was left in Lily's church. Women brought big pots of food and little one-burner kerosene stoves to heat the pots. Mama couldn't cook with her own pots and pans because they had all been boxed up, ready to load onto the trailer. Someone had brought a few of the church benches along so there would be places to sit after the chairs had been loaded.

The men started to carry heavy furniture out of the house. Then they took the boxes. Mama scurried around mopping floors and washing windows as each room was emptied. She wanted the house to be sparkling clean for the new family who had bought Singing Tree Farm.

It didn't take long for the men to move everything out of the house. All that was left was the big heavy cookstove in the kitchen. Papa took the stovepipe down and carried it out. Six men gathered around the stove and lifted it up. Slowly and carefully, they shuffled their way out of the house with the heavy stove and up the ramp into the trailer. Now nothing was left that belonged to them. Nothing at all. The house looked much bigger and sounded funny. As people talked, their voices echoed off the bare walls and floors. Lily shivered.

She felt even worse than she had felt last night. Her house was just a house now. Not a home.

It was time to eat. Men washed up at the water trough outside the barn by pumping icy cold water and splashing it over their hands and face. Lily was glad she didn't have to wash up there. Too cold.

Inside the empty house, everyone gathered in a circle. They stood with their hands clasped behind their backs and bowed their heads for a short silent prayer. After Papa lifted his head, a signal that prayer was over, people started laughing and talking. They formed a line to fill their paper plates with baked beans, potato casserole, and hot dogs. Dessert included fruit tapioca pudding and cookies. There were always, always cookies. But Lily knew that lunches on moving days weren't as good as barn raisings or other times when everyone got together to work.

After lunch was over, the men went back outside. Lily stood at the window and watched as they helped Papa load tools from the barns. They loaded bales of hay and straw. The last belongings that went into the truck were their three buggies. Each one was rolled up the ramp into the back of the trailer. Then Papa closed the doors. Tomorrow morning, they would leave for their new home.

As friends and neighbors said goodbye to Papa and Mama, they said they hoped God would bless them in their new home. Papa thanked them. Lily noticed Mama's eyes glisten. It made Lily feel a little better to know that Mama was sad about the move too. When Lily said goodbye to Mandy Mast, she was surprised to see a few tears trickle down Mandy's cheeks.

As buggies rolled out of the driveway, Lily saw Harold and Helen Young's big car drive toward the house. Harold Young got out of the car and shuffled around a little bit.

"We came to say goodbye before you leave. Sorta hate to see you folks go. You were good neighbors." Reaching into his overalls pocket, he pulled out several lollipops and handed them to Papa. "Thought your kids might like these," he said in his gruff way.

Why now? Why were people like Harold Young and Mandy Mast so nice now that Lily was moving? It was a mystery.

Helen Young gave Mama a hug. She turned to Lily and Joseph. "I'll really miss my little milk delivery people. If you ever come back to visit, be sure to stop in. I keep my cookie jar full and it would be nice to enjoy some together again."

After they waved goodbye to the Youngs, Papa and Uncle Elmer caught the chickens and put them into several big crates. They set them in the back of Uncle Elmer's buggy.

Papa tied Jim to the back of the buggy. He helped Mama up. Then he helped everyone else in. It was crowded in the buggy with Uncle Elmer's entire family and Mama, Lily, Joseph, and Dannie. Papa would lead Jenny over to Uncle Elmer's. A man was coming to pick up Papa's livestock with a cattle trailer. Jim and Jenny and the crates of chickens would get to ride in it all the way to Pennsylvania. Lily was glad the animals would be together. They wouldn't be lonely.

As Uncle Elmer slapped his horse's reins, the buggy started down the driveway. Lily peered out the back window. Papa stood there with Jenny, holding her rope. He wasn't watching them drive away. He was too busy looking at the house and barn. Lily knew he was saying his own goodbye to Singing Tree Farm. And he was not whistling.

Aunt Mary had made a big pot of chili soup for supper. By the time Papa arrived, everyone was ready to eat. Supper was strangely quiet. No one had anything to say. They were feeling too sad to talk.

After everyone had finished, Lily started to help clear the table, but Aunt Mary stopped her. "You don't have to help with the dishes tonight," Aunt Mary said. "You will have to get up early tomorrow morning to travel to your new home. I'm sure you want to be ready for such an exciting day. You can sleep with Hannah tonight."

Lily was happy to not have to do dishes, and even happier to hear she was able to sleep in Hannah's room. Together, the girls ran up the stairs to get ready for bed. They talked for a little while and then Lily got into bed. It felt different from her own. Too soft. She tossed and turned, trying to get comfortable.

After a while, Hannah sat up. "Can't you sleep?"

"No," Lily said.

"Here, you can sleep with my bunny tonight." Hannah handed Lily a lumpy stuffed bunny.

Lily held it. But the bunny didn't feel right or smell right. She was used to sleeping with Sally, but poor Sally was packed into a box and was somewhere in that big dark trailer. Lily would never get to sleep tonight. Never.

Someone was shaking her shoulder. Lily opened her eyes. Mama was bending over the bed.

"It's time to go, Lily," she whispered. "Try to be quiet so you don't wake Hannah."

Lily slipped out of bed and grabbed her dress. Mama buttoned the back. Then they tiptoed down the stairs. Joseph and Dannie were already sitting on the sofa in the living room. They looked groggy, as if they just wanted to go back to sleep.

Uncle Elmer came into the house. "Jim and Jenny are loaded. The driver is here with the station wagon. Everything is ready to go."

Papa had left earlier to meet with the truck driver. Mama said goodbye to Uncle Elmer and Aunt Mary. There was nothing left to do. It was time to go. The longest day was under way, whether Lily was ready or not.

Mama got into the backseat of the station wagon. The cattle trailer was hitched behind it. Lily and Joseph sat next to Mama. Dannie sat in her lap. The driver started the station wagon and drove down the lane. They were on their way. Lily would no longer be Lily of Singing Tree Farm. She wondered what name they might call the new farm.

It was sad to say goodbye to her home—the only home she had ever known. She had been born there, and so had Joseph and Dannie. Jim and Jenny and Chubby had become part of their family there. But Papa said home wasn't a place. Home, he said, could be carried in your heart.

Frequently Asked Questions about the Amish

Who are the Amish? The Amish are a Christian church that traces its roots to the Protestant Reformation in sixteenth-century Europe. They give special emphasis to values such as simplicity, community, separation from the world, and pacifism (which they call nonresistance). They are often referred to as the Plain People because they dress in very distinctive dark clothing (women wear bonnets and men wear horseshoe beards), they use a horse and buggy rather than a car, and their homes aren't connected to the public utility grid for electricity.

Where do they live? How many Amish are there? The Amish migrated from Europe to North America in the eighteenth and nineteenth centuries. Today, no Amish remain in Europe. They live in twenty-eight states and in Canada. Their population totals approximately 261,150—over half are under the age of eighteen. A typical Amish family has five children.

What language do the Amish speak? The Amish speak a dialect of German known as Pennsylvania Dutch. English, typically learned in school, is their second language. Amish people often refer to non-Amish as "English," because they speak the English language.

Do the Amish attend school? Amish children end their formal schooling at the end of eighth grade. Most Amish children attend one- or two-room private Amish schools. An Amish teacher teaches all eight grades. Amish schools play an important role in passing on values, developing friendships, limiting exposure to the outside world, and preserving Amish culture.

How could Lily not have known that her mother was having a baby? The Amish have a very modest culture. In almost all Amish communities, pregnancy is a carefully guarded secret. It is never talked about in front of children. Any preparations for the baby would take place after children are in bed. Even cribs are not set up until after the baby arrives.

Would you like to learn more about Lily? Go to her website, www.adventuresoflilylapp.com, and find out more about her family and her friends. You can play games, download coloring pages from Lily's books, and send Lily an email.

Acknowledgments

From Mary Ann Kinsinger

I would like to thank everyone who had a part in my getting to write this book.

To my parents and brothers for all the happy memories you helped provide.

To my husband and children for all the patience and support you showed and for never complaining of the simple meals I served while my focus was on meeting my word goals.

To the readers of my blog, A Joyful Chaos. Your encouragement to write a book meant so much to me. Together, we are seeing this dream come true.

To my coauthor, Suzanne, I really enjoyed working with you and will always be grateful for everything you did.

A warm thank-you to all the wonderful people at Revell Books.

And finally, a thank-you to God, who makes all things possible.

From Suzanne Woods Fisher

It is with a grateful heart that I acknowledge . . .

My special coauthor and friend, Mary Ann. Thank you for sharing your stories with me, for working so diligently, for being such a pleasure to work with. It's been a joy to get to know you and work with you.

Everyone at Revell. You're simply the best. It's an honor to be a Revell author and see what loving care you give your books. The attention you gave this cover is a fine example of how much you care about each book!

My readers, whose emails make my day. Thank you for giving up hours of your life to read my books, blog, FB updates, and tweets.

My family, especially my two daughters (and first draft readers!) for being such enthusiastic cheerleaders for the Lily series.

Finally, a huge thank-you to our great and faithful God, for giving me the chance to write.

Mary Ann Kinsinger was raised Old Order Amish in Somerset County, Pennsylvania. She met and married her husband, whom she knew from school days, and started a family. After they chose to leave the Amish church, Mary Ann began a blog, *A Joyful Chaos*, as a way to capture her warm memories of her childhood for her own children. From the start, this blog found a ready audience and even captured the attention of key media players, such as the influential blog *AmishAmerica* and the *New York Times*. She lives in Pennsylvania.

Suzanne Woods Fisher's grandfather was one of eleven children, raised Old Order German Baptist, in Franklin County, Pennsylvania. Suzanne has many, many, *many* wonderful Plain relatives. She has written bestselling fiction and nonfiction books about the Amish and couldn't be happier to share Mary Ann's stories with children. When Suzanne isn't writing, she is raising puppies for Guide Dogs for the Blind. She lives in California with her husband and children and Tess, her big white dog.

Visit

www.AdventuresofLilyLapp.com

- Meet the authors
- Get to know Lily and her family
- Learn more about the Amish
- Find fun games and activities

Don't miss any of
Lily's Adventures

Mary Ann Kinsinger
Suzanne Woods Fisher

THE ADVENTURES OF LILY LAPP

A New Home *for* Lily

Book Two

Coming July 2013

Mary Ann Kinsinger
Suzanne Woods Fisher

THE ADVENTURES OF LILY LAPP

A Big Year *for* Lily

Book Three